TUTTLE
IN THE BALANCE

TUTTLE
IN THE BALANCE

a novel

JAY WEXLER

The quotations from the Chuang Tzu are from *Chuang Tzu: The Basic Writings*, by Burton Watson, trans., Copyright © 1974 Columbia University Press. Reprinted with permission of the publisher. The quotation in Chapter Nine from the book of Chuang Tzu commentary is taken from *Chuang Tzu: The Inner Chapters* by A.C. Graham, Hackett Publishing 2001, p. 156.

Printed in the United States of America.

19 18 17 16 15   5 4 3 2 1

Library of Congress Cataloging-in-Publication Data

Wexler, Jay, 1969–
    Tuttle in the balance : a novel / Jay Wexler.
        pages ; cm
    ISBN 978-1-63425-145-7 (hardcover : acid-free paper)
    1. Judges—United States—Fiction. 2. United States. Supreme Court—
Officials and employees—Fiction. 3. Midlife crisis—Fiction. I. Title.
    PS3623.E945T88 2015
    813'.6—dc23

                                2015023422

Discounts are available for books ordered in bulk. Special consideration is given to state bars, CLE programs, and other bar-related organizations. Inquire at Book Publishing, ABA Publishing, American Bar Association, 321 N. Clark Street, Chicago, Illinois 60654-7598.

www.ShopABA.org

In Memory of Sonya Lee

OCTOBER

ONE

ED SITS IN HIS CAVERNOUS OFFICE BEHIND A COLOSSAL oak desk covered with stacks of briefs and papers so high he can barely see the people he is talking to on the other side. They are two of his law clerks—Dawn Fenton and Rick Morrison—and they are discussing *Texas v. Sexy Slut Magazine*, the First Amendment case that several of Ed's fellow Supreme Court justices want to consider this term. It's been nearly forty years since the court issued *Miller v. California*, a decision that placed big time limits on how much the government can restrict pornography, but the early twenty-first century is a far cry from the early 1970s, and Ed senses a growing feeling around the marble palace that maybe it's time to give some power back to the censors. It's not a feeling he particularly shares. Not that Ed is a big fan of *Sexy Slut Magazine* or anything, but censorship has never been high on his list either. Plus, the idea of going back to the era of viewing porn flicks in the court's basement to see if the films are really obscene enough to ban, like the justices used to do back in the "we know it when we see it" era of the 1960s, is something that Ed would like to avoid at all costs. He suddenly imagines having to watch a "money shot" on the court's fifty-six-inch plasma television while sitting on an antique leather couch next to eighty-three-year-old Rebecca Leibowitz, and this causes him to bury his face in his hands and let out a sound like a dying coyote.

"Are you okay, Justice?" Dawn asks.

"Oh, yeah, I guess," Ed responds through the cracks in his fingers. He lifts his head out of his hands, leans back in his oversized chair, and

3

puts his feet up on the desk, right next to the framed photo of his only child Katelyn standing in front of the brand new Manhattan restaurant she opened last March. "What were you saying again?"

Dawn and Rick have only recently started working as Ed's law clerks, and they are trying to deal with the fact that the man they are spending so much time with seems to be very different from the one they expected when they secured this prestigious gig over a year ago. They had counted on someone focused, hard-working, and sure of himself—that's the reputation Ed enjoys with his former clerks—but this Ed seems to be scattered, hesitant, and even a bit of a slacker (at least for a Supreme Court justice). Yesterday, for instance, he left at 4:30 in the afternoon even though preparations for the impending start of the new term kept some of the other justices in the building until after ten o'clock at night.

Dawn takes a look down at her notes, scrawled out in tiny script on a long yellow legal pad, and then looks back at Ed. "What I was saying, Justice, umm, I was saying that it doesn't matter how you vote in conference. There are four votes to grant for sure, right? I mean, obviously Garabelli and the Chief are going to vote to hear it, and what's the chance that the Two Musketeers won't go along with them? So the court's going to take the case no matter what you say. The hard call is going to be when you guys actually decide the case."

Ed nods. Dawn's right, of course. Though it takes five out of the nine justices to decide a case one way or another, it only takes four justices to decide to grant a case, and Garabelli, the old right-wing hothead, almost certainly has at least three other votes to take this one. Ed always cringes when he hears the phrase "the Two Musketeers," but he has to admit the moniker fits. The nickname—conferred by the renowned *New York Times* court reporter Adam Farkas upon justices Arnow and Cornelius, the two dimwitted right-wingers put on the court in the space of a year—has stuck fast in legal circles, and for good reason. The two usually vote together, and when they do, they always vote on the conservative side of the issue; they're about as predictable as an uneaten broccoli floret on a five-year-old's dinner plate. Ed considers himself a fairly conservative justice too, especially on issues like state's rights and affirmative action, but he likes to think that the pundits and court-watchers can't *always* figure out how he's going to decide a case before he actually gets around to deciding it. Ed sighs, tells Dawn she's right, and then suggests—subtly, of course—that it's time for the clerks to go on their way, back to their little offices, to write memos about pending cases, trade gossip about their peers, and spread rumors about the justices' exercise habits or whatever it is they talk about when their bosses aren't around.

After the clerks leave, Ed opens up a brief in the environmental law case that the court will hear Monday, the first day of the term, and starts reading. This is the kind of work that, until recently, Ed would have thoroughly enjoyed. It's a case involving a complicated statute with all sorts of detailed provisions and section three-oh-five-A-one-little-b-little-twos and the like to work through and understand and relate to each other and figure out what the members of Congress could possibly have meant by when they wrote it up—stuff, in other words, that most people would find indescribably boring and horrible, but that Ed, with what one of his law professors once referred to as a "mind uniquely suited to the intricacies and subtleties of the law," relished. But that was before. Now, Ed can't seem to focus for more than thirty seconds on any of the arguments in the brief before he finds his mind drifting back to the summer vacation he has recently returned from—two months of bliss in the Wyoming mountains, a glorious spell of crisp mornings and dry brilliant afternoons, of soaring eagles and scurrying marmots, of white water rafting and fly-fishing on the Snake River, not to mention a good deal of eye-popping sexual intercourse with a series of younger women who, to Ed's great surprise, were just delighted to bed down with an associate justice of the Supreme Court.

Not that he had figured on sleeping with anyone. Meeting women had been the farthest thing from his mind when he boarded the flight from Dulles to Denver. Ever since he and his wife Sarah called it quits, he has given little thought to meeting anyone new. Indeed, he's only slept with one other woman in the past couple of years—an old law school classmate who is now the managing partner of a major law firm in town—and having sex with her was a scotch-fueled mistake that had been about as much fun as filing a motion for summary judgment in a state trial court.

What Ed learned in Wyoming, however, was that when you mention you are a Supreme Court justice to a single woman who has never heard of you, oftentimes that woman will be surprisingly willing to go back to your place "for a drink." Ed met three women this way, and even though the summer kind of ended on a low note, with him being rejected in semi-public by a glitzy pop star (big mistake there, Ed will remind himself for the rest of his life), still the whole trip had been liberating and dizzying and just so much goddamned fun that now Ed is having a difficult time making it through even a single paragraph of the Petitioner's Opening Brief in *United States v. Donald & Hudson Industries* without wondering if he could maybe move out West permanently and participate in oral arguments via teleconference.

After four or five attempts to pore over the brief's Summary of Argument, Ed decides it is time to give up for the day. It's almost five o'clock, and there is plenty of time to get ready before the case is argued on Monday. Ed has already taken a quick look at the bench memo that Dawn has prepared on the case, and if he has to, he figures he can probably read the thing the night before argument and still understand what's going on better than most of his colleagues, which is a testament not only to the fact that Dawn graduated first in her class at Harvard Law School but also to the sad truth that some of his fellow justices are, frankly, nitwits.

***

Greg Bash usually does not like to pick up his office phone when it rings, preferring to let the call go to voice mail so he can return it at his own convenience—often, in other words, never—but when Caller ID shows that the caller is his best friend and old law school buddy and current Supreme Court justice Ed Tuttle, Bash puts aside the student paper he was grading and picks up the phone.

"Oyez, oyez, oyez," Greg announces into the mouthpiece, this being his typical manner of greeting Ed on the telephone.

"Bash, what the hell am I going to do?" Ed asks.

"I don't know. What *are* you going to do? About what?"

"About the fact that I can't concentrate to save my life. I should have never gone to Wyoming. I should have done the Florence gig with Garabelli. This is a nightmare."

"Oh my god, if you say that one more time I'm going to start a movement to have you impeached," Bash responds. He's actually angry. It was partially Bash's idea for Ed to go to Wyoming, and he takes Ed's retroactive rejection of the idea with some offense, particularly because he knows how much fun Ed had out there. During the summer, Bash received emails at least twice a week from the guy about how incredibly, ecstatically happy he was.

"I know, I know," Ed blurts. "What are you doing right now? Do you want to get a drink?"

Greg Bash is always up for a drink. A long-time tenured faculty member at the Georgetown University Law Center, Greg long ago gave up doing anything that couldn't just as well be done the next day. "I don't know," he says anyway, "I have this student paper to grade. Maybe I should just bring it along and you can write some notes in the margin. I'll tell her I was busy so I gave the paper to you to read instead. She'll have a heart attack when I give it back to her. What do you think?"

"What's it about?"

"It's a defense of Garabelli's dissent in *Vogel v. Missouri*," Bash answers. He is referring to the case from two years ago where the court—over Justice Garabelli's dissent—held that gay couples have a constitutional right to marry. Ed had been torn, and initially was inclined to vote along with his four more conservative colleagues, but ultimately, Garabelli's insistence on writing about Jesus in his draft opinion had angered Ed so much that he joined Justice Leibowitz and the three other liberals instead. It had been the first time that Ed was the true swing vote on the court in a landmark case, and the whole experience—including the bags of hate mail he received on a daily basis after the decision was announced—had been harrowing. Much better, Ed thinks, to keep to the more lawyerly, less explosive issues like whether section 209 of the Clean Air Act preempts California's newly promulgated regulations governing taxicab emissions.

"Oh, fuck me," Ed barks, then realizes that he might have spoken too loud and been overheard by his longtime assistant Linda, who sits right outside his office. Linda knows something's been up ever since Wyoming, and he fears that if she hears him screeching profanities into the telephone, she just might call a psychiatrist over for a visit.

"I really like the new you," Bash says. "It reminds me of the old law school Ed Tuttle. Remember that time we all went skinny dipping after first-year spring finals?"

"Of course I remember," Ed answers. "Senator Hatch asked me about it during my confirmation hearing."

"Oh, right. I prepped you well for the constitutional law questions, but I hadn't figured on them knowing about that incident," Bash replies. As one of the nation's leading constitutional law experts—albeit one who has taken it a bit easy, writing-wise, for a while—Bash was one member of a small team who prepared Ed for his Senate Judiciary Committee hearing eight years ago. "Where are we having this drink?"

"Do you want to come over here?" Ed asks. "I have an extremely rare bottle of Japanese whiskey given to me by the chief justice of the Supreme Court of Japan."

The invitation surprises Bash. He can count on the fingers of one hand how many times he's actually been to Ed's chambers. "Really?" he asks.

"Sure, why not?"

"Wow. I guess Wyoming did change you."

"You won't even recognize me."

"I'll be there in half an hour."

***

Ed hangs up, logs off of his computer, throws the briefs for the environmental law case into his black leather over-the-shoulder bag, and peels himself out of the cushy chair that the carpenters in the court basement custom designed for him a couple of years back. He stretches his arms over his head and takes a look around the office. Eight years and sometimes he still can't get over the fact that he's a Supreme Court justice. Who would have thought? The office itself is obscene. For one thing, it's so big he could probably park a small jet in it. There are at least three different sitting areas. He does most of his work at the giant desk, and he often eats lunch at the table by the bookshelves where he keeps the photographs of himself with various famous people (the president, for example, and Clint Eastwood), but there's also the alcove with the dark leather couch and the matching chairs and the glass coffee table topped with a smattering of books he finds meaningful—Holmes's *Path of the Law*, Dostoevsky's *Crime & Punishment*, the issue of the 1968 *Yale Law Journal* that includes his student article on products liability law, his beloved daughter's soufflé cookbook. The office has its own bathroom done up in marble, and thinking about this now, he exclaims softly, "my office has its own goddamned bathroom!" to nobody in particular. He takes a fresh look at the paintings on the wall, all on loan from the National Art Gallery, and they suddenly look too staid and better suited for a funeral parlor or the library of a seventeenth-century fox-hunting nobleman than for the new Ed Tuttle. He makes a mental note to see about trading them in for something a little more modern and lively. A Rothko perhaps? Might there be something by Warhol available? Could he possibly get one of those giant Lichtensteins up there on the wall? *BLAM!*

***

Thirty minutes later, Greg Bash, having been escorted into Ed's office by Linda, is removing his aubergine cashmere overcoat and settling into one of the chairs in the corner alcove. Ed retrieves the bottle of thirty-year-old Japanese whiskey from a cabinet underneath a picture of him and Justice Leibowitz riding an elephant in central Thailand and pours healthy portions into two crystal snifters embossed with the high court's seal. Bash picks up his snifter and puts his nose as far into it as possible. The professor's schnozz is sharp and beaky, descending from a desert-wide forehead traversed by bushy caterpillar eyebrows. A strand of dignified silver hair flips down over the side of the glass as Bash inhales deeply.

"Mmm, nice nose," Bash murmurs. "Smells like Hiroshima."

Ed takes a seat across from Bash and rests his Allen-Edmond-clad size ten feet up on the coffee table. "Well, what do you think of the place?" he asks, fully aware that he has never invited Bash into this particular office—the one he moved into three years ago following the untimely stroke that ended the career of the chamber's previous resident.

Bash looks around, takes it all in. "Big," he says. "Roomy. Kind of boring, though." An unsurprising answer from a guy who adorns the walls of his own office with outsider art purchased from a woman on the precipice of insanity who peddles her wares outside Eastern Market on Saturday afternoons.

"I know, isn't it?" Ed responds. "I've been thinking about replacing some of these old awful oils with something snappier. Maybe I should put up a couple of those finger-paintings from the crazy lady you buy from. Or, now that I think about it, maybe I could get the National Gallery to send over a Warhol or two from their collection. That's such a nice perk of the job. Do you know if they have Warhols at the National Gallery?"

Bash stares down his old friend. "I hate you," he says. "I should have this job. I'd be so much better at it than you."

"Why *don't* you have this job, anyway?" Ed asks. "Why do I have it instead of you?"

"I don't know, maybe because you love and respect the law and I think it's ridiculous?" Bash answers. "You've read my articles."

"Oh, you mean *The Rule of Law as the Law of Whatever Five Guys Say It Is*?" Ed responds, referring to Bash's seminal *Columbia Law Review* article from several decades ago. "I remember it well. Maybe if you had ever actually practiced law, instead of going right to the ivory tower, you could be selecting a Basquiat from the National Gallery instead of me."

Greg rolls his eyes. "I wouldn't have lasted six months in a law firm. I still have no idea how you spent twenty years working in one, much less running the whole place, without chopping your own head off with a homemade guillotine."

"Practicing law was genuinely fun," Ed answers. "Helping clients navigate some complicated statute, arguing an ERISA case at the court of appeals, suing someone who fucked over my client—I actually miss it."

Bash shakes his head in disbelief. "I guess then it's a good thing you have this job instead of me."

Ed smiles and takes a sip of whiskey. Bash follows suit, then takes another look around the office. When his gaze settles upon the old *Yale Law Journal* volume in front of him, he picks it up and flips through it, stopping at the page in the front with the masthead. As Bash stares at the list of names, Ed can see his mind traveling back through time, thirty-five years, a bit more actually, their callow selves with all that hair and their dreams of justice and rolled up shirt-sleeves, trading earnest arguments in a haze of cigarette smoke on the hallowed grounds of Yale Law. Boola Boola.

"Jesus, it's been a long time," he says. "Whatever happened to Norm Thompson, anyway?" Bash is referring to the editor in chief of the volume, the position appearing directly above the list of articles editors, where both Ed and Bash's names can be found.

"Don't you ever read our alumni magazine?"

"I can't bear to. I rely on you for this kind of information."

"He was just named general counsel for the NBA."

This snaps Bash out of his nostalgic haze. "Are you fucking kidding me? I thought he was a partner at Kirkland or something?"

"He was," Ed agrees, swirling around the whiskey and taking a respectable swig. "The NBA was one of his big clients, and he jumped ship."

"God, do you remember what an asshole that guy was? That speech at the banquet? Remember he chided me for 'engaging in a dereliction of duty'?"

"Well, you did insist on publishing your own article."

"It turned out to be the most cited article in the entire volume," Bash adds, accurately.

"True enough. Anyway, I saw him at the reunion two years ago. He's grotesquely fat and on his third wife."

"Good. I hope he dies of throat cancer."

"Lovely," Ed smiles, finishing off the first drink and then pouring them both seconds. "It's good to hear you're chilling out on some of your old grudges. On that note, how's Kelly Anderson's subscription to *Good Housekeeping*?"

Bash pulls out a flimsy postcard from his inside jacket pocket. "I've got his *Cosmo* subscription right here." Twenty-five years ago, a certain Professor Anderson from the University of Virginia had almost, but not quite, ruined Bash's chance for tenure by writing a critical letter that Bash was not supposed to find out about but did. To retaliate, every few years Bash sends Anderson a new anonymous subscription to one of the nation's top women's magazines, something Bash thinks is particularly hilarious given that Anderson is a man sporting a woman's name.

Bash returns the postcard to his pocket and takes a sip. "All right," he says, "give me the lowdown on what's coming up this term. Give me something I can talk about in the faculty lounge tomorrow."

"Since when do you hang out in the faculty lounge?"

"Okay, fine. Tell me something I can use to impress the legal blogosphere."

"Since when do you . . ."

"All right, just give me something that will make me feel cool, like I'm best friends with a Supreme Court justice, for once in my life."

Bash knows that Ed can't and won't tell him anything confidential about the court's business, but that never stops Bash from asking. Plus, if Wyoming has really changed the guy, maybe this is the moment when Ed gives it up. No luck. Ed laughs and points a fake finger gun at Bash. He shoots. Pow.

"Come on, you're killing me. What have you got so far for the term? A bunch of search and seizure cases, some environmental stuff, that ridiculous Second Amendment case? Anything actually interesting coming up this term?"

Ed fights the urge to point out that the Second Amendment case the court will hear in November is actually quite important. Bash, of course, knows this already, so Ed refuses to take the bait. Instead, he engages in his typical response to any line of questioning from his friend regarding the court's work. He starts reciting the Gettysburg Address. He's willing to recite the whole thing, twice even, if necessary. *Four score and seven years ago . . .*

"Wait a second," Bash blurts. "What day is it today? Thursday? That means tomorrow is your big conference. Holy shit. What cases are you going to grant? There must be some juicy possibilities. Are you going to reconsider *Roe v. Wade*? Maybe you could reverse *Marbury v. Madison*, get rid of this whole 'judicial review' thing. If you guys are looking to cut back your already minuscule workload, that might be a good move."

This last suggestion actually makes Ed let out the slightest of chuckles. To tell the truth, Ed is tempted to share with Bash his fear that the court is going to grant the *Sexy Slut* case, but even if the need for confidentiality weren't enough to stop him, the thought of Bash's reaction—Ed figures Bash's head might truly explode all over his office, given what the guy has said and written about the First Amendment—is sufficient to keep him quiet.

Our fathers brought forth on this continent . . .

Bash continues with his prodding. "Well, maybe the president will go through with his threat to attack North Korea without congressional authorization and you can decide whether that violates the War Powers Act. That would be interesting."

A new nation . . .

"All right, fine, forget it. Just shut up already with the speech."

Ed nods his head with delight at this tiny besting of his old friend and takes another drink. "Can we please talk about my midlife crisis now?" he asks.

"Aren't you too old to be having a midlife crisis? Do you somehow think you're going to live to be a hundred and twenty years old?"

"I can't focus on anything at work anymore. I keep seeing myself drifting on the Snake River under an endless sky."

"Yeah, right, and banging some forty-something you just picked up at the Cowboy Bar and Grill."

"And that," Ed admits, putting his head in his hands for a moment before looking up again. "It's true. Also that. I know it's ridiculous, but it was so much fun. And now I have no idea what to do with myself."

"Well, unless you plan on participating in your court duties via Skype, you're going to have to snap out of it. Luckily you have one of the easiest jobs in the world—something any B-plus student right out of law school could do, so I'm not overly worried. Fly out of town on weekends and holidays. It's not like you don't have the money or opportunity."

Ed instinctively recoils at Bash's oft-spoken refrain about the ease of his job, but he knows that, in a way, Bash is right. Reading briefs and deciding cases and writing twelve opinions a year isn't all that hard. Not even close to his former life as a law firm partner, when four days of every week were spent on the road—arguing motions in nowhere towns in Alabama or deposing witnesses in Sheboygan and then working the whole flight home. The work, in other words, that basically ruined his marriage. Being a justice is stressful—the law of the nation is in your hands, after all—but it honestly doesn't take much more work than your average forty-hour-a-week gig. For a moment, Ed considers picking up a second job to keep himself busy. Perhaps something at night. Or maybe he should go back to school, get another degree. He's always been interested in philosophy. How long would it take to get a PhD, anyway?

"Have you been on any dates since you've been back?" Bash asks.

Ed snaps out of his daydream. "No, I haven't. Not one. Somehow it's different here. When I was out West, for some reason I could just go into a bar and meet people. Here either people know who I am, or I think they're going to know me. I'm stifled. What should I do? Go speed dating at the local Holiday Inn? Join a dating service? Do they have one of those things for 'Senate-Confirmed Singles' or something?"

"Why don't you let me set you up with Diana? She's not a lawyer. She doesn't give a shit that you're a fancy justice. Plus, she's not bad looking. You know, for a fifty-year-old divorced mother of two."

"Maybe. Or maybe I should just do what you do and date twenty-five-year-old students."

"Hey, I always wait until they graduate. And they're usually at least twenty-six."

"You're pathetic."

Bash gives Ed a wide grin, his caterpillary eyebrows breaking out in a small dance on the Sahara of Bash's forehead. "I know," he says. "But you still love me." The professor then puts out his snifter for Ed to clink with his own, and after that is done, and both glasses are drained of whiskey, Ed leans back in his chair and declares, a little too loudly, "Oh my god, could I use a good blow job right now."

Unfortunately, this is the exact moment that Linda knocks on the door of the office and opens it, all in one movement, as she is prone to do, having worked for Ed for over twenty-five years, and being quite used to doing whatever she wants around him. Ed hired her back when he was the managing partner at Bloom & Ellwanger, the white shoe law firm where he spent most of his pre-judge career. When the president put him on the DC Circuit Court of Appeals, Ed took Linda with him, and then two years later when he was elevated to the Supreme Court, there was little question she would accompany him. Ed would be totally lost, work-wise, without her, and so he sometimes thinks of her as his own little old lady version of Radar O'Reilly, although he would never tell her that since if she knew that's how he thinks of her, she would probably kick him in the kneecaps and retire.

"Ummm," she stammers, unsure how to react to what she thinks she's just heard Ed say, "is everything all right here?"

Ed, too, is of course flustered, never having before declared his desire for fellatio in front of his sixty-four-year-old assistant. He manages a "no, no problem . . . everything's fine . . . how are you?" as he returns his chair to the floor and places the snifter down on top of his daughter's cookbook.

"Okay, then," Linda says. "I'm going home now. I'll see you tomorrow, right? For the conference? The biggest day of the year? Yes?"

"Right. Have a great night. See you tomorrow, Linda."

"Bye, then," she says, followed by a suspicious glance at Bash, who returns the glance with more caterpillar dancing, and a second suspicious glance back at Ed, after which she retreats and closes the door behind her.

Bash stares at Ed with pure delight. He loves all these new developments in Ed's life. Pointing his own finger gun at Ed, he says, like an eight-year-old who just watched his big sister break their parents' prize ceramic vase, "Uh oh, you're in trouuuuuuuble." *POW.*

***

That night, Ed finds himself alone in his commodious, desolate house in McLean, Virginia, one of Washington's ritziest and dullest suburbs. Too drunk to drive (he and Bash had finished off at least half the bottle), Ed had been driven home in one of the court's chauffeured cars, which means that he's going to have to take a similar car back there in the morning, since his own car is still parked in the lot underneath the court. He makes a mental note to try to get in early so that the other justices don't see his car in the lot before he arrives and figure out it has been there all night. He has a feeling that the conference is going to be tense enough without having to explain that he drank too much the night before the biggest meeting of the year.

Ed stands in his daughter's old room on the north side of the house's top floor, listening to the home's emptiness. The place is far too big for him—he knows he should have unloaded it years ago and bought something smaller in the city, but somehow he's just never gotten around to it. Before his trip to Wyoming, he had mostly confined himself to a small set of rooms on the ground floor—his bedroom (which is not the bedroom he shared with his wife for so many years; he hasn't been in that room, the one that takes up half of the second floor, in as long as he can remember), his study, the kitchen, and the bathroom with the mini-sauna his wife had put in soon after they moved here. Now, however, he often finds himself walking around from room to room, revisiting spaces he hasn't used in forever. Just two days ago, for instance, he had watched an old movie on the television here in his daughter's room, sitting up on the bed with the pink bedspread, gripping a stuffed yellow dog that had been Katelyn's favorite as a little kid. Last weekend, he had cleared some space on his old worktable in the basement and read a bunch of petitions for review down there amongst the screwdrivers and rolls of electrical tape and handsaws. He tells himself that he should make sure to go retrieve those papers before he falls asleep, or he might not remember to get them in the morning before making his way in for the conference.

Ed leaves his daughter's room and wanders down the long corridor toward the main staircase. On the wall he notices, for the first time in a long time, an old picture of him and his wife from ages ago. They are wearing hiking gear and are in some kind of forest, posing in a classic married couple's pose, his arms around her shoulder, her arm around his waist. Ed thinks he remembers the trip—a friend's wedding near Seattle, a side jaunt into a national park or forest, traipsing through light rain to see a waterfall or a lake or some other natural treasure. Someone on the trail must have taken this picture, and as he looks at it closely, he thinks he can see the beginning of their marriage's end in their faces. Is he imagining when he perceives in his own half-smile a preoccupation with some work matter, some motion or brief back home? When he stares at her expression and spies an inkling of despair, is he inventing something that wasn't there? People sometimes ask him what happened, but there's really not much to say. At first they loved each other, and then slowly, gradually, they didn't. If it had been up to him, he probably would have stayed married, but Sarah wanted more, and when she suggested they go their separate ways, he could hardly insist she stay. Maybe if Katelyn had been younger at the time he would have tried harder to make it work, but she was practically out of high school already, so he just signed Sarah's papers and threw himself even deeper into his work.

He can only stand to look at the picture for a short time before turning to the staircase and descending to the kitchen, where he squirts himself a glass of water out of the SubZero's futuristic water dispenser. He is taking a sip and considering whether to take two Advil when he hears an ambiguous squeaking noise coming from outside. At first he ignores it, but when the squeaking continues, he decides to investigate. He stands on the front step, the still surprisingly warm early fall air lightly blowing through his graying hair, and though at first he cannot figure out where the noise is coming from, he soon spots its source—a smallish orange cat, glaring at him with bright green eyes, from fairly far away, over to the left side of the house down the slight decline of a rolling suburban hill, quite close to or perhaps even within the yard of the next-door neighbor, the celebrated long-form journalist whom Ed thinks is the owner of the cat and whom Ed knows, for sure, has just left on an extended research trip to the Guatemalan highlands.

Ed has never been much of a pet person, but he is lonely and still sort of drunk, so he strikes up a conversation with the cat. "Hey, cat. Everything okay over there?" The cat appears relieved to finally have gotten somebody's attention, and it strides bouncingly in Ed's direction on the walk that leads down from his front door to the yard and ends in the empty driveway. When it gets to about twelve feet from where Ed has now taken a seat on the stairs, the cat stops short. Ed takes a sip of the water. "Hey there little guy, why don't you come over here?" he says, following up with a couple of those little *tzzzt tzzzt* sounds that people make when they want to attract a cat. The cat comes no closer to Ed but instead falls sideways onto the grass and rolls onto its back and meows twice as loudly as before. "Okay, so you don't want to play with me, I get that," Ed says. "In that case, what do you think of the *Sexy Slut* certiorari petition? Is this something that we need to be worrying about right now?" The cat completes his roll, stands up, and then sits on its haunches. *Meow?*

Ed wonders what the hell this cat is doing meowing in the middle of the night. Could his neighbor, a flighty individual whom Ed has never liked, have forgotten to make sure the cat was taken care of before he left? No, of course not, how could that be? Surely he's hired a cat-sitter to look after it. But then what would the cat be doing outside? Maybe there's one of those doggy doors somewhere, except designed for felines, which the cat can use to go in and out at his pleasure. But is that safe? Ed has no idea what the answers to any of these questions are, but he's concerned because the cat is at this point meowing mania-cally, like it can smell some delicious food in its vicinity but can't locate it. "Are you hungry or something, cat?" *Meow, meow, meow.* "Do you want something to eat?" *Meowmeowmeowmeow.*

"Okay, okay, stay here," Ed says, and he goes back into the kitchen to find something to give the cat. What do cats eat, he wonders, as he rifles through the refrigerator and the cabinets. Frozen pierogies? Canned straw mushrooms? Figs? Eventually he hits on the mother lode—a can of smoked mackerel, purchased many moons ago after a routine cholesterol check revealed an elevated triglycerides level and a borderline high amount of HDL. The Omega 3 diet has long since given way to 10 milligrams of Lipitor a day, and this can of fish, along with an unopened bag of ground flaxseed, are its only remnants. Ed opens the can, deposits its contents into a small round Tupperware dish, and takes it outside, where he places it down on the walkway a few feet in front of the cat, which doesn't move an inch.

"What? You don't like mackerel?" Ed asks. He figures that maybe it's his closeness to the bowl that is dissuading the cat from eating from it, so he backs up toward the steps and takes a seat where he had been sitting before. The cat keeps meowing, but it does not approach the bowl. Ed shakes his head. Can he do nothing right these days? He stays looking at the cat, waiting for the little animal to take advantage of Ed's goodwill and eat the damned smoked fish, but the cat seems wholly uninterested in the offering. After two more minutes of this, Ed is done. "Fuck it," he says, and then he goes back into the house, takes the Advil, and without gathering the papers from the tool bench in the basement like he had planned, gets into bed and falls asleep.

TWO

THE JUSTICES START THEIR CONFERENCES WITH A GROUP handshake exercise that looks something like the coin toss ritual at the Super Bowl. Every justice shakes every other justice's hand, the idea being that although they might end up vehemently disagreeing with each other on some of the nation's most pressing legal issues, they are, at least in theory, friendly colleagues. Ed has never particularly minded doing the ritual before, but this Friday morning he wishes he could skip it, especially because he is feeling kind of shaky from last night and nervous about what is to come. It has already been a hectic morning; the car that drove him to work was a mile away from his house when Ed remembered the papers in the basement and asked the driver to turn around so Ed could go get them. As a result, Ed arrives at the conference room a couple of minutes after all of the other justices and has no time to settle in before all the shaking begins and the group gets down to business. On the bright side, if anybody suspects that Ed's car has been in the parking lot all night long, they aren't saying anything about it.

The justices' conferences all take place in a space so formal and grandiose it makes Ed's office seem like Fred Flintstone's living room. In the middle of the chamber sits a thirty-foot-long dark mahogany table, flanked by nine tall black leather chairs. Above the table hangs a garish chandelier that could probably illuminate a mid-sized basketball arena. On the far wall, above the fireplace, which the Chief has roaring despite the warmish weather, a portrait of James Madison hangs, the stately visage of the fourth president seemingly keeping tabs on the justices as they work. Nobody is allowed into the room during the conference but the justices, who are now arranging themselves around the table according to seniority. The Chief sits at the head—the room is actually situated within the complicated set of offices that make up her chambers—and Ronald Epps, the most junior justice, sits in the chair nearest the door so that he can answer it if anyone comes knocking with an important message for someone inside or, alternatively, a sandwich delivery.

Ed removes a stack of papers from his briefcase, places them on the table, and takes his seat. As the justice with the third least seniority (the Chief was actually appointed one year after him, but since she's the Chief, she obviously outranks him), Ed sits at the far corner of the table. Epps is to his right. Alistair Arnow, one of the Two Musketeers, is on his left. The justice with the second least amount of seniority but the largest amount of liberal furor, Angelo DeLillo, takes his seat across from Ed. On Arnow's left sits the court's elder statesman and former Democratic governor of New York, John Stephenson. Across from Stephenson is liberal stalwart Rebecca Leibowitz, on whose left is Alan Cornelius, the Second Musketeer. Finally, between Cornelius and DeLillo sits the champion of right-wing legal eagles everywhere, Tony Garabelli, who is quietly immersed in prayer while he waits for the meeting to begin.

After everyone else is seated, Chief Justice Janet Owens takes her seat. The former famed California prosecutor and deputy attorney general of the United States during the last Republican administration, the Chief is a natural at running things and not much one for tomfoolery. She starts with some pleasantries, the slightest bit of chit-chat about everyone's summers, and then it's on to business. Following the practice of one of her predecessors, for each petition on the so-called "discussion list," she introduces the case and then goes around the table, giving each justice two minutes to weigh in on whether the court should take the case. After the initial go-around, there's a little time for open discussion, and then the justices vote.

With machine-like efficiency, the Chief leads the rest of the justices through nearly twenty-five petitions in just short of two hours. They have decided to grant one big church/state separation case, a handful of criminal procedure and habeas corpus matters, and a bunch of cases involving relatively unexciting statutes dealing with things like pension guarantees, arbitration procedures, and banking disclosures. On the other hand, they've decided not to grant the big death penalty case that the ACLU was hoping for and have tabled a couple of the other glamorous petitions pending further briefing from the solicitor general. These decisions have nearly all been unanimous, and the little disagreement they have engendered has been minor. Not so for the next petition on the list—No. 15-178: *Texas v. Sexy Slut Magazine.*

"Okay, folks, here we go," the Chief announces. "As we all know, this is a petition from the state of Texas to reverse the decision of the Fifth Circuit Court of Appeals, vacating the criminal prosecution of the publishers and distributors of *this* magazine as a violation of the First Amendment." The Chief pulls out a copy of the magazine—the June/July issue, to be specific, the one with all the penises on the cover (forty-two of them, all erect, arranged in a collage)—and holds it up for the group to gaze at.

"Is that necessary?" exclaims DeLillo from the far end of the table.

"Why not, what's the problem?" counters Garabelli. "If you think this stuff is protected by the Constitution, why would you object to having it displayed in your presence?"

"I don't want to join the Ku Klux Klan either, but that doesn't mean they can't say what they want. You've heard of *rights*, haven't you?"

"You bet he's heard of rights," injects Stephenson. "The *right* of corporations to contribute to political campaigns. The *right* of businesses to be free of environmental regulation. The *right* of landowners to . . ."

The Chief interrupts, seeking some order: "All right, all right. No pun intended. Let's settle down, folks. We've got plenty more cases to get through today, so let's just treat this like any other case."

"Except with penis props," DeLillo can't resist throwing in.

The Chief stares at DeLillo. There's nobody she dislikes more on the bench than this guy. The day his appointment squeaked by the Senate, she burnt off steam by going on a three-day hunting trip in northern Maine with a couple of old friends from her days at the Justice Department. The rumor around the court is that she bagged two deer and a moose and gutted them all herself, grunting DeLillo's name as she pulled the heart out of each one with her bare hands.

"As I was saying," she continues. "The petition asks us to reconsider our decision in *Miller v. California*, where we held that the First Amendment protects pornographic speech unless it violates community standards of decency, appeals to a prurient interest, and completely lacks any serious artistic, scientific, or literary value. It is suggested in the petitioner's filing that, given how lower courts have interpreted and applied this test, it has become nearly impossible for states and local governments to control the filth that has clogged our newsstands, our radio stations, our cable television stations, and, most importantly, the Internet. With all due respect to one of my legal heroes, Justice Warren Burger, the author of *Miller*, I vote to grant the case, with an eye toward reformulating our test for obscene speech to better reflect the realities of what currently qualifies as 'entertainment' in this country." With this, the Chief hands the magazine to Stephenson. "You're up, John," she says.

Stephenson instinctively takes the magazine, and then looking at it and realizing he doesn't want to be holding it, even for a second, flips it across the table to Rebecca Leibowitz, whose reflexes are not quite what they used to be. The magazine glances softly off the top of her head and lands face down on the pile of briefs in front of her, the back cover's photograph of a giant bald woman's naked ass staring up at her from the table. Leibowitz lets out a horrified squeal and pushes the issue away to her left, where Alan Cornelius picks it up, looks at it for a moment with disinterest, and then passes it on.

"Well, I think we know what I think about this case," Stephenson says, adjusting his red and blue striped bow tie and smoothing back his sparse gray hair across the light bulb of his skull. "If lower courts are making it impossible to regulate this stuff, then all the better. I vote no. But if we take it, maybe we should end up replacing *Miller* with some sort of per se rule against regulation of indecency."

This clearly annoys Garabelli, who out of turn interjects, "The First Amendment has nothing to do with this kind of smut. It's about political speech, and we ought to keep it that way."

The Chief, who agrees with Garabelli's position on the matter, is inclined to let him keep speaking despite the clear violation of conference rules, but her devotion to decorum trumps her feelings about the case. "Yes, yes, you'll have your turn, Tony," she says. "But right now we're up to Rebecca. Rebecca?"

Rebecca is a woman of few words and low volume. When she whispers "no," the rest of the group can barely hear her, but since it's clear what her position is anyway, nobody asks for clarification.

The Two Musketeers are next—Arnow, then Cornelius. Contrary to Dawn's prediction, Arnow is not gung ho to take the case. "I don't know," Arnow says, sighing and rubbing his forehead. The man is clearly confused. "Is this a can of worms worth reopening? We made our decision on this thing forty years ago, shouldn't we just let it stand? On the other hand, I suppose the Internet throws things wide open here. Who knows what Alexander Hamilton would say about the web?"

The rest of the group is not interested in the workings of Arnow's mediocre mind. Garabelli rolls his eyes. Epps actually lets out an audible "Oy."

Arnow concludes with a whimper: "I could go either way. I'm interested in hearing what the rest of you think before I make up my mind. What's your view, Alan?"

Cornelius is no smarter than Arnow, but he is more decisive. "I think the Chief is right here. This is an issue worth reconsidering, and I would like to reconsider it. *Miller* seems to be unworkable at the lower court level, and Alistair is right that the Internet changes everything." This last bit brings a smile to the corner of Arnow's lips. The flattery is intentional. "I'm not sure we can come up with a better approach, but I think it's at least worth a try. I vote to hear the case."

The Chief is pleased. She's got three votes for sure to grant, and if Cornelius wants to hear it, then there's an excellent chance Arnow will ultimately follow. And Tuttle may also vote to take it, she figures. He's a bit of a wild card on the First Amendment, but the Chief is betting that Ed's deeply ingrained conservative streak is going to win out on this one. "Okay, Tony," she says, turning to Garabelli, who is now rubbing his hands in anticipation of getting to speak. "You're up."

Garabelli takes a deep breath. "You all know my position on this issue generally. I wrote about it in my separate opinion in *Loose-If-Her*," he says, referring to a decision several years ago where the court almost, but not quite, got into the Internet porn issue. "I believe it to be quite clear that the First Amendment is about political speech, about the free flow of serious ideas that is needed to sustain a democracy, and not about the unfettered liberty of individuals and organizations to say whatever it is they want whenever they want, no matter how disgusting, no matter how repugnant to the values of a decent society, no matter how perilous it may be to our children. And let's not forget the data showing that pornography is directly linked to increased violence against women." As he makes this last point, he turns his gaze decidedly toward Rebecca Leibowitz. He's trying to get a rise out of her, but she looks back at him with all the excitement of someone cooking a hard-boiled egg.

"But what I'd like to add today in my allotted time has to do specifically with the contents of the magazine at issue in the case," Garabelli continues. "Now, where is the issue? Who's got a hold of it?" He looks around the table to see which of the justices is currently in possession of the magazine, but it does not take long to figure it out. Ed's got the thing laid out before him on the dark table, examining the centerfold and pivoting his head around to get a better look at the young lady in the half-removed cheerleader outfit, sprawled spread eagle across the hood of a fire-engine-red 1986 Pontiac Fiero. Entranced by the image, Ed doesn't notice that the other eight justices are staring at him.

"Ahem, Ed," Garabelli coughs, "if we could trouble you to take a break from Little Miss Cheerleader over there and pass the magazine this way so I can make a point about the future of our nation, that would be terrific."

Ed looks up in surprise. "Oh, oh, yes, of course, sorry," he stammers, and then, awkwardly smushing the pull-out picture back into the magazine, he passes the now bent-out-of-shape issue over to Garabelli, who takes a moment to fold the picture correctly and put it back into its proper place. As Ed pages through his stack of papers to find the petitions and memoranda and other documents relating to the case at hand, Garabelli calmly flips through the porn magazine, licking his right forefinger periodically, looking for a specific page. He pauses at page twenty-eight with an "aha," at a feature entitled "Nasty Move of the Month."

"I thought it might be helpful for our consideration if we were to take a look at exactly what we were dealing with here," Garabelli says, folding the right side of the magazine behind the left, so he can hold it with one hand. With the other hand he puts on his reading glasses and begins to share the contents of page twenty-eight.

"The nasty move for July is, you guessed it, the Bucking Bronco," Garabelli begins, turning the magazine around and rotating its angle so everyone can take a look at the staged picture of a grotesquely hairy man with a bristly mustache and a mischievous grin mounting a buxom blonde from behind and grabbing her enormous breasts with both hands as she tries to rise up angrily from her knees in protest for some unknown reason. The other justices object with a range of everything from Leibowitz's *tsk tsk* to DeLillo's *is this for real?*, but Garabelli insists on continuing, raising his voice above the din of dissent around the table.

"A doggy style technique where the man grasps the woman's breasts tightly and then leans in close to her ear and whispers something infuriating, such as a different woman's name or 'your sister was much better' or 'what is this rash on my DICK?' and then holds on for dear life as the woman tries her darndest to get free. Can you last eight seconds on the back of this bucking bronco? Good luck!" Garabelli looks up at the group and lifts his eyebrows as if to say *what do you think of that?*

"Okay, Tony, we get it. It's gross and demeaning," the Chief interrupts. "Can we move on now?"

"I just think it's important that we understand what the results of our little test have been," Garabelli explains. "The lower courts said that the state of Texas could not fine the publishers of this magazine because on page forty-three there's a discussion of the risks of unprotected sexual intercourse. Serious scientific value, indeed."

DeLillo is actually clapping at this point. "Bravo, bravo, that's beautiful. Very persuasive. Perhaps next you can explain how we will all go to hell if we don't take this case."

"Only if you vote against taking it," Garabelli responds. "I don't think those of us who vote to hear it can be said to be cooperating with evil in quite the same way."

"If only your reactionary religious views had anything to do with your role as a judge," DeLillo counters, "then it might be appropriate for you to raise them here in the conference room at the Supreme Court of the United States."

"Spoken like a true ignoramus," Garabelli responds. "As anyone who has read any moral or political philosophy in the past twenty-five years could tell you, a truly religious person can set aside his views on ultimate reality when deciding a morally charged legal issue about as easily as, well, as say a former public defender can put aside his past experience on the job when thinking about criminal procedure disputes." Here Garabelli is specifically referring to DeLillo's former position as the federal defender for the District of Columbia—a job that has clearly influenced DeLillo's position on several prior cases.

"No, you're absolutely right, those are exactly the same thing," DeLillo answers, shaking his head in disbelief. On most issues, DeLillo and Garabelli can at least pretend to be civil to each other, but on this question of whether a judge should rely on his or her religion, even the tiniest little bit, when deciding hard cases, there has never been any common ground.

"All right, then, I believe Tony has voted to hear the case, yes?" the Chief says. "And he's used up his two minutes, so let's move on. Ed, what say you? Ed?"

Ed has the sense that his name is being called, but he's busy doodling and doesn't immediately respond. He draws a cross on his legal pad, traces it over several times, then adds a head, a face, some long wavy hair, hands on the horizontal points of the cross, a couple of legs, two giant breasts, and now he's got a porn star. Only when Arnow elbows him a couple of times on the upper arm does Ed finally put down his pen and look up. "Umm, what?" he queries absentmindedly.

"The case, Ed. What do you think about the case? Do we grant the porn case?" the Chief asks.

Oh, right, Ed thinks, the porn case. He draws a couple of circles around the cross-turned-sexpot with his pen and then draws a diagonal line through the whole thing. Who the hell knows, he wonders. "I don't know, what do you think?" he says.

"I already said what I think," the Chief answers. "We've got three votes to grant and one maybe from Alistair. Do you want to be the fourth yes? Is everything okay over there?"

Ed notices that on his right Epps is looking at his drawing and so tries to block it with his hand, but the position is awkward so he tears off the page and crumples it up. "Not really," he answers.

"Not really what? Not really you're not okay, or not really you don't want to grant the case."

Ed looks over at the Chief. He tries to pull himself together. "Honestly, Janet, is this something we really need to get involved with at this point?"

"So you're voting not to take the case then?"

Ed sighs, tosses the crumpled paper ball into the air a bit and catches it. "I don't know. I agree that our test is a mess. I just don't know if we can do any better."

"So you're going to do what?" a frustrated Garabelli demands. "Abstain?"

Why hadn't he thought of that himself? Ed's face lights up. "Exactly," he proclaims. "I abstain."

"You can't abstain," the Chief says. "There is no abstaining. Nobody abstains."

"I'm abstaining," Ed answers. "Consider it a new chapter in Supreme Court history." Ed's announcement is greeted with silence and confusion. The other justices look at him, squint, then look at each other. Nobody knows quite what to say. Ed goes back to doodling—this time a small goat. Fifteen awkward seconds pass before the Chief, wanting to get on with things, turns to DeLillo and says, "Well, I guess it's your turn, then, Angelo."

***

Later in the day, after the justices have finished their conference and scarfed down a lunch of grilled chicken and salad, Ed makes his way back to his chambers, where he finds Linda deep in conversation with two of his clerks—Rick and former Stanford Law Review President Sasha Vasvari—about some sort of reality medical show that Linda has recently become obsessed with. Ed barrels through the front door with his unruly stack of papers just in time to hear Rick mention something about a tumor the size of a cantaloupe and Linda respond with something that Ed swears sounds like, "you mean the one with the teeth?" Startled by Ed's sudden appearance, the three stop their conversation, all a bit flustered by having been caught talking about a toothy tumor the size of a cantaloupe when, presumably, they ought to be working on something involving, say, law.

"Justice!" Sasha exclaims, delighted that the big conference is finally over and looking forward to hearing what cases the justices did and did not decide to decide. "How was the conference? You look tired."

The last thing Ed wants to talk about is the conference he's just mercifully left behind. "Does someone have a tumor the size of a small melon? With teeth?" He puts down the stack of papers on a nearby chair that looks like it was carved by elves in the late seventeenth century.

The clerks, being new to chambers and not really knowing what to expect of Ed, or what he expects of them, are reluctant to engage in further discussion with the justice regarding the tumor, but Linda, who has spent most of her adult life with the guy, and who knows that he can't function without her, is not. "It was amazing. The thing was growing in a woman's stomach. They think it must have been there for over a decade. It also had some hair. And something that I guess resembled toenails."

"Wow, that's absolutely horrifying," Ed says. "I hope I make it through my entire life without ever getting a tumor with toenails growing out of it. I would consider my life a success, if I could just do that. Oh, and no worms. I also don't want to get worms."

The clerks stand quietly and nod. "You have a few messages," Linda says, quickly snapping back into professional mode. She walks briskly over to her desk and grabs a small pile of pink "While You Were Out" slips. "A professor from Yale who wants to talk about a clerk applicant. The dean at the University of Texas wants to invite you to judge a moot court in April. And your daughter. She wants you to call her back."

"Terrific. Thanks, Linda. I'll get right back to them." He takes the slips and heads for the door of his private office. Before he gets there, Rick gets up the courage to ask again about what happened at the conference. "Yeah, right," Ed responds. "Umm, I'll come back out in a minute to talk about it. Right now I'm going to take care of these." Ed waves the pink slips in the direction of Rick and Sasha and then disappears into his office, leaving the clerks in the dark. They look at each other and shrug.

"Maybe we should just call the Leibowitz clerks and ask them?" Sasha suggests.

"Sounds like a plan," agrees Rick.

***

Once in his office, Ed puts the pile of pink slips down on the table next to the old *Yale Law Journal* and dials Bash. At the third ring, his old buddy answers with his standard *Oyez, oyez, oyez.*

"Okay, I can't take it anymore. I need to go on a date. Tell me about this Diana," Ed blurts. "Exactly how 'not bad looking' is she exactly?"

"Whoa, there," Bash cautions. "Let's take it easy. One step at a time. Are you hung over? Did you throw up in the middle of the conference? All over the Chief's paperwork, I hope." Bash, the radical left-winger, has never been a big fan of Janet Owens, whom he sometimes refers to as "Chief Redneck."

"Yes, very hung over. No, no vomiting on the Chief. Now, Diana—what's her last name? What does she do? Kids?"

"Wait a second. One more question. Just tell me if you granted this *Sexy Slut* case I just read about on the Internet. Then I'll talk Diana."

"Yes, we granted it. For god's sake, don't tell anyone. Maybe sell all your porn stocks, though."

"Noted. Did you personally vote to grant?"

"No. It was the Two Musketeers, the Chief, and Garabelli. I abstained."

"You abstained? Is that a thing? You can abstain?"

"Look, I abstained, all right? Can we move on?"

"Abstaining at a conference vote? I see a law review article in my future."

"You haven't written a law review article since the Clinton presidency."

"That's not actually true, you know. You do know that's not actually true, right?"

"Whatever. Can we please discuss this Diana character now?"

"Right. Diana Liu. Chinese American. Fifty-two years old. Looks no older than forty-eight. Two kids in college. Divorced several years. Funky glasses."

Ed Googles her as Bash speaks. He likes what he sees. "All right, not bad. Where did you say you know her from? Some university committee, right?"

"We were on the university tenure committee together for two years. We played footsie under the table during deliberations on controversial cases. She's got a dual appointment in Asian Studies and Religion. A Taoism scholar."

"Taoism, hmm. Not exactly sure what that is. They let you serve on a tenure committee?"

"Hey, I'm not a *complete* joke, you know."

"Sorry. So, do you want to fix us up? How would this work?"

"How about I give you her phone number and then email her and tell her you're going to call. I've already talked to her about you, so I think it's a sure bet she'll take you up on at least one date. Whether she goes out with you on a second is out of my control."

"All right. Give me the digits."

"The what?"

"The digits. Her number. It's what the kids say. I learned it from my clerks last year."

"Okay, fine," Bash says, delivering the digits. "You're an absurdity, you know that?"

"It takes one to know . . ."

Click.

***

Ed's next call is to his daughter. She answers on the first ring.

"What's wrong with you?" she blurts. Ed can hear the clanking of pots and pans and the rustling of busy bodies preparing god knows what in the background. Flan? Roux? "What are you doing texting me during one of your conferences? The big one, right?"

"I miss you. I was bored. I don't know. How's it going?"

"Did anybody see you? Seriously, bored? What's got into you?"

"Nothing. Never mind. Everything's fine. I've just been preoccupied. Hey, what do cats like to eat?"

"Cats? I don't know. Cat food? Why?"

"I might have adopted one. Short term. I gave her mackerel last night. At first she wouldn't go near it, but when I woke up this morning it was gone."

"Do I need to come to DC and have you admitted somewhere?"

"Hey, I might have a date. A professor. With funky glasses. I haven't talked to her yet, but I have it on good authority that she's willing to spend at least two hours with me."

"That's what you called me about? To tell me you have a date?"

"No. I'm calling you because you called me. Because I texted you. Because I miss you. But now that I've got you on the phone, where should I take her? I need a good restaurant that's not over the top. Something relatively casual and funky, but really good food. Maybe ethnic. What's the word on the street these days?"

"Umm, the word on the street is that if you want good food you have to come to Manhattan."

"Come on, I'm serious. I need your advice."

"Well, okay, there's Ebisu, the new sushi and sake bar place that's supposed to be fantastic. I know the chef. There are only like six tables, but I could probably get you in."

"No. She's Asian. I don't want her to think I picked an Asian place because she's Asian. That could hurt my chances."

"Your chances? Your chances of *what*?" Ed has only selectively disclosed what happened in Wyoming this past summer, so although their relationship is a familiar one, Katelyn remains largely unaware that Ed has turned into a full-on raging horndog.

"Nothing. I was just hoping to get some kissing in. Or something."

"Kissing. Yeah, right. Look, I have to go. One of my chefs is holding up a five-foot-long squid and gesturing at me like a crazy person. Try a place called The Greedy Llama. It's in the city somewhere, I'm not sure where. But it's Peruvian and supposed to be very cool. I'll call you later. Bye."

"Okay. Hasta la vi . . ."

Click.

***

Peruvian? Ed wonders, as he Googles "The Greedy Llama DC" and pulls up the website. He scrolls through the online menu. Ceviche. Goat. Pisco Sours. This could work, he thinks. And it's actually near Georgetown. Okay, The Greedy Llama it is.

The conversation with Diana goes well. Ed is nervous as he makes the call, but she's been alerted to his plans by Bash and so everything proceeds swimmingly. They chit-chat about Bash a bit, trade tiny tales that they'll review and elaborate over dinner. Ed mentions the funky glasses; Diana seems surprised to hear of their funkiness. She's delighted by the choice of restaurant, though, having read about it in a recent edition of the *City Paper,* the district's weekly newspaper that Ed hasn't read since the turn of the millennium. "I've been wanting to try their ceviche ever since I read about it," she says, and Ed texts the good news immediately to Katelyn, who remains too busy with the oversized squid to respond. The date is set for seven o'clock the next night—Saturday—where they'll meet at the bar, because she lives in northwest DC and will therefore be approaching the restaurant from the opposite direction as Ed.

After the phone call, Ed, flush with enthusiasm, decides to make an early exit from the building, figures maybe he'll take in a movie or watch a ball game over a couple of beers. Packing up the files for the two cases the court will hear Monday into his shoulder bag, he powers down his computer and turns off the lights. His plan had been to zip down to his car without saying anything to anyone, but Linda is at her desk and detains him on behalf of the clerks, who, though they've learned the results of the morning conference, are still confused as to what they should be doing to help Ed get ready for the Monday arguments.

"Oh, I don't know. I think I'll be fine," Ed tells Linda. "Tell them to get some rest, have themselves a little fun over the weekend. I'll look over the cases again tomorrow and if I have any questions I'll give them a call. But I think everything's pretty straightforward."

Linda purses her lips and nods uncertainly. *A little fun?* In past terms, Ed has been full of questions about the cases right up to the moment argument starts, batting around theories and possibilities with the clerks and even with her from time to time. This certainty is disconcerting. "Umm, okay. I'll let them know. Anything else? Is everything all right?"

"Absolutely. Of course," Ed answers, then remembers something. "Oh, actually there is one thing. Do you know if the National Gallery has anything a little snazzier that I can get for my office? I'd like to trade in these dour paintings of horses and old men that I've got up now. Do they have like a Basquiat or something? One of those Lichtensteins maybe? A Warhol?"

Linda finds the question unsettling. "I don't know," she stammers. "I can check. I'll ask the curator's office what they can do. Can it wait until Monday? I doubt anybody will be able to do anything on a Friday afternoon."

"It can wait until whenever," Ed says. Though he doesn't know why, he gives Linda a comically exaggerated wink—something right out of an episode of *Laugh In* or *Hee Haw*—before turning and walking out the door.

THREE

SATURDAY MORNING. SUNNY, CRISP, BIRDS TWEETING. ED wakes up late and full of energy. A terrific night last night, steak frites and two glasses of Chateauneuf du Pape at the bar of his favorite nearby restaurant, then home watching the one game wild card playoff between the Red Sox and Rangers. Ed grew up in a Boston suburb and although he hasn't lived anywhere near the Hub in over forty years, his sports allegiances run deep. In select company and after the requisite number of drinks, he's even been known to declare that the Bruins are *wicked pissah* in a more than passable Southie accent, or to recite verbatim Dick Stockton's famous call of Fisk's miraculous game six blast, complete with dramatic arm-waving motions and all the rest. Last night, with Ed yelling at the television set and pacing around the room with several successive cans of Coors Light, the Sox fell behind early but tied it up in the fifth and then exploded in the sixth (assisted by an unfathomable Texas error), putting the game out of reach and making it possible for Ed to turn in by the seventh inning before things got out of hand, Coors-wise.

The real reason for Ed's enthusiasm this morning, of course, is his impending date, which has rendered him as jitterbuggy as he's been since some of those warm summer nights in Jackson Hole. Ed decides, however, that he will try to think of the date as little as possible until later, instead channeling his nervous energy into final preparations for Monday's two cases. He eats a couple of salt-sprinkled hard-boiled eggs with a slice of marble rye toast and then sits down at his dining room table with an oversized yellow mug of black coffee to take a look.

The first case is the environmental one he was reading through on Thursday, but this time he is able to focus on the details just like the old Ed would have. It's about whether a federal statute on air pollution preempts any inconsistent state law on the same issue, which in this case has to do with a California regulation about taxicabs that is stricter than the federal law. Ed reads the statute himself several times, re-reads the lower court's opinion on the issue, checks out the key parts of the legislative history that Dawn has outlined in her memo, and after about an hour and a half of work concludes—contrary to the court below but probably the same way that he figures most if not all of his fellow justices will—that Congress did indeed intend to preempt state regulation when it comes to air pollution coming from taxicabs. He makes a couple of notes for questions to perhaps ask at oral argument, places a post-it note on a key page of the petitioner's opening brief, and closes the file.

One down and one to go. He gets up and stretches, deciding to get some fresh air. Stepping onto the front stairs, Ed is happily surprised to find his new feline friend sitting in a sunny spot near the bushes on the side of the door, lazily licking the back of its paw and cleaning its face with it. "Oh, shit, furball," Ed exclaims, and the cat jumps to attention. "Are you still here? Your owner not back yet? Your guy? That jackass. Hey, I bought you something. Some food for cats. Wait here." Ed puts up his right index finger to indicate that the cat should wait patiently as Ed goes inside to retrieve this food that he bought for the cat, but the cat does not comprehend the symbolic significance of the raised finger and so runs toward Ed, meowing impatiently all the way, and then, as Ed opens the screen door with his back turned toward the cat, the cat scurries inside.

"Hey, whoa there, cat, this is a private residence," yelps Ed. It's too late, though, because before Ed can figure out what's going on and close the door behind him and put the coffee cup down on the table where he usually puts the mail, the cat has disappeared in the direction of the living room. "Aww, damnit," Ed says, and then he goes in search of the thing. He's in the living room on his hands and knees, scooting around on the hardwood floors in the neighboring dining room, making cat-like noises and saying "here kitty kitty kitty" for five minutes or so before he finds it underneath a china cabinet in between the dining room and the kitchen. The space below the sturdy piece of furniture seems impossibly small to hold a living thing, but there's the cat, staring out at him with glimmering emerald eyes and crying little mews as Ed tries unsuccessfully to cajole it out with idiotic banter that he seems to have borrowed from an eighty-year-old widow.

Two minutes of this, and Ed retreats to the kitchen to retrieve the pricey cat food he bought at Whole Foods on the way home last night. He takes a look at the cans and tries to choose an appropriate flavor for luring a cat out from under a china cabinet. Free Range Hen and Giblets? Filet Mignon Flavor with Shrimp? Halibut Feast? Are they kidding?, Ed wonders. He has a vague memory of a college girlfriend feeding her cat from a bag of what seemed like pebbles. Looking at one can then the other, staring at the little pictures of happy cats on them, figuring that cats like fish, Ed decides on the halibut. He pulls the lid off the can with the handy pull tab and winces with disgust at the slop inside. "This is no halibut that I've ever seen," he says aloud, thinking of the dish he had just two weeks ago for lunch at the Willard, the soft glistening white fish in a sea of watercress coulis, the farm-grown ramps, some sort of heavenly risotto. He dumps the foul stuff into a Tupperware bowl, heads back to the china cabinet, and leaves the food about two feet away from the unit—close enough for the cat to smell the food but far enough away, Ed figures, that if the cat comes out to see what's in the bowl, he might be able to grab it.

He should get back to his work, review the second case for tomorrow, but he needs to call Katelyn first. These days he feels a strong desire to stay in touch with her. If it were possible to keep in constant contact—to shrink her down and store her in his shirt pocket, for instance—he would, for he fears she might be the only thing keeping him from flying off into space like a stray helium balloon at a Fourth of July parade. As he waits for her to answer, he glances quickly at the front page of the *Times*, below the fold, where Farkas has a piece on the biggest cases of the coming term. In the past, he'd probably have devoured the piece first thing in the morning, curious what the experts were thinking about trends at the court and its possible future, but today he has no desire whatsoever to read the article. He thinks: who wants to read about their work when they're not even at work?

"Hi, Dad. How's it going? Sorry I didn't get a chance to call back yesterday. The place was crazy busy, and there was a fuckup with a barramundi shipment and . . .," Katelyn says, by way of a greeting.

"That's fine, no problem," Ed says. "Sounds insane. But 'crazy busy' sounds good, no?"

"Oh, totally. I'd rather it be too busy than too quiet. There's nothing worse than when you can actually hear the silverware sliding against the plates in an empty dining room. And believe me, I've been there," Katelyn answers. "What are you up to today?"

"Well, as I mentioned yesterday, I have a date. Tonight."

"That's right! Where did you decide to take her? The Asian woman. With the funky glasses?"

"I'm taking your advice. The Greedy Llama it is."

"Good choice. It's going to be great. Make sure to have the ceviche. And don't shy away from the hearts. Beef or chicken, both can be excellent if they do them right."

"Delightful. Beef hearts. I'll keep that in mind."

"Hey, doesn't your term start Monday? Shouldn't you be studying?"

"I am, I am, don't worry. I'll be ready. Ready to keep the wheels of justice moving. That's me, mister dependable on the bench. Making the law, so you don't have to. But what's going on with you? How's Bill?" Ed asks, meaning Katelyn's longtime boyfriend who lives with her but does not seem to be interested in getting married anytime soon. Ed thinks again of the helium balloon, this time emblazoned with the word "Grandfather" in dark black ink, floating lazily up into the troposphere, up, up, up, and gone.

"Oh, busy as always. Between my restaurant and his law firm, we see each other about ten minutes a week. From what he texts me, though, things are good, deals are being made." Bill is a high-powered lawyer, but of a very different sort from Ed. A corporate dealmaker at a top-shelf Manhattan firm, practicing mergers and acquisitions, Bill is slick and incredibly rich, but he probably hasn't read a Supreme Court decision since he graduated from NYU law school a dozen years back. Come to think of it, Ed realizes, he might not have read very many Supreme Court decisions while he was *in* law school. From what Katelyn's told him, it sounds like Bill spent most of his law school days drinking and schmoozing. Ed's met Bill only a few times, and each time he's come away from the encounter feeling like his daughter is dating a space alien dressed as a person—one he should seemingly be able to talk to, but somehow never can. "What else is up?"

Ed reaches for something to say. He thinks about inquiring after Sarah—his ex-wife, Katelyn's mother, now remarried to an organic farmer named Harry and living in Marin County—but he knows this is a topic that Katelyn never wants to talk about with him. He settles on a different family-related topic. "Do you remember my uncle Jack?"

"You mean Grandma's brother? The one who lives in Massachusetts? The hoarder guy?"

"Yeah. Though I wouldn't call him a hoarder guy exactly."

"I thought you said that there's only like one and a half rooms in his house that are actually habitable. That the rest are filled with junk from flea markets. Like cuckoo clocks. And old radios that don't work."

"Okay, fine, the hoarder guy. Anyway, he's about to die. I talked to my cousin Jane the other day. She's basically moved into the house to take care of him. I guess he's stopped eating."

"Well, that's too bad. How old is he? Did he ever get remarried?"

"He must be in his mid-eighties. He's been in bad health for a while. No, never got married again. I don't think he ever recovered from Charlotte leaving him. Anyway, I wouldn't expect you to make it up for the funeral."

"Good. I wouldn't expect me to make it up to the funeral either."

"Right."

"So, dad?"

"Yeah?"

"Is everything all right? You seem to be calling a lot more than usual. And you've been sounding kind of weird. Sort of sad, or something."

"What? No, no, I'm fine. I'm really fine," Ed says. He feels a little like he's been found out, silently vows to himself to be more careful, less needy with his daughter. "I'm doing well. I don't know, maybe I've been a little bit lonely lately," he concedes, then winces at having immediately violated his vow of two seconds ago. "But you know, I'm going to try to meet people a little more. Real people, not just people who want to talk to me because of my position. Kind of like I did in

Wyoming. Maybe I'll join a pottery class at the local adult community education center or take a second job at the mall. And I have a date tonight, don't forget."

"How could I forget? All right, then, I won't bring it up again. But if you want to talk or anything, I'm always here. Well, not always. But I can usually scrounge together forty-five seconds for you sometime during the day, in between firing busboys and chewing out Caribbean fish distributors."

"You're too kind," Ed says, happy to be so quickly out of sincere father-daughter talk mode and back into cheerful harmless banter land. "Well, I should get back to work. I am a Supreme Court justice, you know. I have some very important matters to attend to."

"I'm sure you do. It will probably take you an hour just to pick out what to wear on your hot date tonight."

"Actually, what do you think I should wear on my hot date tonight? Do I wear a suit?"

"Dear god no. Definitely no tie. A jacket maybe. So she doesn't see you sweat."

"That's a good idea. Jacket, no tie. I can do that. Thanks, honey."

"You're welcome. Have a great time. Call me tomorrow and tell me how it goes. Unless you're in bed with her all day long. Then don't call me."

"Noted."

***

Ed makes his way back to the kitchen table and takes out the file for Monday's second oral argument. The case is Idaho versus Montana, one of those strange "original jurisdiction" cases where one state sues another directly in the Supreme Court without going through any lower courts first. Ed likes these cases, mostly because they sound like college basketball matchups: Oregon versus Washington, Maine versus New Hampshire, occasionally a non-conference matchup like West Virginia versus California.

The problem, Ed thinks, as he reads through the briefs—the case, like many of these things, is about a border dispute, and it's not that difficult (Montana is clearly going to win this one, will probably even beat the spread)—is that the court always farms out the interesting fact-finding responsibilities to a "special master," some big-time lawyer or law school dean or former judge (even a former justice, from time to time) who gets to hold the hearings and listen to the witnesses and basically decide how the case should come out, subject only to some fairly lenient review from the justices themselves. How much more fun it would be, Ed thinks, if the court could hold the trial itself. It would make for a nice change from deciding everything based just on paper. Back when he was practicing law at the firm, his most exciting times were when he had a case that actually went to trial. It didn't happen often—most of his cases were appeals, and when he did have something that looked like it was going to trial, it usually settled. But those few times were memorable—real people, true emotions, not knowing what was going to happen next, all that tension. A big smile suddenly comes over Ed's face: A trial at the court—maybe he should propose it to the Chief. They could sell tickets! Ed's giddiness, however, is short lived. As soon as he starts imagining the specifics of what a trial at the court might be like, the obvious difficulties present themselves. How could nine people possibly preside over a trial? Who would run the show? Who would make the split-second evidentiary rulings? Would everyone have a gavel?

***

Seven hours later, Ed finds himself seated across from his hot date at a prime table at The Greedy Llama. The place is packed—every table is full, and a line has started snaking out the door. Waiters and waitresses dressed in native Peruvian costumes are bustling every which way, and although they're clearly flustered by the exhausting press of business, they still take their time to make every guest feel welcome and to explain the menu's many items. The room is small and cramped but colorful; bright paintings of llamas (one of which looks suspiciously to Ed like a unicorn) cover the walls, along with the obligatory photographs of magnificent Machu Picchu. Ed is just lamenting never having visited the iconic site when the two Pisco Sours that Diana has insisted upon arrive.

"Hmmm, okay, what's in this thing?" Ed asks, picking up the hefty cocktail glass and examining its pale greenish-yellow contents. He puts his nose right up close to the drink's frothy top and inhales, then cringes.

"Well, Pisco is a South American brandy, and I think they usually mix it with lemon and sugar and an egg white."

"Egg white? Is that what this is? I thought maybe it was steamed milk or something. What's this brown stuff on the top? Maple syrup?"

"I think it's bitters. Try it, it's good. I drank about a hundred of them when I was in Peru a few years ago."

Ed takes a sip. It's not good, he thinks. But this is his first date in six weeks, and he seriously needs the booze, so he takes a big drink. "All right, this is pretty good," he lies. "What was Peru like?"

And so the conversation turns to Diana's trip to Peru—a conference on sacred religious texts held in Lima back in 2007, extended into a pleasure trip to Cusco and the famous ruins with an old friend from graduate school who now occupies a chair in South Asian Civilizations at the University of Illinois. Since the trip lasted only a week, Ed points out that Diana must have thrown down about fourteen cocktails a day, to which she responds, with a clink of her glass, "at least." He laughs out loud, suddenly realizing that he's feeling relaxed for the first time since leaving his house over an hour ago.

The waitress comes over, and they order another round. Ed says he's heard the mixed heart platter is supposed to be good, so they get one of those as well. Diana is impressed that his daughter is a semi-famous chef and asks about her training, which sends Ed reeling into a well-practiced series of riffs on Katelyn's tumultuous early career—the year in Alsace apprenticed to the one-eyed cheesemonger, the arthropod cooking short course in northern Thailand, the tough first few months in New York. Ed inquires about Diana's children and learns that one is in the Bay Area, stuck in an interminable series of neuroscience postdocs, while the other has just moved to London to try out some sort of an international business consulting career. As the second drinks arrive, and Diana finishes describing the outlandish cost of a four-hundred-square-foot flat in Highbury, Ed notices that she has become distracted with something to her left; her eyes—strikingly made up in dark eye-shadow and lurking behind those red-rimmed indeed fantastically funky glasses—keep leaving him and flitting over to the far side of the restaurant.

"Is everything okay?" he asks, taking a bitter eggy sip of the new Pisco Sour that has just arrived. "What are you looking at?"

"I think somebody recognizes you. There's a guy over there who keeps looking over here and then whispering to his date."

Ed takes a quick peek. The guy is definitely looking at him. Probably a law student or something. "Yeah, well, that happens sometimes. Not often, but once in a while."

"I think you should wink at him."

"So he can tweet about it? It will be all over the web that I'm winking at male strangers before our beef hearts even arrive."

"Is it weird? I mean, I feel strange when I see a student in a coffee shop or something. It must be weird getting noticed by total strangers in public."

"It sounds cliché, I realize, but I'm actually used to it by now. And it doesn't happen all that much. I could go on six dates to The Greedy Llama and only be recognized once."

"Have you gone on five dates here already? Is this your go-to first date destination?"

"Ha! I haven't been on a date in six weeks. And I only just heard about this place yesterday."

"So, what's it like? Being a Supreme Court justice? It must be incredible."

Ed's taken back by the directness of the question. He's not sure how to answer. "Yeah, sure, it's pretty great, I guess."

"Pretty great? That's your description? I mean, you're sitting up there on that big bench, making the biggest legal decisions in the country, in the world. You have experiences that almost nobody else in the world has. It must be entirely surreal."

"Doesn't everyone have their own unique experiences?" he wonders aloud. "Maybe my life isn't any more surreal than any other life."

"Well, okay. Fair enough," she says, and the beef hearts arrive. As they place their entrée orders—Ed asks for the classic ceviche, while Diana decides on the rotisserie chicken with fried yucca—Ed feels kind of bad about his short reaction to Diana's question, like he has cut off an interesting conversation for no good reason.

"Don't get me wrong," he says when the waitress has left to put in their order, "it's a fabulous job. I'm unbelievably lucky to have it. There are a thousand people more qualified than I am for it, at least. Bash, for one, which is something I assure you he is quite aware of. And there have been times when I've loved it. Mostly at the beginning. And mostly when I'm working on a case that involves figuring out the answer to some complicated puzzle—not one of these high-profile constitutional things where I feel totally at sea, trying to decide whether people should have the right to look at porn or whatever. How the hell am I supposed to know how to decide that? What am I, fucking Aristotle or something? And then you get piles of hate mail no matter how you decide. No, those cases I could do without."

He notices from Diana's changed expression that he's said something fairly interesting and not particularly expected. *Note to self,* he thinks: Do not take the stage for a public conversation on judging after drinking two hefty Pisco Sours. "Umm, if you wouldn't mind not mentioning what I just said to anyone on earth, that would be great."

Now it's her turn to cackle, and the high-pitched screech that comes out of her attracts the attention of most, if not all, of the surrounding tables. Certainly the young law student in the corner is looking over with great interest. Ed's eyebrows shoot up toward the roof. Diana puts a napkin over her mouth and giggles.

"Sorry. It was just funny seeing you realize that you had said something more or less impeachable."

"Yeah, I guess. Maybe these drinks are stronger than I thought," he answers, draining the last of his glass and looking around for the waitress to get another.

"I find it interesting hearing you talk about this. I'd assumed that you would naturally love every minute of your job. I guess all jobs have their problems, I know mine does," she says, and that, apparently, is reason for her to drain her drink as well.

"I guess it goes to show that even the best job can get you down if that's all you do for eight straight years. Once in a while I even play with the idea of retiring and doing something else. But what's the problem with being a professor? That always seemed like the greatest gig to me—researching whatever you want, teaching some here and there, traveling all summer long. Bash seems to like it, and he doesn't like anything. No?"

"Ppphhh," she says, and rolls her eyes. A small drop of cold Pisco lands on her deep red lower lip, and Ed suddenly wishes he could lean over the plate of steaming beef hearts and slurp it right up. The date, he realizes, is going well.

"What is it that you write about again?" Ed asks. "Taoism? What is that exactly?"

"Don't you guys have cases about religion? Church-state separation, and whatnot?"

"Rarely do we get a case involving Taoism. I think we might have mentioned it once. In a footnote. In 1932 maybe."

"Okay, point taken. It's sort of a mixture between religion and philosophy. Kind of hard to explain. My work these days is mainly on a guy named Chuang Tzu, who's the second most famous of the Taoists. Right after Lao Tzu. You've heard of Lao Tzu, right?"

Ed thinks he might have heard of Lao Tzu once. Maybe not. "Sure, yeah, I think so," he answers.

Diana looks at him funny. She's hip to his jive. "Well, anyway, Chuang Tzu believed that it was impossible to make sense of anything using logic or reason. He believed in the importance of spontaneity and said that you can never know what's truly real. He's lovely, truly lovely. I'm working on a new translation of one of his most important chapters. I'll have to lend you a book—there's no way I could explain him to you here."

"Okay, that'd be great. I need to expand my horizons. But I think you've made my point, haven't you? Being a professor is the perfect job."

"If I could spend all my time writing about Chuang Tzu, maybe. But it turns out that thinking and writing is only about ten percent of the job. If I have to negotiate one more departmental drama, or tenure battle, or worry about some colleague's tender ego, or lead a search committee for two years with no results because the chair suddenly decides he wants to hire an expert in theological ethics instead

of Christology, I think I'm going to quit and get a job at the mall."
Ed's eyes widen. "And the students, oh my god the students. Do you
know how entitled these kids think they are these days? I actually got
an email from a parent the other day asking about her kid's grade. A
parent! What is this, fucking elementary school?"

"*Now* who's going to get impeached?" Ed asks, putting his hand on
hers in what any objective observer would have cautioned is a relatively
risky move. But it works. She squeezes his hand and smiles. "I'm going
to use the ladies room," she says, picking up her empty glass. "Will you
get me another one of these if the waitress comes by?"

"Absolutely," Ed says. He keeps his eyes fixed on her as she folds up
her napkin, puts it on the table, gets out of her chair, and spins around
to look for the bathroom. He watches her closely, admires her shimmery red skirt—whimsically ruffled with the bottom cut at an upward
angle from left to right, exactly the opposite, he notices, as the way her
night-black longish hair is cut in the back at an upward angle from
right to left. She's a woman, he thinks, made out of triangles. And
speaking of triangles, is that the slightest of panty lines he discerns as
she walks away? He eats a beef heart. *Tumescence.*

***

Two hours later, Ed and Diana are in front of her Georgetown townhouse, heading in for a nightcap, and she's fiddling with her keys, trying in the dark to find the one that will open the top lock, when Ed
leans in and kisses her. She's surprised at first but quickly warms to
the idea, turning her head toward him to return the kiss full on. Some
moments later, he steps back, his hands on both of her shoulders, and
murmurs some sort of apology, one that both of them know is unnecessary. They're leaning against the door, trying to take in what's just
happened, when Diana instinctively turns the key clockwise in the
lock. The door opens suddenly inward, sending the two late-middle
aged adults with imperfect knees and creaky lower backs reeling into
the foyer. Diana screeches and drops the leftovers. Ed trips over the
leftovers and careens into a wall. Diana clicks a light switch and looks
to see if Ed is all right. The townhouse now lit up, Ed takes a gander
around and is mightily impressed.

"Wow, this is some place," he comments. "Yeah," Diana responds. "I guess you could say I made out pretty well in the divorce."

While they remove their coats and shoes, a fluffy white cat emerges. "Who's this little four-legged fluffmeister?" Ed asks.

"That's Midnight," she answers. Ed looks at her and rolls his eyes. "Yes, I know it's a cliché joke, but my son insisted."

The cat approaches Ed, and Ed pats its head. "I have a cat," he says. "Really? What kind?"

"Umm, I don't, uhh, know. Orange-ish. Actually I don't have a cat."

"You have a cat or you don't have a cat?"

"I'm kind of taking care of a cat for someone. Except the person doesn't know I'm taking care of it. But the cat seems to like the arrangement. Does that matter?"

Diana smiles and excuses herself to do something up on the second floor. While she's gone, Ed wanders around the living room to see what he can see about this woman he's found himself drawn to so quickly. The room is stylishly—probably professionally—put together. It's fairly minimalist, dominated by a strikingly enormous textured white rug and an onyx-colored grand piano. Inlaid bookshelves surround a slate gray couch that appears to be a place often used—there's one of those comically low coffee tables in front of it with a lipstick-rimmed tea cup and a stack of well-read, post-it-marked books on top. Bending down carefully, he looks at the spines of the books—some appear to be in Chinese, others in English. He's distractedly reading over and over some story about a fish that turns into a bird and flies away into the heavens when Diana returns with two snifters and a bottle of dark liquid and puts them down on the table before him.

"So you've found *The Chuang Tzu* already. Do you feel transformed?"

He puts down the book, feels strangely like he's been caught doing something wrong. "Maybe a little," he says, "but not by the book." He thought the line was smooth, but looking at Diana's blank reaction, he's not so sure.

"Before I forget, let me give you a copy. A good translation. I can't give you any of these, because I need them for my work, but I have others." She pads over to one of the bookshelves farther away and starts thumbing through their contents. "Pour us some brandy while I'm looking."

He looks at the bottle, opens it, takes a sniff. He's not a big brandy drinker, but the Pisco worked out fine, and apparently that was brandy, so he figures why not. He pours them small portions and re-corks the bottle. "Aha," she says from the other side of the room near the piano, pulling out a small book with a solid burnt orange color and waving it high over her shoulder. "This is perfect. A great early translation of the Inner Chapters. I'll put it by your coat so you won't forget it."

When she returns to the couch, they sip brandy and quickly fall back into kissing. Before long the kissing accelerates to include some hair caressing, a little button fiddling, and even a bit of neck nibbling. When they come up for air, they pause, smile at each other, laugh a little. Diana takes off her half-already-removed jacket and then leans back in to Ed, who is disappointed to learn that removal of the jacket has not gotten him all that much closer to Diana's bare skin. She's done the thing that so many women do these days—the wearing of many thin layers between their breasts and the outside world—something Ed has always found unattractive and distressing. As the kissing resumes, he runs his fingers over the various fabrics on Diana's shoulder and counts three. There's a bra down there somewhere, but it's underneath a white blouse and, worst of all, a white tank top, the kind that always reminds him of his grandfather, his mother's dad, a/k/a Paw-Paw, a/k/a Grandpa Artie from Long Island.

Uh oh, Ed thinks, as memories of his childhood take up unwelcome residence in his head. He tries to banish the images as best he can, but the terrible tank top makes it impossible. Ed flashes back to hot summer weeks spent with family at his grandparents' modest old-fashioned split-level, splashing around in their round above-ground pool, listening to the hated Yankees on a transistor radio, guzzling copious amounts of iced tea, playing board games until late in the evening. The whole summer his grandfather wouldn't put on a proper shirt a single time, always wandering around the yard in his yellowed ribbed tank top undershirt and maybe a hose to spray the flowers or a beer to cool down from the steaming heat.

As Ed's hands wander over Diana's body he cannot shake the image of ol' Paw-Paw, that bushy bustle of hair blossoming out over the top of the frayed undershirt, the way that after dinner he would usually remove his similarly tattered canvas shorts and spend the rest of the night in his decades-old underpants, burping. Suddenly, Ed realizes that his cock, which had been on alert all night long (at dinner, Ed had worried it might actually rap up against the bottom of the table and spill the pisco sours all over both of them), has lost its mojo. He suddenly wonders whether maybe he had hallucinated that panty line he thought he spied at the restaurant. Perhaps under that shimmery red skirt, Diana is actually sporting a pair of loose-fitting yellowed boxer shorts originally purchased in a three-pack from a department store in the mid-1950s.

This image is the last straw, and Ed suddenly pulls away. Diana clearly realizes that something is up.

"What?" she asks, with some urgency. "What's wrong?"

"Umm, uhh," Ed stammers, tries to think of what he should say, quickly rejects the notion of explaining that she reminds him of his half-clad dead grandfather. "I don't know, maybe we shouldn't do this yet."

"What? Are you sure? Why?"

"Would you hate me if I said that I thought we should take it slow?" he asks, channeling some cheesy television drama he might have watched a lifetime ago. "I had a great time with you tonight, and I feel sort of like we might ruin it if we move too fast. I know I sound like a sixteen-year-old girl, sorry."

"No, no, I understand, okay," Diana says, disappointed but not overly so. She reaches for her jacket and drapes it around her shoulders. "All right. Maybe you're right."

"What if I promise to call you tomorrow and make another date, maybe for next week sometime?"

"Well, only if you want to."

"Absolutely, I totally want to," he says, and he means it. He kisses her, and it's a good kiss, and this eases her worries somewhat. "I promise I'll call you tomorrow."

They both get up and straighten themselves. Ed walks to the foyer and slips his shoes on. As he bends over to tie them, Midnight strolls by. Ed pats the cat's head, and she takes a swipe at him. "Whoa," Ed exclaims, standing up quickly. Diana misses the encounter, but when she inquires about his yell, Ed doesn't feel it's the right time to be dishing out shit about her cat. He murmurs something about stubbing his toe before putting on his coat and slipping the orange book into his pocket. A few last words of farewell, one last kiss, and then Ed is out the door and into the night, in search of a cab that will deliver him home.

FOUR

IT IS THE FIRST MONDAY IN OCTOBER, AND SO THE NEW
term of the Supreme Court of the United States officially begins. Following the morning-coated Marshal's opening call of *Oyez Oyez* and
his bit about all those having business before the court being admon-
ished to come near and then the constitutionally questionable piece
about God saving the honorable court, the robed justices emerge from
behind thick red velvet curtains and take their seats behind the grand
bench in the court's ostentatious main chamber. This is the room that
the architect Cass Gilbert designed in the 1920s with marble secured
from Italy with Mussolini's help and mahogany stripped from fragile
Honduran rain forests. Twenty-four thirty-foot-high marble columns
circle the chamber's perimeter; lines of dark wood pews sit on rich red
and gold rugs in the room's center. Enormous marble friezes flank the
room from atop the columns, depicting a veritable parade of lawgivers
from Confucius to Moses to Mohammed to Napoleon on the north
and south walls and allegorical representations of justice and virtue
and all sorts of other top-notch stuff on the east and west.

By tradition, the justices are seated by seniority. The Chief is in the
middle. Ed sits in the second to last chair on the Chief's left, between
Cornelius on his right and Epps on his left. He places his materials
down on the bench before him and looks out over the courtroom. It
is always a bit of a rush to come out here for the first time after the
long summer, to look out at the sea of spectators—hushed silent by
intimidating officers, chewing gum practically snatched out of their
mouths by these uniformed bullies—sitting expectantly before him,
the members of the press huddling together in their appointed bullpen

to the justices' right side, looking up at the bench to see if any of the judges have changed appearance over the past few months. Is Cornelius sporting a beard this fall? Does Leibowitz look even frailer than usual? How's Epps handling that extra weight? Ed turns toward the bullpen and smiles. He sees Farkas and Julie Anderson from the *Post* and gives them just the tiniest of waves, for which they seem grateful. For the moment, anyway, Ed feels content, almost happy, sitting up here on his grandiose juridical perch, settling in for the beginning of his ninth term on the high court.

After a few preliminaries—the court clerk swears in a group of lawyers to the Supreme Court bar, the Chief notes with sadness the passing of the court's eighty-two-year-old barber over the summer—the argument begins. The first to argue in the environmental case is the acting solicitor general, a baby-faced forty-one-year-old named Bill Crenshaw whose meteoric rise through the government ranks has court watchers pegging him as a possible future pick for the bench, although Ed happens to know that the guy has stepped on so many toes on his way up that the Senate probably wouldn't confirm him even if he were nominated. Crenshaw approaches the lectern, smooths his starchy morning coat, and begins to speak.

"It is the government's position in this case that the state of California's program for giving financial subsidies to cities that adopt low-emission taxicab fleets constitutes a 'standard' under section 209 of the Clean Air Act and is therefore preempted by the federal law," Crenshaw begins.

"Ahh, yes, well," DeLillo interrupts. These days a lawyer is lucky to get out a single sentence before one of the justices butts in. "The question is what does the word 'standard' really mean? I looked it up myself, and the dictionary said it was an old jazz tune, like something Ella Fitzgerald might have scatted."

At this, the gallery erupts in laughter. Not to be outdone, Justice Cornelius breaks into his version of an Ella Fitzgerald scat. "A rat-a-tat bah bah boo beeee shmooo bap yeah," which causes the audience to laugh uproariously.

Ed can hardly stand the inanity and shakes his head in disbelief. A few years back, a law professor with too much time on his hands wrote a "study" of how many times each justice got the gallery to erupt in what the argument transcript refers to as "[laughter]" and ever since, DeLillo and Cornelius have been openly competing for the mantle of funniest justice, a title that Ed thinks is about as meaningful as sauciest economist or fattest astronaut. In recent terms, the two dimwits have stepped up their game, shamelessly making so-called "jokes" that have nothing whatsoever to do with the case at hand. Ed wouldn't be overly shocked if one day DeLillo responded to some lawyer's weak argument by screaming "for me to poop on," only to have Cornelius follow up by pulling out a mallet and smashing a watermelon to smithereens all over the lawyers and the first three rows of the gallery.

Having argued before the court over fifteen times already, Crenshaw is used to such shenanigans from the bench, and he continues his argument unfazed, without himself falling prey to the idiocy. Soon, the discussion turns to a serious parsing of the statute's language and the Act's legislative history and some fine points of preemption doctrine, and before long Ed has tuned out. He is thinking about his date with Diana and how he needs to call her to set up a second date just as soon as the morning's business is over. He had arrived home by taxi late Saturday night and tried in vain to masturbate to an image of the back of Diana's head bouncing up and down on his lap, her silky black hair tickling the whites of his inner thighs, but he couldn't keep the vision of her head from periodically morphing into the back of Paw-Paw's head instead, with its meaty red neck folds and wiry curls of ear hair and that dark brown chunk of a growth, practically a mushroom, protruding from the top of his misshapen skull. Luckily, though, by late Sunday afternoon, a long day of case preparation and football watching behind him, Ed was finally able to banish his grandfather back to the deep dark mental crevasse from where he had emerged. Managing an uninterrupted and surprisingly complicated fantasy involving not just Diana but also the super hot weather lady from the metro Washington area ABC affiliate and some chocolate cookie dough, Ed ejaculated magnificently all over his six-hundred-thread-count navy blue fitted sheets and immediately vowed to call up Diana just as soon as Monday morning's arguments are in the books.

On the bench, Ed drifts in and out of the argument, occasionally able to focus on a point or two, but for the most part hearing only the *waahh waahh waahh* of a Peanuts cartoon grownup. He does manage to tune in for long enough to ask California's lawyer a technical question about how her state's voluntary emission incentive program works, not because he is truly curious about the program's operation—indeed, Ed pretty much knows the answer to his question already—but rather because he wants to make sure his colleagues understand this key aspect of the program. It is a little-known fact among those whose lives do not center around the court that most of the questions the justices ask are attempts to persuade their colleagues of one thing or another and not sincere attempts to figure out how they should rule in the case.

Soon, the first argument ends and the second begins. Although Ed generally likes these border dispute cases, he can't keep his mind from wandering, and soon he is doodling pictures of Idaho on the back of the petitioner's brief. Quickly he realizes that he can't remember whether the part that sticks up toward Canada is on the east or the west side of the state. Does the fat part stick out toward Oregon or Montana? He draws them both ways and still isn't sure. The arguing attorney worriedly glances in Ed's direction when she sees Ed shaking his head; she has no idea he's dismayed at his own geographical stupidity and not whatever she's saying. Ed draws faces on both of the Idahos—cartoonish eyes, wide silly smiles, button noses—and dialogue bubbles so they can talk to each other. "Are you facing the right way or am I?" asks the Idaho with the thin part sticking up on the left. "How the hell do I know?" the other one responds. "I hate myself," replies the first one.

It's because I don't have to actually know anything about Idaho to decide this case, Ed thinks, almost aloud, and he comes back to what he was thinking about on Saturday—his idea that the justices should take a more active role in resolving these state versus state controversies. The real questions in the case are actually interesting—how far from the original banks of the river between the two states are the banks now, did the people on one side of the river think they lived in Idaho back in the nineteenth century, and so on—but only if you're the one actually doing the research out there under the big sky and definitely not if you're just sitting inside behind a giant bench (even if that bench *is* carved from the last remaining trees in the Honduran rain forest) and reading about them in thick sheaths of paper filled with citations to other thick sheaths of paper and so on and so on. At least if the court were actually holding the trial itself instead of reviewing the report of the guy who heard the witnesses and looked at the maps and probably even camped out by the river in the early fall as the tourists headed back to their offices on the East Coast and the days got shorter and just a little chillier—then Ed could feel like he was having an actual experience, like he was *present*, wouldn't that be nice? The idea excites him. He puts down his pen, and without any regard for the fact that Justice Epps is in the middle of asking one of his typically convoluted and unilluminating hypotheticals—one that nobody in the gallery, not even his colleagues, and certainly not the arguing lawyer, is following in the least—Ed blurts out the question he's been thinking about now for days.

"Umm, excuse me, counsel," he starts, and his voice comes across so clear and sure that Justice Epps, perhaps sensing that his question wasn't going to help anything anyway, stops mid-sentence and yields the bench without complaint. "What would you think if we stopped relying on special masters to prepare recommendations on these original jurisdiction cases and heard the facts ourselves? Would you support that change in practice?"

The question throws the lawyer—the attorney general for Montana, a short-haired woman in her fifties sporting a fairly conservative blue suit punctuated by an alarming turquoise necklace—for the proverbial loop. "I'm sorry, Justice Tuttle," she says, swiveling her head from one side of the bench to the other to address Ed. "Could you restate the question?"

"My question is whether you, as an attorney general of a state, would support us—the justices of this court, that is—if we were to reassert our role as the primary fact-finders in these original jurisdiction state versus state cases?"

The lawyer crinkles her forehead. Is this a joke? she wonders. "Well, Justice Tuttle, do you mean that the court would sit as sort of a trial judge in the case? Hearing testimony? Ruling on evidence? That sort of thing?"

"That's right," Ed answers. "Why not? That's what the Constitution seems to call for, doesn't it? Usually, when we say that a court has 'original jurisdiction' over a matter, it means that they hear the evidence themselves, right? Why shouldn't we do the same thing?"

"I, well, umm . . . I don't know," the lawyer stammers. "I've never thought about it. I'm not sure how it would work." For a moment the courtroom is entirely quiet. The gallery doesn't seem to know what's happening. Over in the journalist bay, Farkas looks at his colleague from the *Post* and silently mouths "what's going on?" To which she noiselessly responds, "I don't know."

DeLillo breaks the silence. "Justice Tuttle has raised an intriguing suggestion. Irrelevant, certainly, but intriguing nonetheless. I wonder, though, how my brother Tuttle would have us rule on evidentiary objections? Would it take a majority to overrule an objection? Would we each have our own gavel? *Bang, bang*?"

The laughter that explodes at DeLillo's question—and the gavel-banging pantomime that goes with it—is probably worth two "[laughter]"s in the professor's standings, at least if the laughing is measured in length and the number of times that people in the gallery look at each other and mimic DeLillo's *bang bang* with great mirth. Ed throws his hands up in the air in frustration, but nobody notices. When the laughter finally dies down, Justice Epps continues with his unhelpful hypothetical, and from there the argument proceeds, and then ends, without anything much further of interest.

***

After oral arguments, the justices retire to the conference room to discuss the cases. The senior member of the majority—usually the Chief, but sometimes these days Justice Stephenson, as the senior member of the court's left wing—decides who will write the opinion in the case, which means that the justices with the most seniority end up writing the most interesting cases and the junior people write the opinions in the boring cases involving, say, whether the Clean Air Act preempts certain state laws about taxi cabs. Then there's usually lunch. Today, however, Ed is in and out of the conference room quickly—the cases are easy to decide and assign, and Ed has little appetite for lunch, especially because his colleagues keep giving him a hard time about his line of questioning at oral argument, and also because he is eager to get back to his office and call Diana. When Cornelius puts his arm around Ed's shoulder, hammers the air with his free hand, and yells *bang, bang* in a far too loud voice directly into Ed's left ear, Ed decides that's his cue to leave, so he makes an excuse about an appointment and takes off.

Back in chambers, the clerks and Linda have clearly been talking about Ed, as he can tell since they all immediately stop talking and turn to look at him, sitcom style, when he walks through the door and puts his files down on the first table he sees.

"Oh, no, not you guys too," Ed says. "The first person to say *bang bang* gets fired immediately."

"What? Oh, no, no, we weren't talking about that," Dawn the law clerk says, unpersuasively.

"No, we were talking about, umm," Linda flounders, "the umm . . ."

"The response in the blogosphere to the *Sexy Slut* grant," Rick offers. "The pundits seem genuinely surprised."

"And worried," Dawn interjects.

"As they should be," Ed says. He's not convinced that they were talking about the *Sexy Slut* case, but he plays along anyway. "I have a feeling the world might be coming to an end, and it's all going to start right here. Any messages?"

If Linda finds Ed's premonition alarming, it's impossible to tell from her professional demeanor, as she takes a pink slip from out of a shirt pocket. "Yes, Greg Bash called," she reads. "He says you should give him a call, and also he says to tell you *bang bang.*"

"I'll kill him."

Ed grabs the pink slip away from Linda and crumples it up, shoots it at a faraway trash can, hits the rim and out. Then he wordlessly scoops up his files and disappears into his inner sanctum. Linda and the clerks look at each other, shrug their shoulders, and head back to work.

Diana is not in her office, so Ed leaves her a message, one that he's quite pleased with. He apologizes for the previous night, but not pathetically, then asks her out on another date, perhaps for Wednesday night, when the week's arguments have ended and McCoy Tyner is in town for a show at the Howard Theater, and ends by saying "please say hi to Midnight for me" in such a perfect deadpan that he's tempted to go buy a bottle of champagne and toast it.

Ed considers calling Bash back, but he's not in the mood for the cranky nutcase. What to do instead? He walks to his desk and scans the piles on top. Files for the rest of the cases this week. A stack of clerk- ship applications. Pages of a draft for a talk he's giving to the American Bar Association in a couple of weeks. The sight of it all nearly makes Ed weep. What does interest him, though, is the slim orange volume that Diana gave him Saturday night. Some sort of abstract picture of an ancient horseman graces the cover and reminds him of the rodeo he went to over the summer with one of his young Wyoming lady friends. Ed had managed to live sixty-some years without ever having attended a rodeo, so when forty-three-year-old divorced mother of three finan- cial analyst Amy suggested they check it out, he agreed. They drank cans of Bud Light and rooted on the bull riders, cheered for the rope throwers, gasped at several near-death experiences, then went home and fucked like bucking broncos. Ed's decision is made. He grabs the book and zips out of his office. A quick farewell to Linda, and a minute later he's outside, striding briskly through the crisp autumn afternoon without any clear idea where he's going.

After a few minutes' walk down Maryland Avenue, he finds himself in a small park where he takes a seat on a bench. He closes his eyes and lets what's still left of the October sun warm his face; Ed Tuttle is tired. Thinking about it for a bit, he decides that what he really wants to do is lay down. The bench would be uncomfortable, but the ground is grassy, seems to be free of used hypodermic needles, and so would do fine. He takes off his dark suit jacket and balls it up a bit, puts it down for a pillow, stretches out on the ground, closes his eyes, and breathes.

Maybe a minute goes by before Ed opens his eyes. He looks up at the sky, plays the "what does the cloud look like?" game. There's a duck, a horse, Maine's northern coastline. He closes his eyes again and tries to fall asleep but quickly realizes it won't work. What the hell am I doing lying on the ground in the middle of a park, he says to himself, then calls an end to the silliness. He stands up, drapes the suit jacket over the back of the bench, and sits down. A few minutes pass and a young woman, maybe early thirties, sits on a bench across the path from him. She's got a book in one hand and some kind of wrap in the other. Ed immediately thinks: *she is hot.* Mid-length smooth blond hair, khaki skirt, stylish royal blue button-down shirt, sleeves rolled up slightly to reveal creamy forearms, a jangle of silver bracelets on one of them. Ed's got a thing for forearms, and so he imagines caressing hers with his fingers, playfully twiddling the bracelets, picking the arm up and rubbing it lightly on his forehead and cheeks and closed eyes, kissing it gently. He's got to stop; his erection is visible through his dark slacks if anyone cared to look. For a minute, he consoles himself with the thought that other sixty-year-old-men (okay, fine, sixty-two) need a blue pill to get what he can achieve these days just by glancing at a relatively nice-looking female for half a second.

What could dispel an unwanted boner faster than a little ancient Chinese philosophy, Ed figures, so he takes his eyes off the young lady and opens his book.

Once Chuang dreamt he was a butterfly, a butterfly flitting and fluttering around, happy with himself and doing as he pleased. He didn't know he was Chuang Tzu. Suddenly he woke up and there he was, solid and unmistakable Chuang Tzu. But he didn't know if he was Chuang Tzu who had dreamt he was a butterfly, or a butterfly dreaming he was Chuang Tzu. Between Chuang Tzu and a butterfly there must be some distinction! This is called the Transformation of Things.

Ed lifts his gaze back to the blonde on the bench and wonders how one would go about trying to pick up a woman such as this without any shared experience to talk about or alcohol to move things along. She's not married at least; the first part of any woman he looks at these days is always the left ring finger, and this one's naked. He figures he should just say hello, and that's what he does. She looks at him curiously and says hello back through a mouthful of lettuce. "What's your book?" he asks. "Just some novel a friend recommended," she answers, showing him the front cover. "Any good?" he asks. "It's okay, I guess," she says.

She shows no interest in carrying on a conversation, so Ed returns to the *Chuang Tzu*.

> *There is a beginning. There is not yet beginning to be a beginning. There is a not yet beginning to be a not yet beginning to be a beginning. There is being. There is nonbeing. There is a not yet beginning to be nonbeing. There is a not yet beginning to be a not yet beginning to be nonbeing. Suddenly there is being and nonbeing. But between this being and nonbeing, I don't really know which is being and which is nonbeing. Now I have just said something. But I don't know whether what I have said has really said something or whether it hasn't said something.*

There's got to be some way to capture this cutie pie's interest, Ed thinks, but he doesn't know how. He considers blurting out that he's a Supreme Court justice, but he realizes how obnoxious that would sound. Probably she wouldn't even believe him. But then again he could tell her to look him up on her little smartphone, and in five seconds his identity would be confirmed. But still—obnoxious. And yet. "I guess the Supreme Court started its term this morning," he says. His object of interest looks up. "Ugh," she says. "I wish they'd all retire, so we could start over."

Ed thinks this is a bad sign. "Not a fan, huh?"

"Can't stand them. Did you hear they're probably going to ban pornography now? Just what we need, a bunch of old fogies deciding what we can read or watch."

He's tempted to explain that they've decided no such thing, but he restrains himself. "Some of them are okay, though, don't you think? The old lady's pretty good, right? And that Tuttle guy, he's not bad."

"They're all terrible," she says, putting up her hand and waving it around like the court is a mosquito that needs to be swatted away. She looks at her phone, taps it a few times. "I better get back to the office. Nice talking to you."

That went well, Ed thinks to himself. "Have a good rest of the day," he says, as she packs up her stuff and walks away.

Chuang Tzu and Hui Tzu were strolling along the dam of the Hao River when Chuang Tzu said, "See how the minnows come out and dart around where they please! That's what fish really enjoy."

Hui Tzu said, "You're not a fish—how do you know what fish enjoy?"

Chuang Tzu said, "You're not I, so how do you know I don't know what fish enjoy?"

Hui Tzu said, "I'm not you, so I certainly don't know what you know. On the other hand, you're certainly not a fish—so that still proves you don't know what fish enjoy!"

Chuang Tzu said, "Let's go back to your original question, please. You asked me how I know what fish enjoy—so you already knew I knew it when you asked the question. I know it by standing here beside the Hao."

"Oh, shut the fuck up," Ed says out loud, and he slams the book closed.

***

Wednesday night, Ed and Diana are at a bar in Georgetown, where they've headed after McCoy Tyner has finished tickling the keys at the Howard. Ed has a hankering for a top-notch single malt, so he orders a glass of twenty-five-year-old McCallan, despite the forty-five-dollar price tag. What good is it to be a Supreme Court justice, he reasons, if you can't from time to time spend a small fortune on two ounces of old brown liquid? Diana claims that she prefers bourbon to scotch—actually that she can't stand scotch—and orders some kind of single barrel something or other that Ed has never heard of.

Five minutes later the drinks arrive, and Ed takes a deep sniff of his, then grabs Diana's glass and sniffs that.

"It's like a nightmare in a glass," he says, returning it to her with a grimace.

"No, it's delicious," she says, taking a sip. She savors it for a moment, then picks up Ed's scotch and takes a drink.

"Hey," he exclaims. "You owe me eight bucks for that sip."

"It's actually not bad," she says.

"Maybe your aversion to scotch stems from drinking too many Passport and sodas in frat house basements back in the seventies."

"Yeah, lots of frat houses at Smith."

"Fair point."

Diana reaches across the table and takes Ed's hand. "That piano player was incredible," she says. "Thanks for taking me. I know almost nothing about jazz."

"Tyner is amazing. I've seen him a few times, but not for a while. He's gotten so old. When he was talking to the audience, it seemed like he was about to keel over and die right in front of us. Then he sits down at the piano, and it's like *whoa*."

"And he's playing another show right after? I teach one class and I need to take a two-hour nap."

"I tried to take a nap on the ground in a park the other day. It didn't work."

"Too bad. You might have woken up surrounded by gawkers pointing at the Supreme Court justice sleeping on the ground. Your picture would have been on *Huffington Post*. Drooling all over your cheek."

"I think you greatly exaggerate the extent to which anyone knows who I am or gives two shits about it."

"I think maybe you greatly underestimate your *Huffington Post* worthiness."

"So after I got up from the ground I started reading your *Chuang Tzu*."

"Yeah? What did you think?"

"I don't know. Chuang Chou who dreams he is a butterfly but thinks he might be a butterfly dreaming he's Chuang Chou? I dreamt I was being attacked by a lion last night, but when I woke up in my bed I was definitely me who had been dreaming of being attacked by a lion and not me being attacked by a lion dreaming I was in my bed."

"Maybe you are the lion."

"I think I'm just a guy who is worried about what to do with the cat that is apparently now living with me."

"I still don't understand. This is not actually your cat?"

"I'm taking care of it for a while. Well, I guess 'taking care' of it isn't quite right. I kind of stole it."

Diana: wrinkled brow, look of concern. "You stole it?"

"Stole it, borrowed it, something like that. But the guy who owns the cat is out of the country. He's my neighbor. I'll give the cat back to him when he gets home. Maybe."

"Who's the guy?"

His name is Savin LaPierre, he writes articles for *The Atlantic* and places like that, written a couple of books criticizing basically everybody who works for the government. He's a real prick actually, very earnest type, thinks of himself as the last bulwark against the corruption of the modern world. Or something like that. Have you heard of him?"

"I don't think so."

"He doesn't like me at all, of course, because I'm part of the problem. Upholding the oligarchy of the privileged white man and everything."

"Doesn't he live in a big house in McLean?"

"Exactly," Ed says, tipping his glass in Diana's direction as if to toast her prescient remark, then tipping it back to take a drink. "The worst story about him is when Katelyn was about to graduate from high school, and she messed up and got caught drinking with some friends during a school event, maybe three days before graduation, and it was a big deal, and the principal decided that she couldn't walk during the ceremony but that she could graduate. This was when my wife and I were first separated, and of course Katelyn was kind of a mess because of it and was acting up. Anyway, this Savin guy actually came up to me to tell me that he thought Katelyn should have been expelled on principle and that she should have had to do her senior year again at some other school and reapply to college. I wanted to punch the guy in the fucking throat."

"You didn't actually punch the guy in the fucking throat though?"

"I didn't. I just turned and walked away. We've barely said ten words to each other ever since. Well, except for the oak tree lawn mowing border incident of 2011."

"Hmm." Diana drinks from her bourbon. "Just to play devil's advocate for a minute, isn't deciding how to deal with problems according to principles sort of like . . . umm . . . your job?"

"In a way, sort of, but not really. I mean, if you're a buffoon like Tony Garabelli, and you think that every dispute should be decided according to the principle of what a bunch of dead guys would have thought about it in the late eighteenth century, then yes, we decide cases according to principle. But, you know, judging really involves making the best and most pragmatic decision you can given all the circumstances. Is that a principle? Maybe. But that's not what I mean when I say that this Savin jerk insists on his principles regardless of whether they might ruin some eighteen-year-old girl's life. Or result in the destruction of my oak tree, for that matter."

Diana nods and looks at Ed with obvious pleasure. She's delighted to see him get animated about his job, or at least sort of about his job. "You know," she says, "you're kind of hot when you get all . . . judgy."

Ed finishes his drink. "Is it time to go back to your place?"

"No objection here, your honor," she says. And winks.

"Check, please!" Ed bellows.

***

This time when they arrive at Diana's townhouse, they are careful to walk slowly through the front door to avoid a repeat of last weekend's tumble. Shoes kicked off, they are quickly into hot necking—literally, she's biting his neck—when he mutters, "bed, bed, bed" into her ear. "Right," she answers, pulling her head away from his and leading him down the hallway into the bedroom. More necking, some unbuttoning, Ed is over the moon to learn that only a bra this time separates him from her breasts once he's removed her blouse, and what a bra it is!—colorful, some sort of lovely green-blue color, fancy as all hell, it probably cost her upwards of two hundred bucks, although really, what does he know about how much a fancy bra costs, basically nothing he figures, his mind going a mile a minute as more and more skin sees the soft light of Diana's exquisite bedroom.

"Do you like to talk dirty?" Diana asks, surprising him, as she fiddles with his belt.

"Dirty? You mean like, *oh baby your tits are so hot*, or *that's one sweet looking vulva you've got there, sugar*?"

Diana spits with laughter all over his face, for which he's actually relieved—for a second there as he was making the joke he panicked that this was going to turn into a *Seinfeld* moment from 1992, and she was going to throw him out. Instead she's let go of his belt and is practically choking with her chortles. She playfully throws him down on the bed and removes her bra. "I guess the answer to that is no, then?" she says when she finally recovers. She starts tugging at his pants, pulling them halfway down over his also-not-too-inexpensive-thank-you-very-much Brooks Brothers red tartan pattern boxers, when suddenly she stops and declares that she has to go pee. Turning around quickly, she springs for the bathroom on the far side of the bedroom and shuts the door behind her.

"Hmm, okay," Ed thinks, as he takes his pants off the rest of the way. As he's folding them and draping them over a nearby chair, because that's what you do when you're sixty-two and your pants cost 325 dollars, he feels his phone in one of his pockets and takes it out. There's an email from his cousin Jane.

"Oh shit," Ed says. He reads the email, and it's just as he feared. Uncle Jack is dead, and the funeral is in two days. Jane wants to know if Ed would say a few words at the service. Again: "Oh shit."

He's emailing her back with his condolences and a promise to be in Massachusetts within twenty-four hours with a eulogy of sorts in hand when Diana returns. She's unpleased.

"You're on your *phone*? What are you, tweeting this? Live blogging my boobs?" As she says this, she grabs one of her breasts and lifts it sort of toward him, but she can quickly tell from his serious expression as he types that something is wrong. She returns her breast to normal position and asks if everything is all right.

"Oh, sorry, yeah, I just got a message that my uncle Jack died. I have to go to Boston tomorrow for the funeral. I'm just emailing my cousin that I'll be there."

Diana gasps. "Oh, no, I'm so sorry. Were you close?"

"No, not especially. Maybe a little when I was a kid, but not for a long time. He's been sick for a while and kind of crazy. A hoarder type. I can't remember the last time I actually saw him. He's the last of the older generation."

He finishes typing and sighs, shakes his head. Diana comes over and puts her hand on his leg. "So, does this mean we're once again not having sex?" she asks.

Ed looks up. Diana is rocking nothing but a pair of shimmery light blue panties, and suddenly Ed pretty much forgets the email, the funeral, everything but her. "No," he says, tossing the phone on the ground and inviting her into his embrace. "No, it definitely does not mean that."

FIVE

ED CAN'T ARRANGE A LAST-MINUTE FLIGHT TO BOSTON, so he's boarded a high-speed Acela train at Union Station and settled into a comfortable seat in the quiet car, where so far only two people have violated the rule against talking on their cell phones. He wonders whether Supreme Court justices should be able to give tickets to people who are being assholes. "I'm sorry sir, yes you sir, the guy with the blue shirt with the awful white collar and cuffs yelping like a beagle into your cell phone in the quiet car," he would say, writing out a hundred-dollar ticket, "but you're an asshole, and as a member of the high court of the land, I've determined that as punishment you should pay an asshole fee of one hundred dollars into the general treasury to benefit public schools and repair crumbling bridges." He quickly imagines some of the difficulties. For one, he would be constantly handing out tickets to his colleagues on the bench—DeLillo, for example, for making an idiotic joke, or Garabelli for insisting on showing everyone the magazine cover with all the penises on it—and then they inevitably would issue him citations in return. It would be a never-ending cycle, angry justices slapping ticket after ticket into the pockets of all of their co-workers—every one of them would owe the government millions of dollars within months and have to quit the bench to take jobs in the private sector, resulting in the total collapse of the American justice system. No, Ed figures, the asshole citation idea, attractive though it may seem at first glance, is not going to work.

It turns out that having seven hours to kill on a train trip isn't so bad. For one thing, Ed has a lot of reading to do for the following week's cases. The court will be hearing a couple of Fourth Amendment search and seizure cases and two complicated statutory cases involving the federal pension law that he hasn't even looked at yet. Plus, he plans to break up the work by reading more of this *Chuang Tzu* book. He likes Diana so much that he figures if she finds something compelling in it, it's probably worth looking at some more, even if he's skeptical that he'll ever be able to embrace a third-century BC Chinese weirdo pitching spontaneity and the pointlessness of reason.

Another good thing about taking seven hours to get to Boston instead of two is that he won't have to spend as much time with his family. Or with what's left of his family anyway. It was never a big family in the first place—Ed's an only child, and his parents had only one sibling each—but now the people still alive that he can realistically refer to as family can probably be counted on his fingers. He will be surprised if more than five actual family members make it out East to attend his uncle's funeral.

It's not that Ed dreads seeing what's left of his family, or even that he doesn't like them—he likes them fine. It's just that since becoming adults they hardly ever see each other or even talk on the phone or trade emails or follow each other on Twitter or anything else, so that when they do get together for an occasional wedding or funeral (the last get together, Ed recalls, must have been his own mother's funeral five years ago), things are usually awkward. And since nobody else in the family is much of a drinker—his cousin Jane's daughter Alex, Ed knows, might have a few glasses of wine from time to time, but the rest are of the one beer a night type at best—Ed can't even rely on the liquor lubrication that gets so many other families through uncomfortable moments. The later he can get to Boston and the earlier he can leave, Ed figures, the better. He'll go to the funeral, and even say a few words about his uncle, but he doesn't expect to find any meaningful connections with this group of people whom he hardly knows at all.

Ed opens the *Chuang Tzu*. A random page.

Cook Ting was cutting up an ox for Lord Wen-hui. At every touch of his hand, every heave of his shoulder, every move of his feet, every thrust of his knee—zip! zoop! He slithered the knife along with a zing, and all was in perfect rhythm, as though he were per-

forming the dance of the Mulberry Grove or keeping time to the Ching-shou music.

"Ah, this is marvelous!" said Lord Wen-hui. "Imagine skill reaching such heights!"

Cook Ting laid down his knife and replied, "What I care about is the Way, which goes beyond skill. When I first began cutting up oxen, all I could see was the ox itself. After three years I no longer saw the whole ox. And now—now I go at it by spirit and don't look with my eyes. Perception and understanding have come to a stop and spirit moves where it wants. I go along with the natural makeup, strike in the big hollows, guide the knife through the big openings, and follow things as they are. So I never touch the smallest ligament or tendon, much less a main joint.

"Oh, I can follow things as they are," Ed says to himself, closing up the book and pulling a case file out of his briefcase. "You better believe it. *Zip. Zoop.*" He opens up the Brief for the Petitioner in Delaware versus Mulholland, one of the search and seizure cases, and grabs a pen. "I'll carve an ox. I'll dance the Mulberry Grove. Just watch me, baby."

***

Ed arrives at the funeral home early in his rented sedan. His stomach is queasy, and not because of the undercooked Belgian waffle and two cups of sludgy black coffee he just threw back at the Marriott's "hot breakfast." Ed speaks in public a lot, of course, but giving a eulogy for his uncle in front of family members whom he hardly sees is more nerve-wracking, it turns out, than speaking about constitutional theory in front of an auditorium full of high-powered lawyers. As predicted, though, attendance at the service is light. Ed greets people when they enter. He hugs Jane, with her drippy eyeliner, and her brother David, who smells just so slightly of the Camembert cheese that he crafts in northern Vermont, and a more disheveled and weary-looking Alex than he remembers. Handshakes and man-hugs are exchanged with Jane's spindly husband Peter, whose beard has gone nearly white, and Alex's husband Chad, a burly Chicago type who is some sort of banker and who seemingly enjoys his bratwursts a little too much. Ed makes small talk with Alex, asking about her law practice, to which Alex simply shakes her head and says, "it's bad, I'll tell you about it later, I need your advice."

Soon, they are all seated—these few family members plus maybe ten people Ed does not recognize, old friends most likely, perhaps a nurse or two who treated Jack in his last days. Ed's mother's side of the family is Jewish, so the men are wearing yarmulkes, which Ed hates wearing, they make him feel like an awkward schoolboy—and a rabbi is conducting the service. Since the rabbi never even met Jack—if Jack had set foot in a synagogue more than three times in his entire life, Ed would be shocked—he is parroting a few tidbits about Jack that Jane and Alex shared with him when they met briefly the evening before, trying to weave them into some sort of a narrative that everyone in the audience knows is mostly false because even if the facts are accurate, the nuance is all wrong. Ed is sitting in the front row next to Chad, who looks particularly ridiculous in his yarmulke, which resembles a bottle cap on top of his giant square head. No matter how stupid the Jews look in these little hat scraps, Ed thinks, the Christians always look stupider.

It's not long before Ed is called to the lectern to deliver the eulogy. He brings a page of notes and a water bottle, which he drinks from several times while struggling through the opening of the speech, causing several members of the audience to involuntarily recall the State of the Union Republican Response Small Water Bottle Fiasco of 2013. After a couple of minutes, though, Ed settles down and gets to the heart of the talk, the stories he remembers from his youth, those days when the family was more or less a real family, holiday get-togethers and all the rest. He recalls the time that Jack brought a cheesecake made out of Velveeta to a New Year's Eve party, the crazy sideburns he sported throughout the 1970s, the time he put his arm around a tiny Ed and comforted him throughout the scariest thunderstorm Ed had ever witnessed. The stories are having the desired effect, Ed assesses, sending the small crowd on the same roller coaster ride of emotions that Ed himself feels—vaguely, anyway—as he speaks.

As he nears the end of his speech, Ed looks up and notices an attractive older woman in a simple black dress quietly sneaking into the back of the room and taking a seat by herself in the final row of folding chairs. At first he thinks it is strange, maybe even impolite, for someone to creep into a funeral service after it has already started, but as he looks at her, it dawns on him that the woman might in fact be Tammy, his now-dead uncle's stepdaughter from his ex-wife's first marriage and the girl who was Ed's favorite cousin growing up, even if she wasn't technically his cousin at all. The woman's long hair is gray, practically silver, and her face is wrinkled, though not unpleasantly so, and thus it is hard for him to match her with the memory of the fourteen-year-old girl he used to know, but when she catches his eye and gives him the smallest of waves, he is sure. The smile that seeing her brings out in him is incongruous with the eulogy's sorrowful finale, but it is doubtful that anyone in the small assembly has noticed it, either because they are crying or because they're thinking about what their email will have in store for them once the service is over.

Afterward, the group gathers in the lobby of the funeral home and makes plans to get to the cemetery for the burial. People praise Ed for his eulogy, call it "touching," "moving," "true." Alex asks if she can ride over to the cemetery with Ed, and Ed agrees. Before they leave, he asks Jane if the woman with the gray hair standing over by the mint tray is in fact her ex-stepsister Tammy, and Jane assures him that it is, explaining that she's recently been in touch with Tammy by email and let her know about the arrangements for Jack, figuring that since he had been Tammy's stepfather for about eight years (albeit forty-plus years ago) she might want to come pay her respects. "Holy shit, she looks great," Ed says in return. Jane, who does not look so great these days, especially today, Ed thinks, in her hideous black pantsuit with the weird purple shirt, winces and reluctantly agrees.

Ed walks up to Tammy and gives her a playful punch on the shoulder. "That's you, isn't it? I can't believe it," he says, bending his knees a little so he can look directly into her eyes. It is hard sometimes to see the child in someone's face you haven't seen for years, but with Tammy Ed can manage it. In an instant, he remembers the fun they had during their short time together as kids before Charlotte left Jack and took Tammy with her—playing hide and seek for hours in the backyard of Jack and Charlotte's house in Ipswich, marathon ping pong sessions in the basement of Ed's house on the South Shore, the time that Tammy and Jane dressed him up as a girl, escorted him into a living room filled with grownups, and introduced him as Shelly.

"It's me, yes, it's true," Tammy answers, returning his little punch. "And you? You are . . . *you*, I presume? My former sort-of-cousin now turned Supreme Court justice? Wow. And to think that I knew you when."

"When I was just a little girl named Shelly," Ed replies, and Tammy's face lights up. "I haven't thought about that in forty years. I can't believe you remember."

"Some things are kind of impossible to forget," Ed says, recalling the best he can the titillating feel of Jane's white cotton tights gripping his boy-thighs. "What in the world have you been up to these past forty years?"

"That is a long story," Tammy says. People are starting to exit, and Tammy can tell that Alex is waiting by the door for Ed. "Are you going to the thingamajig after? At the restaurant?"

"Of course. Will you be there?" Ed asks. Jane has announced that family and friends will gather at a local favorite restaurant of Jack's after the funeral, which everyone agrees is a good idea since Jack's house is uninhabitable and set to be bulldozed within the week.

"We can talk then. It will be great to catch up," Tammy says. "I think they want us to get moving now."

"Okay. It's great to see you. I look forward to talking."

"Thanks," Tammy says. "It's great to see you too." And then they leave.

***

In the ride over to the cemetery, Alex laments her life as a young lawyer at one of Chicago's top law firms. Her complaints are hardly unique; indeed, Ed has heard them a million times before. Too much work, not enough responsibility, a partner she works for who has the social skills of a marmot, rude secretaries, not enough pens. "Not enough pens?" Ed interrupts, because this in fact is a complaint he has never heard before. "All right, maybe that's not a big deal," Alex concedes. "But I swear to god I could not find a pen the other day. I think all the secretaries steal them." Ed is trying hard to keep pace with Jane's Honda Civic. He's following her to the cemetery, but she seems oblivious to her leadership responsibilities and keeps moving lanes and passing slower cars, which requires Ed to do the same.

"What is your mother doing?" he asks. "Does she think she's in a race or something?"

"She's becoming nuttier by the day, I don't know what's going on. Anyway, this partner . . ."

Ed zones out as Alex continues her rant about the law firm. What's he supposed to tell her? That's life at a law firm. Some people naturally thrive in that atmosphere. He did. But most don't. So maybe she should leave. Ed wonders what advice Chuang Tzu would give in this instance. He has no idea. Probably he'd tell her to go play in the mud. Might not be such a bad idea.

"Do you know anything about Taoism?" he suddenly asks her.

"Huh? What?"

"I've been seeing a woman who is a professor of Chinese religion, and she lent me this Taoist text called the *Chuang Tzu*. Do you know about this book?"

"The *Chuang Tzu*?" Alex says, confused. "No, I've never heard of it. Does it have something to do with this problem I'm talking about? Like the Tao of Law? Or the Tao of Getting a Pain in the Ass Partner off My Back?"

"No, not really," Ed admits, and then realizes that Jane is making a right turn into the cemetery. He follows, and parks the car in the spot next to Jane's Honda. "Well, here we are," he blurts to Alex, who gets out of the car without having received one iota of advice about the practice of law from her Supreme Court justice uncle.

***

The part of the funeral where the casket is lowered into the earth is always the most poignant one for Ed. He is standing six feet in front of the hole in the ground. Tears well up in his eyes as the rabbi starts chanting the dramatic prayer that proceeds the lowering. There are maybe a dozen people congregated here on this broad green lawn on a lovely autumn New England day to see this corpse in a wooden box descend to its final resting place. Ed thinks about what his own funeral will be like. If he had remained a private lawyer, then his funeral would have looked a lot like this one, though probably with a few more people—young lawyers looking for a good networking opportunity most likely. Even if his career had stalled at the lower court level, the funeral wouldn't have been anything particularly special. But as a justice, his death will be a news item, his funeral an event. The idea of it is surreal. He imagines the networks interrupting their regularly scheduled programming to announce his demise (would they actually do that, he wonders—maybe only if he dies while still on the bench, unexpectedly), lying in state in the court's grand foyer, his dead body being visited by mid-level bureaucrats, perhaps a visiting foreign dignitary or two, an official burial service in the National Cemetery, his magnificent coffin draped with the American flag, the weeping of the First Lady (okay, that might be a stretch). Jack's body is now six feet under, as they say, and the rabbi has invited the guests to shovel a small scoop of dirt onto the coffin in the traditional Jewish way. Jane goes first, saying "rest tight, Dad," as her dirt rains down upon Jack in the box. David wordlessly follows, then Alex, and then it's his turn. He grabs the small hand shovel from Alex and digs into the small pile of dirt and stones provided by the cemetery. How thoughtful of them, he thinks, as he scatters the contents of the shovel over the length of the casket below. Good bye, Uncle Jack, he says, and that's a wrap on the generation that raised his own.

***

At a local seafood restaurant, perched on the edge of a wetland dotted with large birds that occasionally take to the sky, dangling their long legs behind them like kite strings, Ed manages to sit next to Tammy at the end of the table of mourners, where they can talk. They are both drinking a beer—they're the only ones at the table drinking anything but water—and giving each other the five-minute version of the last forty-five years of their lives. He learns that Tammy has always lived on the North Shore of Boston, that she works as an office manager for a team of orthopedic surgeons, and that she rides a motorcycle.

"Really?" Ed exclaims. "A motorcycle?" He's pretty sure that he doesn't know anybody at all who rides a motorcycle. He may never have known anyone who rides a motorcycle.

"It's true. I started about three years ago. After I was done with my skydiving phase. It's super fun. I even ride with a group of other old ladies on the weekend. We call ourselves the Gray Ladies. We had a ride scheduled for today, but, well, you know."

"Wow, that's impressive," Ed offers, and he is indeed impressed, though not entirely surprised. Even as a kid, Tammy was a notch wilder and braver than he and his other cousins. "I think the scariest thing I've ever done is go white water rafting this past summer in Wyoming. But even that was with a guide. And a few eight-year-olds."

"You should try it. Maybe I'll give you a ride later, you'll see what I mean."

"It could happen," Ed says, though he doubts it. "What else?"

Tammy brings him up to speed on her mother Charlotte, who has completely lost her mind and lives in a nursing home, and Ed tells Tammy about his mother's death from cancer a half decade earlier. Tammy is a toucher, and she keeps her hand on the back of Ed's wrist pretty much continuously as she relates the story of her two divorces— one from Mark the contractor after fifteen years and two children, and the more recent one from Josh the community bank loan officer after only two.

"So now what?" Ed asks. "Have you sworn off men for good?"

"Hah, I wish," she answers. "Those fuckers."

"Yeah," Ed says, taking a sip of his Sam Adams. "We fuckers. Wait, why are we fuckers?"

"Because you're all so fucking full of yourself, it's like you live in your own worlds. Hello? Hello? There are other people here in the universe also."

Ed, who remembers hearing various versions of this refrain many times in the years leading up to his divorce, finds it hard to disagree.

"You'd think I would have figured this out already after all these years. I mean, take my most recent relationship," Tammy starts, then stops. "Shit, I can't talk about this without smoking a cigarette. Do you want to come outside while I smoke?"

Ed's not sure the last time he talked to someone who smoked. People still smoke? "Sure, yeah, why not," he says. He finishes his beer and with a few quick words to Chad about where they're going, follows Tammy outside. She's got a big purse, practically tote-bag size, and she rifles through it looking for her smoking accoutrements. Ed leans back against the brick wall of the restaurant and watches her. She looks sort of like a cute hamster rummaging through a pile of seeds looking for just the right one. Eventually she finds what she's looking for, pulling out a lighter and a pack of cigarettes with a name on it that Ed doesn't recognize. "Found it," she exclaims, and then lights up.

"Have you always smoked?" Ed asks. "Or did you take it up when you started riding the motorcycle?"

"These things are my lifelong nemesis," she answers, shaking the lit cigarette in front of her face. "I started for real the year I dropped out of college, but I've quit maybe five times. There was a ten-year period in there somewhere when I didn't smoke a single time. That's long gone, obviously."

"Well, that's good. Otherwise you wouldn't be able to talk about this most recent guy," Ed nudges.

"Right. Eric. Talk about fuckers." She takes a drag and lets the smoke out slowly, just to the left of Ed's face, but the soft wind blows some of it back in his direction. He inhales a bit of it, likes it, vaguely remembers the one year of law school when he actually smoked, sort of, well he bought a few packs of cigarettes that year anyway. "We lived together for two years. *Lived together.* And then one day he tells me he's going back to his ex-wife. We even bought a dog together. A dead dog, now."

"He killed the dog?"

"No," she laughs. "Well, sort of. He left the goddamned fence in the backyard open and the dog got run over by a truck. It was a stupid dog. So fucking stupid. But I loved him. Just like I loved Eric. Who was also stupid. Fucker."

"Can I have a cigarette?" Ed suddenly asks. The question surprises himself, but then again, thinking about it a little, it doesn't.

"Really? Are you sure?"

"Yeah," he says. "I smoked a little in college. I haven't been a total geek my whole life."

Tammy takes the pack of cigarettes out of her bag, hands one to Ed, and lights it for him. He inhales—a little—and lets the smoke out. Now who's fucking stupid, he thinks. But what the hell.

"I remember you and I went to see a concert together," Tammy says. "I don't even know who was playing. We must have been about fourteen. Just about the time Jack and my mom split up. I was drinking some sort of awful alcohol concoction out of a canteen, but you wouldn't drink any of it. You were too worried about getting caught."

"I remember that," Ed says. "It was Fleetwood Mac I'm pretty sure. It was the first concert I ever went to. I thought I was real groovy just going to see a rock band. You were my cool cousin."

Tammy smiles. He's right, she was the cool cousin. "It's great to see you again," she says, and touches his arm. "I almost didn't come to the funeral—I mean, I haven't seen Jack in ages—but Jane said you were going to be there so I decided to come. I think it's terrific that you've done much with your life. I was the cool cousin, but you were the one who was going places."

"Never rode a motorcycle though."

Tammy takes a drag on the cigarette. Ed follows. They're quiet for a few brief moments, contemplating the sum effect of the choices they've made for the past sixty years in the span of maybe thirty seconds tops. Tammy speaks first. "Do you want to do it? Let's do it. We could just take off and go back to my place and we'll be on the road in fifteen minutes. I've got an extra helmet. It'll be fun."

Ed considers this. Would it be a good idea? Does it matter if it's a good idea? Should he even be considering whether it matters if it's a good idea? He doesn't know. He doesn't even know how to go about knowing. "All right, yes," he says, to Tammy's surprise, to his own. "Let's do it."

***

The next thing Ed knows he is opening the passenger side door of Tammy's pickup truck and jumping down onto the driveway of her gray split-level house somewhere deep in the anonymous maze of suburbia. His shiny Allen Edmonds clickety clack over the blacktop as he follows Tammy to the front door past a couple of empty trash cans and a shabby pink tricycle that Ed figures (hopes) is something her granddaughter uses when she visits, although Ed seems to remember from the conversation at the restaurant that the granddaughter is ten, so who knows. Tammy picks up three old *Boston Globes* in blue plastic bags from the doorstep before fishing her keys from her giant bag and opening the door, tossing the bags down into the cluttered foyer. "I don't know why I still get the paper delivered. I almost never read it," she says, and then motions for Ed to come in. "Sorry about the state of this place. As you know from the truck, I'm not particularly tidy." Ed looks around, and the place is indeed about as big of a mess as her truck had been; it had taken her a good five minutes to throw away all the crap—food containers, magazines, piles of orange peels from a prior century—that had colonized the passenger side of the cab.

Tammy excuses herself to go change out of her funereal dress into something more motorcycle-worthy, so Ed makes himself at home, more or less, in the upstairs living room. The house is stuffy and dark, a *Cosmo* sits on the coffee table. Ed smiles at the thought of Bash's nemesis receiving his first copy down there in Charlottesville and picks it up. Why is a sixty-year-old woman reading *Cosmo*, Ed wonders, opening to an article about how to use a thong as a ponytail tie. Ed thinks: *Eww.* But the four-page "Hard Ass Workout" spread is a different matter. He scans a line of barely clad nineteen-year-old asses, turns the page to another line of barely clad nineteen-year-old asses, and . . . yup, there's the erection again. Reluctantly, he closes the magazine, puts it back down on the table, thinks about how to organize the Clean Air Act preemption decision that he's been assigned. And the erection is gone.

Tammy's back, wearing jeans, a black top, and fresh makeup. She plops down on the chair next to the couch he is sitting on and starts pulling on her long black motorcycle boots. "Did you read the *Cosmo*?" she asks. He says yes, yes indeed, that he's happy after all these years to have finally learned how to hold his hair back with a thong.

"I know, I know, it's silly, I can't read the newspaper but I read every issue of that barely disguised pornography without fail. Hey, didn't I hear on the radio that your court is going to ban porn?"

The last thing Ed wants to talk about right now is work, much less the term's biggest, most impossible case, so he stands up and declares himself ready and excited to get going on this new adventure. "So where are we going, anyway?" he asks.

Tammy stands up. She looks good. The boots make her three inches taller, and in a way she looks like an actress who has aged pretty well despite some hard living. "I thought we'd take some pretty back roads, zip through some of these old tiny little Massachusetts towns. It'll be nice and we won't have to hit the highway. And then I have a little surprise destination at the end."

"Another surprise. Oh goody," Ed says in a deadpan.

"You better believe oh goody," Tammy adds.

SIX

THEY ARE GLIDING OVER SOFT HILLS AFIRE WITH THE COLORS of autumn through quaint towns that date back to the seventeenth century, the crisp New England fall air slapping their cheeks as they pass roadside stands selling pumpkins for the upcoming holiday and white clapboard churches with steeples sticking up into the bright blue sky like miniature rockets. It had been a beautiful day for a funeral, and it is an even better day for a motorcycle ride. Ed grips Tammy tight around her waist, his crotch jammed up against her ass. This was weird at first, but no longer. He trusts her on the bike. She may seem generally scatterbrained and a bit of a mess off the motorcycle, but on it, she is totally in control. The ride is glorious. Ed feels happier than he has in a long time, maybe since his rafting and fishing days on the Snake River under the giant Western sky this past summer. He wonders whether he should look into learning how to ride one of these things himself when he gets back to Washington. How sweet would that be, pulling into the court parking garage on a Harley and parking it next to Garabelli's Lincoln or Stephenson's Mercedes? Has a justice ever ridden to work on a motorcycle? He makes a mental note to Google this important question just as soon as he gets back to the hotel.

They stop at one of the farms along the way for bottles of water and two freshly picked apples. The fruit is juicy and giant; the one that Tammy is eating is almost as big as her head. Ed tells her how great the ride is, how genuinely happy he is, how he's going to look into motorcycle riding justice history when he gets back home. He even leans in and gives her an impromptu hug and kiss on the cheek, a kiss that

perhaps lingers just a little too long, though if Tammy minds there's
no way to tell.

"Okay, are you ready for the final surprise destination?" she asks
him, when it seems like his awkward little affection fest has come to
a close.

"Not particularly," he answers, "but you're in charge."

"All right. So have you ever had a pet that you loved completely?
Like, felt a serious kinship with?"

"No," Ed says. "I'm not a pet person. Although I do have a cat at the
moment. It's not my cat. Not really. It's orange. And furry. I'm taking
care of it, for a neighbor, kind of. I put out a bowl of food for it when I
came up here. That's what you're supposed to do, right? I wonder what
the cat's name is. I stole it."

Tammy looks at Ed for a moment in silence, trying to figure out
whether he's making fun of her or something, whether he in fact is taking care of a furry orange cat with no name that may or may not be his.

"Right. Well, I had this kind of relationship with my last dog. The
dog that my ex and I had together. I mentioned that Eric the fucker
left the gate open and the dog—his name was Romeo—ran out into
the street and got hit by a car. A stupid kid driving fifty miles an hour
in a neighborhood. That's a whole different story. Anyway, we put him
to sleep—the dog, that is, not the kid—and got the ashes. Eric has the
ashes in his house. I want them. He doesn't seem to want to give them
to me. Out of spite or something, I don't know. He probably keeps them
in the garage next to the motor oil. I've been wanting to go over and
confront him about it, but I'm too nervous to go over by myself. Do you
mind coming along? I'm just going to ring the doorbell and ask him for
the ashes. I think he'll give them to me if I actually go over there and
ask for them. You just have to be there and hang out for moral support.
What do you say?" She looks up at him with the sixty-year-old twice-
divorced grandmother version of puppy-dog eyes. "Please?"

This seems to Ed like more than he bargained for. It's kind of stomping on his buzz. He considers declaring it *out of his jurisdiction*. But
then again, this is family. Sort of. He should step up, lend a hand, come
through in a pinch. He'll do it. Chuang Tzu would be proud. "Sure," he
offers. "Anything for a non-cousin I haven't seen in forty years. I'm in."

Tammy rolls her eyes, but she's grateful. They finish up the fruit, hurl the cores into the forest, and get back on the hog. They are not far from their destination; she had brought them pretty close, clearly figuring Ed would say yes when she asked him for the favor. Tammy coasts in next to a squat maroon single-floor house with black shutters and a crude addition built onto the back that has been painted a slightly different shade of dark red. The place is worn down, down-at-the-heel, ramshackle. She turns off the bike, dismounts, and removes her helmet. Ed gets off the bike too. "Okay, you can just stay here. I'm hoping this doesn't take long," she tells him, and then strides off toward the front door.

Ed watches as she rings the doorbell and waits. From behind, with her long hair and motorcycle getup, Tammy could be in her forties, maybe even younger. He looks around at the yard—it's unkempt, the grass hasn't been mowed probably since late summer. The fence where the dog must have been kept, unsuccessfully, is on the right side of the house, and it's half fallen down. Suddenly Ed has a thought about one of the Fourth Amendment cases he's hearing next week—the case is about fences, actually, and seeing this fence in disrepair gives him an idea for a question he might ask at oral argument. He feels around in the inside pocket of his black suit jacket for a pen and something to write on. Luckily, he's kept the program from the funeral service, and there's space underneath a sad Jewish poem for him to scratch a few notes that will remind him later about the question he's just thought of—that is, if he doesn't forget about the notes and throw the program away before Tuesday. Once the note is scratched out, and the pen and paper returned to his pocket, Ed looks up to see an obviously impatient Tammy, still waiting on the stoop of her ex-boyfriend's crappy-ass house for someone to answer the door.

"What's going on? Is anyone home?" he asks.

"Nobody's answering. I thought he was here. The car's here, that usually means he's here," she says, pointing to the navy blue beater in the driveway. The car is slathered with right-wing bumper stickers— GOP candidates, NRA slogans, libertarian jingles. "He's probably out with his slut wife whore, Donna."

"Yeah," Ed says. "Probably he's out with his slut wife whore Donna. Maybe we should leave."

"Oh, no. Now that I've come all the way over here, I'm not leaving without the ashes. I think I know a way in to the house through the back window." Tammy hops off the front step and tiptoes through the front yard, trying to peek into the picture window to see if anyone is home, but the dreary off-white drapes keep her from getting any information. She scoots around the side of the house and disappears from sight.

"Ummm," the associate justice mutters. "Not sure if this is a good idea."

All of a sudden, Ed is nervous. Their little outing has apparently just passed the line from exhilarating expedition to potential low-level felony. Is she really going to break into the house? Maybe the house is still in her name somehow, he tells himself, so it wouldn't be breaking and entering. And in any event, he certainly doesn't know that the house is *not* in her name, so he's not at fault, right? For a moment, these technical defenses to criminal liability make him feel better, but then just as quickly he realizes how pathetic they will look in Farkas's front-page article about the break-in and is back to worrying again.

Minutes pass. He has no idea what to do. Should he go in back of the house and try to talk Tammy out of whatever she's doing? It's probably too late for that. Most likely she's already in her ex's bedroom, stealing his watch. Maybe he should walk away. Leave his helmet on the seat, make it clear that he will not be a part of these hijinks. That's what a good justice would do; Felix Frankfurter wouldn't be caught dead hanging out by a motorcycle while his former cousin-by-marriage breaks into her ex-boyfriend's house to steal her beloved dead dog's ashes, right? Oh, stop being such a wimp, he chides himself, it's not like she's stealing a plasma television from a stranger. No, he should stay out here with the bike and help out his cousin while still maintaining reasonable deniability for when the cops show up. That's the best option. He looks around at the neighboring houses to determine if anyone's noticed what's going on. He sees nothing. The homes in the vicinity are for the most part just as run down as this one. He figures that the people inside these places have their own problems—not a nosy crew, in all probability. But then again: What does he know?

Ed is still arguing with himself when Tammy comes trotting back into the front yard, triumphantly holding aloft a small cylinder that presumably contains the remains of her recently passed pooch.

"Mission accomplished!" she declares.

Ed is glad to see her, but is still a little disturbed by the turn of events. "Uhhh, yay? I guess?" he responds.

"What? What's wrong? I got the ashes," she says, shaking the container kind of close up to Ed's face.

"I didn't know this surprise destination was going to involve breaking and entering."

"Oh, don't worry. I'm actually still on the lease," Tammy says, "so it's not breaking and entering, right? You can't break and enter into your own house, can you?"

"Well, I guess that's better," Ed says, and he's in fact somewhat relieved. "Were the ashes hard to find?"

"No. They were in the garage, just like I figured. That idiot."

"What do you think he'll do when he realizes they're gone? Will he freak out? Is he, umm, you know, violent?"

Tammy looks at Ed like he's a bit of a dope. "What do you think this is, the *Sopranos*? Plus, the jerk never cared about the dog, and he's too busy calling in to moron right-wing talk radio shows to ever notice that the ashes are gone. It could be the perfect crime."

Ed stares at her.

"Well, not crime, technically," she says. "But you know."

Tammy and Ed's back and forth is interrupted when the front screen door of the house swings open with a bang. A wiry shirtless man with a tanned chest steps out onto the stoop. The gray hair on his head is alternately matted and poking out haphazardly; it would seem that his ex-girlfriend's shenanigans have interrupted some kind of a nap. Eric shakes his head in equal parts disbelief and an attempt to jar the cobwebs from his still half-sleeping brain. "What the fuck, Tammy? Did you just break into my house?" he demands.

"Oh, shit," Tammy mutters to Ed under her breath. She turns to face Eric. "Yeah, that's right. I went and got what's mine," she yells back, shaking the canister of dog dust in his direction.

"What's that? That stupid dog's ashes? You stole them? What the hell are you thinking? Jesus Christ, you're a fucking nutjob. If I believed in government I'd call the cops on you."

"It was my dog, you asshole. You wouldn't return my calls. I knocked on the door, but you didn't answer, so I took them. You don't want them anyway. Why don't you just go back to sleep, you lazy shit-for-brains."

The angry swearing is making Ed uncomfortable. "Maybe we should . . . go?" he suggests.

"I didn't answer because I was fucking my wife. I should shoot you is what I should do." At this, a similarly disheveled red-haired woman in a long white t-shirt appears behind Eric's shoulder. "Is that your ex-girlfriend?" she asks. "What the hell?"

"Go ahead and take a shot at me, dickface," Tammy screams back. "You couldn't hit the side of a barn from twenty-five feet. You're an embarrassment to all right-wing militia freaks everywhere. You'd probably shoot yourself in the back of your thigh somehow."

Ed is not sure what to do. Nothing in his life has prepared him for anything like this particular oral argument. But he has to give some credit to Tammy for that last bit about the back of the thigh. Pretty quick thinking there. Would definitely earn her a "[laughter]" if anyone was transcribing this little brouhaha. Ed doesn't want to snicker, but he does.

"Who the fuck is this guy? Is this your new gigolo?" Eric asks. "How much do you have to pay him to let you suck his dick?"

"This is my cousin the Supreme Court justice, you asshole. Maybe he'll put you in federal prison where you belong."

Ed coughs. "I can't, umm, I can't actually do that, so . . ."

The news that he's been wildly cursing in front of a justice of the United States Supreme Court gives Eric pause, but only for a moment.

"I thought you hadn't seen this guy in forty years. What are you, fucking your famous cousin now?"

"Yeah, maybe I am," Tammy says, and Ed almost chokes. "Maybe I *am* fucking my famous cousin. You got a problem with that?"

"We're not actually, uhh . . . fuh . . . fornicating or anything," Ed says, wanting to die.

"Yeah, we're fucking all right," Tammy bellows, then looks back at Ed, her face crimson with rage. "How many times did we fuck this morning, Ed? I can't even remember, it was so mind-blowing. Plus, with all the cunnilingus, I get mixed up. You know what cunnilingus is, Eric? No, you don't actually."

Neighbors, a few here and there, have started peeking out from behind their drapes and front doors. Ed wonders whether he could maybe climb into his helmet and disappear. No luck; he's too big. Donna steps out in front of Eric on the stoop. The stained t-shirt she's wearing—it must be Eric's—is just long enough to touch the top of her cellulite-colonized thighs. "He knows what it is, you bitch. He just wouldn't go down on you because you're too fucking nasty." She bends down, picks up a small rock, and hurls it in Tammy's direction. The throw is errant, and it pings off the front of the motorcycle.

"Did you just throw a fucking pebble at me, you whore?" Tammy screams. She takes a step forward, as though she's going to attack the woman. Ed thinks that this isn't so far from the *Sopranos* after all. He puts his hand on Tammy's shoulder. "Come on," he says, "let's go. This is ridiculous. He's going to let you have the ashes. Let's just get out of here, relax, go have a drink or something."

Ed's pleading has the desired effect. Maybe it's also his touch. Tammy regains a smidgen of composure. "All right, you're right, sure, let's get out of here, take this," she says, handing him the container of ashes. Tammy puts on her helmet and sits down on the bike, revs it up.

"Yeah, get the fuck out of here you lunatic. And take your fucking Supreme Court justice with you," Donna screams. Ed looks around, his helmet in one hand and the dog's ashes in the other. The neighbors next door are now fully out on their front lawn, gawking. Ed sees them and gives them an awkward wave with the hand holding the ashes. "Hi there. Hello," he squeaks.

"Get on the bike, Ed," Tammy demands, and Ed is happy to comply. It takes them a few seconds to figure out the best position for him. He tries holding the container with both hands in front of her body, against her stomach, but that's uncomfortable for both of them, so he switches to holding her with his right arm, the container with his left hand out to his side. It's not great, but it works. With the eyes of the neighborhood staring them down, Tammy puts the bike in gear, and the two of them lurch off and away, another rock whizzing behind Ed's head as they go.

***

"Wow, that was crazy," Ed says, when they're back in Tammy's living room, relaxing on her yellow leather couch, sipping Narragansetts from tall cans, recovering. Tammy has transferred the ashes from Eric's generic container to an ornate ceramic one in the shape of a golden retriever that she purchased just for this purpose. She has placed the ceramic dog that holds the ashes of the real dog in a small shrine prepared weeks ago on the mantel of the fireplace that is built into the wall perpendicular to the couch. The shrine consists of several pictures of the apparently playful pup, one where Romeo is trying to pull a long white rubber bone out of Tammy's grip; the bone itself—along with a chewed and mangled stuffed rabbit—is also part of the shrine. Ed finds the whole thing both inexplicable and a little nauseating, but he keeps this to himself and even nods solemnly when Tammy tearfully asserts that now her beloved dog can finally rest in peace.

"I am so sorry about that," Tammy tells Ed, for about the fortieth time since they sped away from the house. "I'm completely mortified. I don't know what came over me. Something about that asshole brings out the worst part of my personality. I can't control myself around him. I'm incredibly embarrassed."

Ed has already told Tammy that it's okay, that he doesn't mind, that the adventure was fun and exciting in retrospect, however horrifying it might have been while it was going on. And indeed, this is no lie, it's how Ed feels. He is confident Chuang Tzu would in fact be proud of him. He tells her this again, but she's clearly still not sure.

"I mean, have you ever been with someone who you know is terrible for you, who you know is a bad person, but there's just nothing you can do to stop yourself because you're so fucking attracted to them?"

Ed has not been with such a person. Ever. He's read about them in books, though. "Kind of," he says, "I guess."

"That's how it was with Eric. I knew he was bad news, but fuck if that's ever stopped me before, right? I should have just taken off the first time he called into Rush Limbaugh."

"You hadn't mentioned that he was a, hmm, how would you put it, ideologue?"

"Yeah, *ideologue*, that's a kind way of saying it. More like *fucking lunatic*. I think he would actually dissolve the government if he could. Well, except for the military. He was a fan of yours, you know, for a while anyway. Of course I told him we were sort of related—I tell everyone—and then you wrote some decision that said Congress couldn't do something or other . . ."

"The Commerce Clause decision—*City of Rudolph*, a couple of terms ago."

"Whatever. Anyway, for a couple of weeks you were his hero. I'm pretty sure he even said so on Limbaugh. Of course, then you went ahead and upheld gay marriage, and that was pretty much the end of the love affair."

"Hah," Ed says, as a way of laughing, and then finishes his beer. "Can I have another beer?" he asks. "This beer is terrible. But it's fun drinking out of a can."

"It is fun drinking out of a can, isn't it?" Tammy replies, finishing her own beer and heading to the kitchen to retrieve two more. "It keeps me young. That and getting rocks thrown at me by the wife of my insane ex-boyfriend."

Ed tries to crush the empty can with his hand, but it doesn't budge much so he uses both hands, making only slightly more progress. Wiggling his fingers around, he vows to get back on the tennis court asap—back when he was playing twice a week with Bash a few years ago his right hand was a sinewy machine, but now it's like five Twinkies attached to a Ring Ding. Tammy comes back with the new beers and sits beside him, closer than she was before. They crack open the cans, and Tammy clinks Ed's can with her own. "What should we toast to?" she asks.

"To not getting hit by flying rocks," he says back.

"To not getting hit by flying rocks," she affirms, and then she leans in and kisses him.

Whoa, Ed thinks, but he doesn't pull away. Instead, he lingers, remains passive for a moment, enjoys her lips, cold from the can, on his. Some seconds pass, and she backs up. "Was that too weird?" she asks. "I'm sorry if that was too weird."

He smiles at her. "It was weird," he says, touching her forearm gently with one of his Twinkie digits. "But I wouldn't say it was *too* weird."

"I had a crush on you when we were kids," she says. "I'm not even sure I knew what a crush was back then. But it was definitely a crush."

This makes Ed instantly ecstatic. "This may fall under the category of too much information," Ed says, "but since you just kissed me and then confessed to having a crush on me when you were twelve, I feel like I can tell you that I had my very first wet dream about you. Back when I was thirteen."

Tammy's eyes widen at the news. She takes a big drink from the new beer and nods her head. "Wow. That really may be too much information. I don't know. I guess I should be flattered, right?"

"I think so," Ed says. "I didn't even know what sex was back then. In the dream we were just rolling around on your mother's bed. Then I woke up, and well, there it was."

"And there it was!" Tammy exclaims.

"There it was!" Ed yelps back.

Tammy and Ed look at each other. They are both holding their tall boys, nodding. Awkwardness. Tammy breaks the silence. "So, umm, now what?" Ed looks at her some more.

He's trying to decide what to do next, how to weigh the pros and cons. Should he keep kissing his cousin? His *cousin*? But of course she's *not* his cousin. What would Jane say? Although . . . who gives a flying fuck? But then again, he just slept with Diana two days ago, and *wow* does he like her a lot. But on the other hand, looking at Tammy, seeing an ancient fantasy lying open for the taking in front of his eyes, thinking about what seemed like really, *really* expert lips, and—he has to admit—a damn nice soft forearm in his hand, he has a hard time even conjuring Diana's face up in his head. And when it does flit into his consciousness, he immediately banishes it. It's not like they're an item or anything, they hardly know each other, she doesn't have to know anyway, what she doesn't know won't hurt her. And yet . . . she will know, he'll have to tell her, she won't like it, why mess up something that seems like it could turn out so incredible? All this goes through Ed's brain in the space of about a second-and-a-half. His head throbs. Then, the image of a cook. Cook Ting. And an ox. An ox and a knife. *Zip, zoop,* Ed thinks, and suddenly his mind is made up.

"I think if we're going to do this," Ed says, "I'm going to have to drink this entire can of beer first."

"Yes," Tammy says, "I agree."

Another clink of the cans, some mutual college-kid-esque lager chugging, and then the two old friends fall into each other's arms.

***

Holy fucking shit, Ed says to himself, over and over, the next day, as a car takes him back to his house from Union Station. *I can't believe I fucked my cousin.* It's been like a mantra from the moment he woke up in his hotel bed. Hot breakfast. *I fucked my cousin.* Shower and shave. *I fucked my cousin.* Morning dump. *Fucked my cousin.* Drop off the rental car. *I. Fucked. My. Cousin.* Get on the train. *Fuckedmycousin-ohmygodIdid.* He can't take it anymore.

Not that the actual fucking of the cousin had been bad in any way. In fact, the cousin-fucking had been downright scrumptilicious. Ed and Tammy had taken their time, as those in their seventh decade tend to do, and as it happens, one-hundred-and-twenty-three years of experience can make up for almost any amount of drooping and jiggling. He had been right about her lips, surprised by her thighs, nearly blown away by her exuberance. She reveled in the idea of making love with a judge. More than once he balked at one of her more erotic suggestions, but his objections were overruled, his further hesitancy declared "out of order." At one point Ed dilly-dallied when Tammy demanded that he bite her nipple, so she threatened to call the bailiff and hold him in contempt. No matter how many times he explained that these were the actions of a lower court judge, a trial adjudicator, a lowly district court toiler, she insisted on calling him to the bench for a sidebar and threatening to keep him on a *tight leash*, like pretty much every judge she had ever seen on any episode of *Law and Order*. Eventually, he had to reverse her on appeal, but it turned out that she loved even that in the end.

After several hours of this, Tammy gave Ed a ride back to his hotel. They were quiet, mostly, on the way; Tammy had seemed particularly distracted. At the hotel, awkward kisses were exchanged, as were phone numbers and emails, halfhearted promises to stay in touch that neither one expected to keep. Regret did not descend upon Ed immediately. He walked to the Applebees down the road and drank two Budweisers while watching the end of the first game of the Boston-San Francisco World Series with thirty locals and a garrulous bartender named Sheila. When the Sox dropped the game 5-2, the fans tried to make their peace with the loss, said things to each other like *it's just one game* and *just wait until they get to Fenway*, and *give me a fahhh-hkin fried clam roll, Sheila.* Ed walked back to the hotel and then fell asleep nearly immediately, had one of his recurring dreams, the one where the law school registrar informs him two days before graduation that he did not complete enough graded credits to be the class valedictorian. In the dream, Ed always goes over the math, sure that he had taken just enough credits to squeak over the limit, but the numbers never line up right. Like usual, he had woken from the dream in a heart-thumping panic, only to realize within seconds that graduation was thirty-something years ago and that nobody was going to force him to relinquish his seat on the court in disgrace.

Only this time, a new horror had quickly replaced the dissipated panic: *Holy shit, I fucked my cousin.* The horror has haunted him all day, hiding behind some neurons in his cerebellum, jumping out and assaulting him at random moments, in the middle of reading a brief, for instance, in the quiet car, just when Ed thinks he has figured out the puzzle of the pension statute's use of the term "fiduciary." *Boo!* the horror shrieks, and Ed loses his train of thought, thinks back to the previous afternoon, his bare limbs intertwined with a woman who, forty-five years ago, was his uncle's stepdaughter. He knows there's nothing wrong, of course there's nothing wrong, with what he's done, but yet, but yet. And then, when he has convinced himself once again that he has done nothing wrong, right when he's about to return to the brief, or Dawn's bench memo, or the newspaper to see what the Russians are up to or who the Red Sox might send to the mound in Game 5 if they get that far, he remembers that in fact he has done something wrong, and it has nothing to do with the fact that he and Tammy used to sort of be related. Diana. What will he tell her? What will she say?

The car lets Ed off at his house. He opens the door and throws his bag down in the foyer. The orange cat trots over to greet him, meows a few times, does a figure eight between his legs, rubbing against his khaki lightweight wool pants while he bends down to scratch her on the cheek, behind an ear. "Hi, cat," Ed says. "I fucked my cousin."

He fills the cat's bowls with fresh food and water, then collapses on the couch and re-reads, for the final time, the key parts of the briefs for Monday's cases. He's ready—neither of the cases involves any Fourth Amendment violations as far as he's concerned, though he knows that Stephenson and Leibowitz will see the issues differently. He closes his eyes and falls lightly asleep to visions of Tammy and Diana, their grinning faces floating around his dozy brain, one's head on the other's naked body, then the other way around and back again, and he is everywhere, an imaginary ménage a trois bringing an involuntary smile to his lips, an erection to his still weary penis.

The fantasy is busted up, shattered into smithereens, by loud repeated banging on the front door. "Oh, shit," Ed says, as he gets his bearings, sits up cautiously on the couch and rubs his eyes as the banging accelerates, grows louder. "What the hell?" As he makes his way to the door, he realizes that his erection is poking his pants out so he stops short, conjures an image he often goes to in this situation—his grandmother's naked buttocks, circa 1961, surreptitiously and regrettably viewed, the less said about the context the better—and the erection withers to nothing. The banging on the door is so intense that when Ed finally opens it up, the frazzled guy at the door—whom Ed immediately recognizes as his neighbor Savin LaPierre—comes pretty close to punching Ed in the chest; in fact, Savin's forward momentum when the door is opened practically sends him lurching into Ed's house. It takes a moment for Savin to recover, to step back, regain whatever composure he can muster. He actually smooths down his white oxford button-down shirt before embarking on his tirade.

"Did you steal my cat, Tuttle?"

Ed recognizes what's going on right away, of course, but there's still a small part of him that can't believe it, so he says some words simply to fill the void, put off the inevitable. "What? What the hell are you talking about, LaPierre?"

"You what I'm talking about, Mister Justice. I came home yesterday from Central America, and my cat was missing. I took a walk around the neighborhood and saw him sitting in your window. I can't believe you stole my cat!"

"It's a him? Hmm. I did not know that."

"Yeah, Mr. Fluffy is a him, that's right. Hard to believe, I know."

"Look, Savin, I'm sorry, I didn't steal your cat. He was meowing one night and keeping the whole neighborhood awake, so I gave him some mackerel and then he came back the next day and ran into the house. I've been feeding him. He's fine. I thought you had forgotten about it or something, so I took care of it for a few days, what's the big deal?"

"You fed Mr. Fluffy *mackerel*? Jesus. He's on a strict dry food diet special for cats with urinary tract problems. Probably you've killed him."

"He was outside. How could he eat his precious urinary food if he couldn't get into your house?"

"The garage has a little door for him, you idiot."

"Oh," Ed manages.

Presumably at the sound of his owner's voice, Mr. Fluffy trots out into the foyer, past Ed and toward Savin, who is delighted to see him.

"Hi, Mr. Fluffy," Savin squeaks. "How are you? Are you okay? Did this Supreme Court justice hurt you? He thinks because is a big shot judge that he can go around stealing his neighbors' pets. But we know he can't. Don't we?"

Ed shakes his head, rolls his eyes, would like nothing more than for this guy to get on his way. "Just take the cat and go," he says.

Savin bends down and picks up the cat, holds Mr. Fluffy in front of him so he can look into the cat's big green eyes, its legs dangling helplessly. "Let's go home, buddy," he says to the cat, then turns back to Ed. "Since I'll have to take him to the vet to make sure you haven't done any irreparable damage with the smoked fish diet you've put him on, you'll be getting a vet bill in the mail. If you're lucky I won't write something about this incident for the *Atlantic*. It might help me to not write something if you would trim your damn oak tree like you're supposed to."

"Great talking to you, Savin," Ed responds. "Like always."

As Savin turns and walks away with Mr. Fluffy still in his arms, Ed watches them for a few moments. He feels a bit of sadness at the cat's departure but a more palpable relief at Savin's. "Bye, Mr. Fluffy, if that is your real name," he says, then purposefully slams the door as hard as possible, the shot of noise sending Mr. Fluffy flying maniacally from Savin's arms and into a mad dash in exactly the opposite direction from where Savin wanted to take him.

Ed stands, staring at the inside of the now closed door, smirking, listening to Savin scream. "You're a total asshole, Tuttle," the neighbor yells, fruitlessly. "You are such an asshole!"

**

Deeply satisfied by his encounter with Savin, Ed retreats to the couch and returns to his nap. This time he sleeps deeply, for hours, until he is woken by the ringing of his phone. He fumbles for it, finally answers on the fourth or fifth ring. It's Tammy. Ed is surprised to hear from her, and he sits up on the couch, opens his eyes wide to wake himself up, runs his hand through his messed up hair. "Tammy," he says. "What's up?"

At first she says nothing, which makes Ed think that maybe the connection has been lost. "Tammy? Tammy? Are you there?" he asks.

"Yeah, I'm here," she says weakly.

"Is everything all right? Are you okay?"

"Yeah, well, no, I mean I'm all right," she says, incoherently. "I just need to tell you something. Something I should have told you about before."

"What's going on? You're scaring me, Tammy."

She collects herself and sighs. "What do you know," she asks, "about Chlamydia?"

JANUARY

SEVEN

"THIS ISN'T A GRADUATE-LEVEL SEMINAR IN CHINESE HISTORY,"
Andy says to Jim after Jim has explained to the group his view of the
relevant *Chuang Tzu* passage. "We're not trying to figure out what the
text meant in the third century BC. We want to know what this guy
has to say to us *today*, living in the modern world. It doesn't help us
to know that Chuang Tzu was reacting to the Mohist school or the
Confucians or whatever."

"I totally disagree," Jim responds. "I mean, unless we're just going to
say that the *Chuang Tzu* means whatever we think it means regardless
of what it actually says, then I think we need to know what it really
says. And you can't understand what it says unless you know the historical context."

"I think there's got to be some sort of a middle way," Ed interjects.
"I agree that the language and history put a basic limit on what we can
take from the book, to the extent we can understand them, which is no
easy matter when it comes to a Chinese guy writing 2,500 years ago,
but at the same time, we're not going to get anywhere in learning how
to make our own lives better if we get too bogged down in this stuff
that obviously we can never get to the bottom of."

Jim shakes his head back and forth at a strange angle that suggests
both disagreement and frustration, but the other five members of the
group seem at least mildly persuaded by Ed's moderate position. None
of them have any idea that they have a Supreme Court justice in their
midst. This is Ed's fourth time at the local DC "Chuang Tzu for Modern Life" meetup group, and, as usual with these things, he's taken
extra steps to ensure that nobody here recognizes him. He's wearing

the new casual getup he's been wearing everywhere recently—pajama-soft, three-hundred-dollar dark blue jeans, black v-neck t-shirt, thick black Alden boots, navy sport coat from Boss—and he's added a pair of completely fake oval eyeglasses with a distinctly striking hunter green frame and a blue Red Sox cap that in addition to the classic "B" in the front also features a little pennant in the back that boasts of the team's freshly won World Series championship. Additionally, he's told everybody that his name is Ralph.

The meetups take place once a month in Andy's one-bedroom apartment on Capitol Hill, not five blocks from the court and less than two blocks from the tiny Spartan apartment that Ed has been renting for the past month while he gets his McLean home ready (new paint, fixing the deck, a hundred other small things) to put on the market. Five guys and two women have arranged themselves around a cramped living room smelling faintly of incense and cigarette smoke on a few shockingly mismatched chairs, a handed-down overstuffed Pottery Barn couch, and a stained red ottoman. Most of the discussants are drinking either cheap red wine or bottles of microbrew beer, but although Ed has dutifully brought a six-pack to the gathering, he drinks only soda water; for the past few months, except for a glass of wine here and there at fancy functions, he has cut out booze altogether.

"I had a totally Chuang Tzu moment the other day," blurts Stuart, a nineteen-year-old business administration student at a small college in the suburbs, whose stated goal in life is "to make a ton of scratch" and who pretty much all the other members of the group agree doesn't understand the first thing about Chuang Tzu. "I was working downtown at my internship, and after work I'm walking down K Street and there's this homeless guy who asks me for a dollar. So I look at him and tell him that he has a nice nose. He's like, *what did you say?* So, I say it again: *You got a nice nose, you got a nice nose* over and over in this ridiculous falsetto voice. He had no idea what was going on at all. It was awesome!"

"That's not you being Chuang Tzu," says Emily, a thirty-something painter-slash-barista at the Starbucks on the corner of Pennsylvania and 3rd. "That's just you being an asshole." Ed likes Emily and finds her to be pretty consistently amusing, although he's not sure that her reason for being here—to "channel the sage" so she can "become a better and more successful painter"—is necessarily a good one.

Indeed, Ed's not at all sure what he's doing here with these people. He had come on a lark to the first one as part of his "Rethinking Ed" project back in mid-October, and the newness and weirdness of it had appealed to him. Plus, with Diana out of the picture, Ed liked being able to talk about this book that had wormed its way into his consciousness with a bunch of people who were also interested in it, even if they had not been particularly insightful about the text. Emily made him laugh, and both Jim and Andy were smart and decently trained in their disciplines (Andy in philosophy, Jim in Chinese history, both currently working on their dissertations). Ed came to a second meeting and then a third, took what he could from the scholars, ignored Stuart the dingbat, wondered about what the always-silent Sadie—mid-fifties, dressed consistently in mostly purple, sipping wine, but never adding anything to the conversation apart from an occasional chuckle or cluck of dissatisfaction—was getting out of the group. But by halfway through the third meeting, Ed had decided he wouldn't be coming back. Emily wasn't *that* funny, and he had come to recognize that the constant bickering between Andy and Jim about the right way to go about interpreting the book was terrifyingly similar to the debates he'd been witnessing day in and day out around the Chief's mahogany conference room table for the past eight years.

And he wouldn't have come back, either, if it hadn't been for the presence of a new member at the third meeting. Mister Wong, as he had introduced himself, seemed almost like a Chuang Tzu meetup cliché, if such a thing could possibly exist. The little old bald guy wearing plain gray slacks and a white button-down shirt had shown up about halfway through the meeting and, with hardly a word to anyone, taken a seat cross-legged on the floor. After pulling out a thermos of hot tea and a well-worn, dog-eared copy of the *Chuang Tzu* (in both English and Chinese) from his backpack, he had motioned with a wiggle of his hand that the group, which had of course stopped talking while watching the new guy settle in, should continue its deliberations. Jim and Emily had then resumed talking about the passage where Chuang Tzu suggests that maybe there is no difference between words and the chirping of baby birds (one of Ed's favorites), at which point Mr. Wong took out a beanie with a propeller on the top, put it on his head, and spun the propeller around. When Andy asked Mr. Wong what was "up" with the hat, Mr. Wong had simply looked at Andy and squawked, "it's a spinny hat!" which made everyone, including Ed, burst out in nearly uncontrollable laughter for several minutes. Over the course of the rest of the meeting, Mr. Wong had spoken only a few times, but each time Ed found himself laughing like he hadn't in months, so even though Ed couldn't tell whether Mr. Wong was a standup comic, a spiritual guru, or just a run-of-the-mill crazy person, he figured he'd give the group one more try before swearing it off for good.

It is getting toward the end of the meeting, and they have been discussing a question of great interest to Ed, though one that also makes him somewhat agitated: Can a true Chuang Tzu-ian serve as a government official? Emily had suggested the topic at the end of the prior month's meeting because it had struck her as particularly Chuang-Tzu-ianly absurd and/or possibly appropriate that they were convening a Chuang Tzu meetup group within a mile of the nation's Capitol Building. Ed had responded that he wasn't sure it was totally off the wall to think that one could be both a Chuang Tzu-ian and a government official, and so the group decided to discuss the question at the next meeting. According to Emily and Jim, a passage from a chapter called "Autumn Floods" basically cemented their "No True Chuang Tzu-ian as Government Official" position:

Once, when Chuang Tzu was fishing in the P'u River, the king of Ch'u sent two officials to go and announce to him: "I would like to trouble you with the administration of my realm."

Chuang Tzu held on to the fishing pole and, without turning his head, said, "I have heard that there is a sacred tortoise in Ch'u that has been dead for three thousand years. The king keeps it wrapped in cloth and boxed, and stores it in the ancestral temple. Now would this tortoise rather be dead and have its bones left behind and honored? Or would it rather be alive and dragging its tail in the mud?"

*"It would rather be alive and dragging its tail in the mud," said
the two officials.
Chuang Tzu said, "Go away! I'll drag my tail in the mud!"*

Ed had to admit that this was some pretty strong evidence that Chuang
Tzu didn't think a true sage should serve in the government; if this
were a constitution they were expounding, a piece of evidence like
this from the constitutional convention would be enough to convince
even Justice Leibowitz—about as far from an originalist interpreter as
you could find on the court—to concede the point. But still, this isn't
a constitution they are expounding, is it, and so Ed is trying to come
up with something creative to counter the passage's obvious meaning.

"Even without understanding precisely to whom Chuang Tzu was
responding," Ed adds, ignoring Stuart's dumb story and following up
on his previous point about the middle way, "we might be able to say,
right, that at least this part of his philosophy is limited to the specific
context in which it arose. Just because one shouldn't be an official in
third-century BC China doesn't necessarily mean that I can't—I mean,
one can't—be an official in twenty-first-century America."

"Hah!" Mr. Wong, who had been silent throughout this part of the
discussion thus far, exclaims. "Saying you can be a disciple of Chuang
Tzu and a government official at the same time is like . . . it's like . . .
saying that the best route between two points is the shortest one!"

At this, the whole group, other than Ed, breaks out into great guffaws and chuckles. *But wait,* Ed thinks, *the best route between two
points is not the shortest one?*

"Hi, I'm a person. I need to get from Point A to Point B," Emily says
in a mocking tone, shaking her head around like a doddering fool. "I
know, I'll go in a straight line!"

More guffaws all around. *Bah ha ha ha ha.*

"I need to get to my destination very, very fast," Mr. Wong says, don-
ning a silly expression and spinning the propeller on his hat. "I have to
get there very quickly!"

Yuk yuk yuk yuk.

Ed wants to inquire about the point, but he can see that if he does,
they'll all mark him as a moron, so he restrains himself, even forces

himself to laugh a little alongside them. "All right, all right," he says, adjusting his Red Sox hat a bit and sipping a little soda water, "I guess I'm in the minority on this government official thing."

"Better give up those plans of running for mayor there, Ralph," Stuart says.

"Back to the grind, then, I suppose," Ralph says, referring obliquely to the accounting office where he once told them he works.

"My father was a panda bear, you know," says Mr. Wong, to great fanfare.

***

When the meetup is over, Ed says his farewells and starts walking to the court building to do some last-minute reading and thinking about the *Sexy Slut* case, which the justices are finally set to hear first thing in the morning. Although the court is only a few straight blocks down Constitution Avenue, Ed decides to try out the lesson he's just learned and walks there in a route that takes him a few blocks out of his way—down Fifth Street for a bit, then a right turn on East Capitol, and another right on First Street before making his way to the side door into the building. It's not bad, he figures, this *not going in a straight line* thing. He passes a gray cat and says hello, thinks wistfully for a moment about Mr. Fluffy, whom he hasn't seen for months. At the corner of East Capitol, he goes into a convenience store that he's not sure he's ever noticed before. Although Ed thinks about buying a six-pack and taking it to his chambers, he resists. Keeping the drinking to a minimum these few months has been tough, and he knows it won't last forever, but it's given him a clarity of mind he knows he needs. He's got a huge decision ahead of him, one he has been seriously considering for months now, and it's not one he can afford to make while under the influence: Will he or won't he retire from the court once the term is through?

As he chews on the single piece of beef jerky that he bought at the store instead of the beer, Ed thinks about the question in light of the *Chuang Tzu* passage they were just discussing at the meeting. It's not like Ed has become a Taoist or anything—although he's had a few moments here and there when he's felt a sort of oneness with nature (while gliding a rented kayak on the Potomac for instance or, more recently, on a day of learning how to cross-country ski with his daughter in upstate New York over the holidays). He still wasn't buying into the idea that there's some force out there that he can tap into and find perfect serenity. But yet, there's something about the book that has changed how he thinks. The idea that words might be nothing more than the tiny peeps of chirping little birds is one that he was starting to come to anyway, however inchoately, but the book has brought it front and center. All these briefs he reads, the arguments he hears, the sentences he writes, the distinctions he so carefully draws—his life's work, in other words— these days they all seem so much more like a thousand squawks in a crowded aviary than anything he can put his trust in.

As he makes the turn onto First Street and walks by the front of the court, with its imposing marble staircase and gleaming golden doors and massive pillars and the two disappointingly crappy fountains on either side, Ed pauses, takes it all in, ponders his future. It's probably been years since he's just stopped and considered this grandiose view; taking the circuitous route indeed has its virtues. The building, despite the fountains, is magnificent, and Ed knows how important the work he does inside it is. He is still proud of that work, and he still feels humbled to have been entrusted with it. It's just that he's not sure he wants to do it anymore. There are so many other things to do, so many other places to see, so many other people to meet. These days, Ed feels far too much like the unhappy turtle, all wrapped up in cloth and stuffed in a box. He is seriously thinking about taking his Brooks-Brothers-clad tail out into the forest somewhere and dragging it through some serious mud.

It's a lovely clear night despite the cold temperature, and Ed is in no rush, so he climbs the grand staircase and takes a seat on one of the steps near the very top. He gazes northward out toward the Capitol dome and breathes the fresh air, turns his coat collar up to protect his neck from the chill. It's been a strange few months. The mid-October cousin-fucking, Chlamydia-contracting fiasco had really thrown him for a loop. At first he'd hoped maybe he hadn't in fact caught the STD, but his wait-and-see game came to an end one morning when it suddenly felt like he was peeing fire, like his penis had turned into Godzilla overnight. It actually turned out not to be all that bad, physically—a strange analgesic that turned his piss bright orange soothed him until the Doxycyclene worked its magic—but the psychic wound has taken longer to heal. How stupid he felt, sitting in his doctor's office, a justice on the Supreme Court, his dick throbbing, as he explained to his physician how he'd had unprotected sex with a virtual stranger, as though he hadn't heard the word on the street that such activities might be dangerous. How stupid he still feels thinking back on it— somehow it's one of those mistakes whose sting doesn't much dissipate over time. *Dimwit. Nitwit. Dumbass.*

Plus, of course, Diana had been, to put it lightly, displeased. It wasn't so much that he'd had sex with Tammy that bothered her, though she wasn't exactly thrilled about that either. It was more the Chlamydia that had set her off. He still remembers quite clearly her response to that particular revelation: *Oh my god, that's disgusting. If you had to go fuck a skanky cousin, couldn't you have at least worn a condom?* What could he say? Her logic was unassailable. "Yes, I should have. I'm sorry. I'm an idiot," was what he'd said, and she had agreed, with gusto. She had sent him away, not necessarily for good, but with instructions to leave her be, to give her time, to let her do some thinking. He hasn't seen her since. Probably he should have called her, redoubled on the apology, laid it on thick—Bash tells him this every time they talk—but he's decided to take her at her word and let her be. And so now he sits, on the court's marble staircase, celibate, alone, sober, sad . . . and *cold*. *Damn*, Ed thinks to himself, wrapping his arms tightly around his torso. *It's fucking cold out here.*

A couple of minutes later, Ed arrives in his chambers and says hello to Dawn, who is hard at work in her office despite the fact that it's Sunday evening. As far as Ed can tell, Dawn is never not in the office; it is certainly the case that whenever he's in the office, she is as well. He's explained to his clerks that they don't have to work their asses off on his account, but most of them do it anyway. He understands it—when he was clerking here after law school thirty-plus years ago, he had spent practically every waking minute at his desk working on something. It is no surprise that the clerks, who are only here for a year, would want to spend as much time in the building as possible. Only a jaded curmudgeon like Ed would actually yearn to be somewhere else.

"What are you working on?" he asks Dawn.

"I'm still poring through the data on the pornography-violence link. I think it's pretty weak. Or at least inconclusive. You should take a look at the amicus brief filed by these law professors at Northwestern. It's even better than the ACLU's brief."

She hands the brief to Ed, who takes a quick look at the page Dawn has marked. It's got all sorts of handwritten notes all over it and at least two post-its stuck to the side, with even more handwritten notes on those. Ed knows what's going on. Dawn wants Ed to vote with the liberals and hold that the First Amendment protects the kind of stuff in *Sexy Slut*. Everyone knows that Ed's the swing vote in the case, but Ed has been tight lipped about what he's going to do in the case, primarily because he truly doesn't know how he's going to vote. On the one hand, he figures he should just stick with the precedent, go with the status quo, apply the doctrine of stare decisis and be done with it. But on the other, he's always believed that judges should interpret and apply the Constitution in a limited way, to protect the democratic process, let the people decide what to do, keep the courts out of it unless there's an extremely clear reason for them to get involved. Why shouldn't Texas be able to prohibit some guy from making money by plastering a collage of penises all over the cover of a magazine? What does Ed care? It's not like the Constitution says "the right to publish penis collages shall be sacrosanct" or anything.

Meanwhile, he's read all the briefs on both sides, even the one he's currently holding in his hand, and nothing in any of them has persuaded him one way or the other. Pornography causes violence. Pornography doesn't cause violence. Pornography decreases violence. The First Amendment was intended to protect personal expression. The First Amendment was intended only to protect political speech. The court should always adhere to precedent. The court doesn't always have to adhere to precedent. Blah, blah, blah, squawkedy-squawk-squawk, peep peep cheepedy fucking cheep.

"I know, I know, I've read it," Ed says to Dawn, handing her back the brief, heading for the door to his own office. "I've read it all. Every last word. Of everything."

"How are you going to vote?" Dawn calls after him.

"I wish I knew," his voice trails back as he disappears into his inner sanctum.

Once in his office, Ed sits down on the couch, closes his eyes, lets out a deep sigh. When he opens his eyes after maybe a minute he looks at the wall over his desk at the two minor Lichtensteins that Linda was able to scrounge up from the National Gallery and then scans down to the desk itself, where he sees the ukulele that he's been learning how to play for the past two months. His mood brightens immediately—it's like a rainbow has sprouted from his trash can and spread its multi-colored glow over the office. Ed gets up, retrieves the uke, along with the chord sheets for "Under the Rainbow," and returns to the couch, where he starts playing. It's a fairly easy song, but Ed's still new to the instrument, and he has almost no natural musical talent whatsoever, so it's still tough going. The first line usually goes smoothly, but the tricky E-minor in the second line nearly always trips him up. More-over, even when he does nail all the chords, he can't sync his singing with the music, so he ends up sounding terrible anyway. But Ed doesn't care. It's not like he's planning on going on tour or becoming the next incarnation of Tiny Tim or anything, so he just plays and plays and tries to do the best he can and enjoys engaging in an activity that is about as far from what he typically does as anything he can imagine.

He's been working on the rainbow song for maybe fifteen minutes when the chief justice pokes her head into his office. "Umm, hello? Excuse me? Mind if I come in?" she says hesitantly, poking the door open a bit more with her right index finger.

Ed is startled. He puts the uke down on the couch and stands up awkwardly, feeling almost like the time when he was fourteen and his mother caught him jacking off in the family room.

"Oh, hi, yeah, sure," he stammers. "Come on in, Janet."

"I was just walking by in the hallway and I heard something that umm, sounded sort of like music coming from in here," she says, pointing to the ukulele.

"Right, yup. Oh, that? That's my ukulele. I've just started taking lessons. I thought it would be a good way to reduce stress, take my mind off things for a little while at a time. I'm still not that good."

"No, no. You're not. Dear, sweet Lord, no. Not good at all. Are those new glasses?"

"Oh, these?" he asks, removing the glasses from his head and handing them to her, inexplicably. "No, those are purely cosmetic. Sometimes I wear them when I don't want people to recognize me."

"In your office?" she asks, refusing to take the glasses, pushing them back toward him. "Do you get a lot of strangers coming into your office these days? Maybe we should beef up security around here. I'll make a note of that."

"Yeah, good idea," Ed says, like an idiot.

"When they come in—the strangers, that is—when they come into the office that says 'Ed Tuttle, Associate Justice' on it, do the glasses work to confuse them? Do they think, hmm, this guy wearing the glasses and working in the office that says 'Ed Tuttle' must not be Ed Tuttle. Because Ed Tuttle doesn't wear glasses?"

"Yeah, no, right. I was just wearing them earlier, when I was outside the building. I forgot to take them off."

"Is everything okay, Ed?"

"What? Sure, yeah, everything's fine. Just came in to do some last-minute thinking about the case tomorrow."

The Chief looks conspicuously at the ukulele on the couch.

"I do some of my best thinking while I play," Ed offers. "While I try to play, anyway."

"Well, good," she says. "Any idea which way you're leaning? I think you're the decisive vote on this thing."

Like anyone had to tell him that. "No, not quite sure. Going into the oral argument and conference with an open mind."

"All right, then. If you end up agreeing with us, I can assign the opinion to you," Janet says. "You could write it as narrow as you want. I'm sure you could still get together a majority for a measured change in approach, even if most of us prefer something a little more radical."

"Perhaps," Ed answers, though he knows that regardless of how he comes out in the case, he'll likely get to (*have to*, is more like it) write the opinion. If he decides with the libs, Sutherland will probably assign him the opinion too.

The Chief stares at Ed, waiting for him to say more, to give some hint of how he's leaning, what he's thinking about the case, but to no avail. When she realizes that he's not going to say anything more on the matter, she changes the subject.

"What do you think about this Pledge of Allegiance petition we're talking about Friday? I think we pretty much have to take it, right?"

Ed realizes, sadly, that yes they do have to take the case. Once again, a court of appeals has held that the "under God" part of the pledge is an unconstitutional establishment of religion under the First Amendment, and that's exactly the kind of case that the Supreme Court has to decide. The justices had taken up the issue a few years ago, the first time an appeals court had struck down the pledge, but that time there was a technical problem with the lawsuit that let the court get rid of the case, and preserve the pledge, without reaching the thorny issue at the heart of the case. This time, everyone agrees, the justices will have no choice but to rule on the merits.

"I guess that's right. Marvelous. Another case where we have to decide moral policy for the nation. I can't wait."

"Well, this one's pretty easy, don't you think?" the Chief asserts. "It's not like the Pledge is a prayer or anything. It'll be good to get this resolved once and for all."

"Maybe," Ed answers. "Though I do think it's a problem that Congress added 'under God' to the Pledge in 1954 to distinguish us from the so-called godless communists."

The Chief grimaces. "You were with us on the merits last time around, if I remember right," Owens says, quite clear that she remembers correctly. "You haven't changed your mind since then I hope."

Ed pauses, hesitates. "I don't know," he says. "There isn't much I know for sure anymore."

The Chief stares at Ed, then looks around—at the glasses that Ed's twirling in his hands, the ukulele on the couch, the strange new paintings on the wall that have replaced the traditional fox and hound hunting ones that she used to admire. "Well, I think you'll come around. The Ed I know isn't going to declare that the Pledge of Allegiance is unconstitutional. Judicial restraint, and all that. Anyway, have a good night." And with that, the Chief pats Ed on the shoulder and leaves.

Ed watches her go. "See you tomorrow," he mutters, but the Chief's long, no-nonsense strides have already taken her too far away to hear him.

***

The next morning, Ed takes his seat on the bench between Cornelius and Epps and prepares for the beginning of the dreaded argument about pornography. This is the first case of the term that the public and the media are paying any real attention to, and the plaza in front of the court is packed with protestors and sign-carriers of all kinds. One poster has the cover of the *Sexy Slut* issue reproduced on it twenty times; at forty-two times twenty, that's 840 penises being paraded around the front of the nation's highest tribunal. Not to be outdone, some of the people on the other side—the "let pornography be free" crowd—have come dressed up as giant penises and have been doing cartwheels and dancing to swing music next to the fountain on the east side of the plaza. It's exactly the kind of constitutional circus that makes Ed cringe, although if this were a reality show and he had to vote for one of the groups to move on to the next round, Ed pretty much knows that he would vote for the dancing Johnsons. At least they have a sense of humor.

The solicitor general for the state of Texas is the first to argue, and the liberals unshockingly give her a hard time. "What's wrong with the test we've been applying for the past forty years?" Epps asks. "How can you say that pornography isn't expressive?" demands Stephenson. "What's the alternative?" wonders Leibowitz. Sharon Cox answers the questions without hesitation—the test is too strict, the expression is dangerous, the alternative is to let the states do what they want. The conservatives are mostly silent, once in a while even peeping up to support Cox's position, to make clear they agree that hardcore porn should not be protected. The Chief asks about the pornography-violence link; she poses her comments in the form of a question, but it's clear she's just giving the lawyer the green light to wax eloquent on the dangers of too much smut in the public square. Wax she does, and Garabelli practically gets out of his seat to applaud her efforts.

Ed stays silent for the entire argument. Among other things, he doesn't want to give the reporters anything to talk and write and blog about. They know that the case will likely turn on his vote, so everything he says will be dissected endlessly, put through the prognostication mill, misconstrued. Instead of asking questions, he tries to sketch the lawyer's profile on the back of the petitioner's brief. The perspective is difficult because Cox is at an angle and constantly turning her head to answer a different justice's question, but by the end of her twenty-eight-minute argument (she's reserved two minutes for rebuttal), and with the help of a good deal of erasing and redrawing and closing of one eye and then the other to get better focus, he thinks he's got something worth showing his sketch drawing class when it meets next Sunday afternoon at the Adult Education Center in Foggy Bottom.

The magazine's lawyer is up next. He's one of the nation's top First Amendment experts, but he's more of a scholar than an appellate advocate, so the court's conservatives eat him for lunch, make him wish he was back in his office at Harvard grading papers. The Chief mocks him. Garabelli ties him in knots. Cornelius gets two "[laughter]"s at his expense. The lawyer can't make a straightforward argument that appeals to anyone's common sense; he's too wrapped up in his esoteric theory and obscure scholarship to score any points. Ed almost feels bad for him, considers jumping in to his defense, but then decides such an intervention would be fruitless and unnecessary. The guy should have practiced more. The client should have hired somebody else. In any event, since the justices are almost never moved to change their minds by anything any lawyer ever says during oral argument, the advocate's poor performance has no real effect, except on the professor's future ability to secure high-profile oral argument gigs.

Meanwhile, Ed's brain is bouncing around the inside of his skull like the blue die in the middle of a Magic Eight Ball. How will he finally make up his mind? *Try again later.* What argument will end up moving him the most? *Outlook is cloudy.* How can he do the least amount of damage to the democratic constitutional system he has taken an oath to uphold? *It is uncertain.* Ed considers what an Eight Ball designed by Chuang Tzu might say, and he writes down the possibilities under his drawing of Sharon Cox. *All signs point to Yes and No. How should I fucking know? Go eat a sandwich.*

The state's lawyer approaches the lectern for her rebuttal. She begins on the stare decisis point—in response to her counterpart's position that the court only reverses course in extraordinary circumstances, she draws the court's attention to several recent cases where the justices have reversed their long-term positions without much fanfare. "In *Edmond versus United States*, for instance," she says, "the court issued a holding—a government officer who is supervised by a higher officer is an inferior officer for purposes of the Appointments Clause no matter how important his or her duties—that was a 180 degree reversal from its earlier holding in *Morrison versus Olson*. The circumstances there were hardly extraordinary; the court simply changed its mind. And in *Oregon v. Smith*, the court . . ."

Ed fidgets. She's citing cases, but there are others on the other side. Sometimes the court does one thing, sometimes another. Sometimes the justices say one thing, sometimes they say something else, so what? It's all just words. He's had it up to the proverbial *here* with all the words. He interrupts Cox's string of citations.

"Counselor," says Ed, "I can't help but notice that, like your opponent, you insist on framing your argument with words. Does the strength of your argument rely on the presumption that words mean something rather than nothing?"

Ed is looking intently at Cox. The lawyer blinks. Once, then again. Ed imagines he can hear her eyelids close and open, like in an early morning cartoon. *Blink, blink.* The question, understandably, has thrown off the cool nerve of Texas's top arguer. In all the many practice arguments she had staged to get ready, not once did any of the lawyers playing the justices ask her to defend the human race's shared assumptions regarding the capacity of language to convey meaning. It just hadn't come up.

The silence in the courtroom, if possible, is even more silent than its typical silence. In the pews, members of the audience look at their companions with cocked heads and raised eyebrows. The journalists scribble notes on their little pads and punctuate them with exaggerated question marks. Ed's colleagues are quiet too. Not even Cornelius can come up with anything to get a laugh. The Chief is fuming. Cox stammers. "Umm, well, I suppose . . ." She keeps looking down at the light on the podium, hoping it will turn red, signaling that her argument time is over. Soon it does. The Chief wastes no time. "The case is submitted," she declares, and to everyone's relief, the court is adjourned.

In the argument's aftermath, the court-watchers and journalists and bloggers are astir, trying to make sense of Ed's enigmatic query. Most assume he was making a joke, one that went flat, one that didn't even register a single laugh much less a "laughter." Of the people in this camp, a minority admire Ed's pluck, but the majority find the attempt at mirth inappropriate. Then there's another group—the right-wing alarmists, mostly—who think that Ed was making fun of the Texas lawyer and her position in the case. Concerned that the question foreshadows a 5-4 loss, some of these outliers call for Ed's immediate impeachment, demanding that Rick Santorum be appointed to his seat. Finally, a couple of the larger media outlets go for the ratings and see what they can do with the merits of Ed's question. Chomsky is consulted. *What is Language?* asks MSNBC. CNN wonders, *Are Words Empty?* Jake Tapper's got Steve Pinker on the air within the hour.

In the conference room, where the justices decide how the case will come out and who will write the opinion, the Chief gets right down to business. "Okay, let's try to get through this as quickly as possible," she says. "I've got lunch plans with the Speaker and his wife. And if it's all right with everyone, I propose we proceed with the presumption, controversial as it may be, that words mean something rather than nothing."

This breaks the tension. The justices all laugh, each in his or her own way. Cornelius guffaws, Stephenson chortles, Leibowitz cracks a light smile. Even Ed has to chuckle. What else can he do? If he's going to stay on the court—and for now at least, here he is—what choice does he have but to put aside his doubts and place his faith in the god of reason, which, after all, has done him pretty well in his life so far.

The justices go around the grand table and state their views one by one, but it's all a formality until they get to Ed, because they have all made their views on the case clear before now except for him. When

Ed's turn comes around, he honestly does not know what to say. He had thought maybe the answer would have come to him by now, but it hasn't.

"I'm afraid I'm still undecided," he says.

"Well," the Chief begins, with a tone that reveals a frustrated lack of patience. "I'm afraid you're going to have to decide. What would you like us to do? Announce that we can't make up our minds? *Sorry, the case is too hard for us, we give up.*"

The Chief intimidates Ed, but between last night's visit and this little invective, which has the court's right wingers smirking, he's had enough of her. "You can't make me decide, Janet," he says. "I'll decide when I'm ready to decide. Send me the opinions on both sides, and I'll choose whether to join one of them or write my own. Sorry, but that's where I stand."

The Chief knows her blustery bluff has been called. Ed's right. It's not like she can force him to reach a conclusion if he's not ready. The Chief has some administrative powers beyond what the associate justices do, and she runs the meetings, but ultimately they're all equal when it comes to deciding cases. "All right, then," she says, "I will write up a draft of the opinion on the right side of the issue, and John, I presume, will write up something on the wrong side." She gestures toward Justice Sutherland, who nods in assent. "And we'll see which one of us is lucky enough to convince our indecisive colleague to become the majority."

"Perhaps, Chief, you should consider preparing a painting instead of a written opinion," Garabelli interjects. "You might have a better chance persuading him that way. What, with the inadequacy of language and all."

"We could issue a symphony!" Cornelius pipes in.

"Or maybe a collage!" Arnow can't help but add.

"Okay, okay, very nice," Ed says. "Are we done now?"

"I believe we are," says the Chief. "It's now lunchtime. Thank you for coming."

EIGHT

IN THE OAK-PANELED LOCKER ROOM AT THE CLUB WHERE they have resumed their weekly game, Ed and Greg Bash are changing into their tennis getups and preparing for what Bash has termed the "afternoon of revenge." Although the two old friends have always been roughly equal in athletic ability and usually more or less split their games here at the club, last week Ed crushed Bash so thoroughly that Greg demanded they both undergo steroid testing.

"Are you ready for the afternoon of revenge?" Bash asks, as he starts undoing the buttons on his shirt.

"I have a feeling that today's drubbing may in fact be even worse than last week," Ed answers. He's feeling more confident in his game than he's ever been—mostly because cutting out the booze has both left him thinner and improved his reflexes. Bash, who's still on his three-drink-a-day-at-least program, is as out of shape and slow as ever.

"Did you get your urine tested like we agreed? I'd like to see the results. By the way, look at this bruise you asshole." Bash pulls his pants down and shows Ed a tennis-ball-sized black and blue mark on the side of his left thigh into which Ed had mashed an overhead slam. "You can't do something like that without the help of some prohibited substance. What are you on? HGH? Tiger penis? What?"

"Tiger penis, actually, yes, you got me. How'd you know? Can you remove your thigh from my vicinity now please?" Ed is one of those guys who is not thoroughly comfortable in a locker room. He's not a lingerer. He doesn't like to sit around naked, snapping towels at his friends' hairy asses, studying his toes and making jokes about whores or whatever it is that the lingerers like to joke about. Indeed, Ed's pretty much already fully dressed for tennis—other than his shoes—while Greg is still in a state of half-dress. Greg *is* a lingerer. "Hey, speaking of tiger penises," Greg says, "I think my balls are getting bigger. Will you take a look at these? I don't know what's going on. I need some advice."

Ed turns his head and puts up an outstretched hand to block the sight just in time, as Bash pulls his scrotum out from his threadbare briefs and tries to present it to Ed for inspection. "Jesus, get those things out of here, god," Ed says, and he gets up and starts making his way to the courts, shoes in hand.

"Okay, okay, never mind," Greg says, and he puts his genitals away. Still, though, as Ed reluctantly returns, Greg seems to be weighing each testicle individually, trying to compare them to his memory of how they used to feel. "Do balls typically swell up as you get older?" he asks Ed. "Is that normal? Do you think I should see a doctor?"

"I think you should see a doctor," Ed answers. "In fact, for you, I'd suggest seeing a doctor every single day of your life. You should move one into your house."

"Ahh, this from the guy who five hours ago made the most public display of craziness since Dan Rather left the set."

"I was wondering how long it was going to take you to bring that up." Ed reaches into his bag and checks the time on his phone. "Twelve minutes. Not bad, actually."

"It would seem that the consensus so far is that you were making a joke."

"That's what my clerks tell me."

"Were you? Was it really a joke? Somehow I think it might not have been."

"I don't know. Maybe both a joke and not a joke."

"Well, I think it's the best thing you've done since you've been on the bench. *Does the strength of your argument rely on the presumption that words mean something rather than nothing?* Brilliant! And what's even better is that she couldn't answer you. She couldn't even bring herself to concede that her argument, made with words, would fail if words meant nothing. Now that's sticking to your guns."

"Thanks, I think. You're probably the only person in America who understands what I was getting at. You, the professor who once simultaneously published two articles on the same issue in two separate journals arguing exactly opposite positions."

"The high point of my career, thank you very much."

"Didn't you get shit for that? Did the dean reprimand you?"

"Who, Treanor? No, he would have probably given me a grant for that research. He loved it. He even considered featuring it in the alumni magazine, but someone talked him out of it. There was that one professor who had a temper tantrum on his blog about it, though."

"Right. Who was that again?"

"Oh, that tool from the University of Chicago."

"A tool from the University of Chicago? You'll need to be more specific."

Bash cackles. "True enough. This was the guy who ranks everything. Top schools. Number of citations. Associate dean dick sizes."

"Dear Lord. Reason number eighty-three I don't read law professor blogs."

"You know," Bash says, his tone one notch more serious as he changes the topic, "as soon as I read about your question on Twitter— I think Above the Law posted about it like four seconds after you said it—I sent a link to Diana. She was very impressed. Said it sounded like some Taoist she introduced you to has gotten into your head."

Ed's heart leaps. "Oh, shit. Why'd you have to go do that?"

"Why not? You should have sent it to her yourself, but since I knew you weren't going to do that, I thought I should do it."

"I wouldn't have sent it to her because she told me to stay away from her."

"It's hard to believe that three months later, your dick all fresh and healthy again, and you still think she doesn't want to hear from you. How'd you make it to your age knowing so little about women?"

"How about when I need your advice regarding the opposite sex I'll send you a letter soliciting it?"

"Your time is running out, buddy. I think she's dating someone. Not particularly serious yet, but . . ."

Ed cringes involuntarily at this news, not that it's by any means surprising. "Look, I liked her, maybe I even liked her a lot, but I fucked it up, and it's over, so forget about it."

"You know, for a justice on the US Supreme Court, you really are a dope."

"And you're just mad because you can't beat me in tennis anymore."

Bash finishes tying up his shoes. He grabs his racket and shakes it in Ed's direction. "I can't believe you just said that. All right, commence the *afternoon of revenge.*"

***

After about twenty minutes of tennis, it is clear that Bash will not be enjoying anything close to an afternoon of revenge. Even though all the stuff they've just talked about periodically bubbles up and breaks his concentration, Ed has no problem vanquishing Greg on point after point after point. Indeed, Ed has only lost three points in the entire first set, and each of those have been on shots that he simply hit too hard, too far. Ed is enjoying making Bash run around the court like a confused Dalmatian. He follows up down-the-line forehands with backhands to the court's far corner, sending Greg dashing toward the net with little volleys and then scuttling back to the baseline with lob shots over his head.

As they trade sides for the beginning of the second set, Ed worries that his winded, red-faced friend may have a cardiac infarction and die right there in front of him, so he asks Bash if he'd like to take a break. Bash waves him off with his racket, but while slowly making his way to the opposite baseline, he pretty much concedes that he's no longer Ed's equal on the court. "I would like you . . . to start drinking again," he says, through throaty, canine pants.

Ed smiles, bounces a ball up and down on top of his racket, and strolls slowly to his own baseline. While he does certainly enjoy his newfound tennis acumen, he has to agree that he would like to start drinking again. And fucking, for that matter. Bash is right about one thing—his dick is fresh and healthy, and he ought to start using it again. And he will, soon. But not yet. He hasn't shared with Bash that he's thinking about quitting. Hasn't told anyone. Except for his daughter, to whom he mentioned it on their skiing trip. She had been surprised but supportive, although he doubts she knows how serious he is about stepping down. In any event, this is a decision he's got to make by himself. And he's got to make it with a clear head. He only hopes that he can reach the decision sooner rather than later, before his liver shrivels up and his penis falls off from neglect.

It's Ed's serve. He takes the ball in his left hand, leans forward, then back, tosses the ball aloft, and brings the racket up at the perfect time and angle. He comes down over the ball, connects with the heart of the racket, follows through like a picture in a textbook. The ball sears only inches over the net, pings the back corner of the service box like a lightning bolt. Bash can't even come close to hitting it. Fifteen-Love.

***

The next afternoon, the day's arguments and conference over, Ed takes Linda and his clerks to an animal shelter in southeast DC to pick out an office cat. It won't be a permanent office cat, he makes sure they know. It's just that he wants a pet cat, and he wants it now, and the apartment he's renting while getting the McLean house ready for the market won't let him have pets, and he doesn't want to violate the terms of the lease even though it's unlikely the landlord would ever know because he is, after all, still a justice on the Supreme Court, so he's decided—after consulting with the others who work in his office, checking for cat allergies and the like—that he'll get the cat and let it live in his chambers until he can bring it home. Linda, Rick, and Dawn are thrilled; Sasha is not particularly enamored with cats, so she's not thrilled, but she doesn't object either, and since she figures that a little non-work time with her boss the justice looking at potential pets would be a unique way of spending the afternoon—one she might be able to tell her grandkids ("I went to help Ed Tuttle pick out a cat just as he was starting to go bananas")—she goes along as well.

As they enter the shelter, Ed is surprised by the cacophony inside. He has never been to such a place and for some reason had assumed that it would be quiet and orderly, the little animals all lined up and smiley, putting on their best behavior to entice some kind human to take them home. Instead, it is chaos, dogs of all sizes and shapes and colors barking and wailing at the visitors, at each other, at nothing at all. One couple has a weird little mutt out of its cage. The man and the dog are playing tug of war with a frayed green rope; the dog seems to be winning, and the female member of the couple is not persuaded this is the pup for them. A lot of kids are in the room, and they're almost as loud as the dogs. Two little girls, twins it would seem, are banging on the side of a cage holding two small brown and white rabbits that appear to be scared out of their wits. These children, Ed immediately concludes, should not be trusted with so much as a fish or a Madagascan hissing cockroach for a pet, much less something with four legs, warm blood, and a set of lungs.

The cats have their own room, apart from the maniacal canines, thank goodness, and Ed leads his coterie into it as quickly as possible. Two full walls are devoted to kitty cages, and the cats inside—fat, scrawny, normal-sized, gray, orange, black, white, solid, mixed-up-colored, calico, old, not-so-old, fully-eared, missing-part-of-an-eared, green-eyed, gray-eyed, blue-eyed, furry, very furry, super-duper furry, and one with no fur at all—fill the room with their mews and cries, and Ed thinks, like many who enter the room, that he'll just take them all home with him. The feeling passes in a moment, and it's down to the business of choosing one. Dawn goes right for a little guy (not an actual kitten, there are no actual kittens here) that looks like a miniature Tom from the old Tom and Jerry cartoons—he's grayish blue with some white on his face and a white belly—and as soon as Dawn goes up to his cage he tries to brush up against the hand that she puts on it. She sticks a blue-fingernail-polished index finger into a hole in the cage and scratches the cat's cheek, the top of his head. "Hey, look at this guy, justice. What do you think about this one?"

Ed, who is kind of overwhelmed by the choices, is happy to have his concentration narrowed on one particular cat, so he goes over to Dawn and takes a look. "Oh, hi, Tom," he says, because the resemblance is that strong. "How are you today?" As he tickles Tom underneath the chin, Ed marvels at how his brief time with Mr. Fluffy has changed his mind about cats. The things are so damned cute! How could he have not liked them before? "Where's Jerry? What are you doing in a shelter? Did that stupid mouse get you kicked out of the house? Did he drop a frying pan on your head? Your head is a little flat, actually." Ed pats Tom on the top of his head, but instead of purring appreciatively, the cat takes a halfhearted swipe at Ed's hand. "Hey, what's up with that?" Ed asks, but rather than answering, the little cat retreats to his food bowl and bites into a nugget. Not a match.

"All right, this guy's kind of cute. But who else do we got around here?"

Linda is a few cages down, wiggling a feather toy in front of a rambunctious gray tabby with a glimmering pair of green Mr. Fluffy-ish eyes. Ed comes over to take a look. "Ooh, this guy's super cute," he says, with such exuberance that Rick and even Sasha come over to see who he is talking about. They all watch as Linda flicks the pink feather around the cage, and the cat, whose name, according to the information card attached to his cage, is Freddy, launches himself after the toy, bouncing off the bars and tumbling on the floor before standing up and launching himself again the other way as Linda changes the feather's direction. This goes on repeatedly, leaving Freddy's audience in a state of near-hysteria that hits its high point when Freddy tumbles into his food dish, tipping it over and spilling its contents all over the cage, and then stands up and looks at his admirers, squeaking out a tiny meow as if to say "What? What did I do? What are you all looking at?"

"Freddy, you are crazy," an enamored Ed says, putting his finger into the cage and petting the cat lightly. "Do you need a new home? Would you like to come live at the Supreme Court for a while?"

A shelter volunteer comes over, a girl with a ponytail wearing jeans and a gray George Washington University sweatshirt, and introduces herself as Tamara. "If you want," she says to Ed and his group, "you can take him out and play with him over in that pen." She points to a fenced-in area in the corner of the room.

"Really? That would be great, yes, thank you," Ed says.

"Okay, then, one kitty cat coming up," Tamara says. She inches past Ed to the cage and opens the little door at the front. Freddy seems confused but willing to go with the flow, as Tamara reaches in, picks him up, and hands him to Ed, who is kind of unsure about how to hold a cat. Freddy is excited to be out of the cage and starts squirming in Ed's hands; the justice almost drops the cat but with a couple of *whoa whoa*

*whoa*s reconfigures his grip at the last second and manages to hold on, grasping Freddy on both sides of his upper body, Ed's thumbs hooked around the cat's front legs, leaving Freddy's lower legs dangling below helplessly. Ed is staring right into the cat's green eyes. "All right, big fella," he says, though he has no idea why he'd call this little cat a *big fella*, "let's get you in the pen before you run away to China."

In the pen, everyone takes turns petting and playing with Freddy. Ed goes last. He takes a seat on a little stool and wonders what to do. Freddy wanders over, and Ed bends at the waist to pat him. Ed's tie—a yellow one with blue elephants all over it, purchased in Bangkok one summer years ago in a rare free moment between lectures—grazes Freddy on his face. Freddy figures the tie is a bird or maybe a toy that's supposed to look like a bird, so he swats it with his front right paw, snagging a claw on the tie and pulling a yellow silky thread out of it, a half-inch at first, then an inch, maybe more, as the cat continues to swat and pull and more-or-less dance with the tie in an effort to free himself. Ed realizes at once that the tie is ruined, though while this may at one time have annoyed him greatly, now he could not care less—why does he even wear ties these days, he wonders, it's not like he needs to impress anybody with his sartorial elegance, maybe he'll wear jeans and a velour sweater, or overalls with no shirt to the next conference—so he unknots the tie from his neck and drapes it over the cat. Linda and the clerks watch giddily as Freddy, who is still attached to the tie, rolls around the pen, wrapping himself up in the yellow and blue silk until he looks like a half-opened Christmas present. The cat, realizing he needs help, meows plaintively. Ed kneels on the ground and unwraps him, frees Freddy's paw from the tie. Freddy rubs his face thankfully on Ed's thigh. Ed picks Freddy up. Up, up, up, high over his head, the cat's tail grazing his forehead. "I think we've got a winner!" Ed declares, and his followers, even Sasha the doubter, applaud with delight.

***

At the conference on Friday morning, the justices take their seats and discuss which cases they should hear during the court's last sitting in April. As is her usual practice, the Chief keeps the juiciest case for last. So, after the justices dispose of the first eight cases on the list—denying five and granting two more criminal procedure cases and an obscure dispute about judicial deference to administrative agency decisions—the Chief announces the day's big matter: *City of Philadelphia v. Downey*, the much-anticipated case about whether the phrase "under God" violates the First Amendment, which says that the government may pass no law "respecting an establishment of religion."

"Well, I doubt this will take very long," the Chief begins. "By finding that the Pledge violates the Establishment Clause, the Third Circuit has departed from every other court to decide the issue and has, in my view, clearly misunderstood our own precedents in this area. I vote to grant."

Next to speak is Justice Stephenson, who, though he concurs with the Third Circuit's conclusion, agrees that the court needs to take the case. "Well, I suppose we have no choice but to hear this one," he says, rubbing his ancient eyes with wrinkled fingers. "Groundbreaking fundamental decision on federal constitutional law. It's our obligation. Plus, we can't have one rule in Pennsylvania, New Jersey, and Delaware, and a different rule everywhere else. If a public school teacher in Pittsburgh can't lead her students in the 'Prayer of Allegiance,' then the same thing has got to apply everywhere. I vote to grant."

Even though it's not his turn, Garabelli can't stop himself from taking Stephenson's bait. "Did you hear that everyone? The 'Prayer of Allegiance,' he said. Get it? Do you get it? He said the 'Prayer of Allegiance.' Oh, that's good stuff, John. Real rich."

Stephenson looks over at Tony Garabelli, takes in his jowly red face, his thinning hair, his crumply, profoundly unstylish blue blazer with its stupid gold buttons, and shakes his head in some combination of misery and disbelief. "Janet," he says, turning to face the chief justice. "Do we need to have this fire burning all the time? The building is, after all, heated with electricity."

The Chief scowls at Stephenson, turns a bit and scowls also at Garabelli. "If we could please focus on the case at hand rather than the interior climate of the building, and if perhaps we could speak in the proper order, we could get out of here in time for my eleven o'clock rock climbing class," she says, and the conference quickly comes back to order.

It takes only a few minutes for the justices to unanimously decide to hear the case. Even Ed, who looks forward to deciding this issue about as much as he looks forward to his yearly prostate examination, votes to hear it, because Stephenson's right—this is an issue that has to be decided the same way everywhere, and only the Supreme Court has the power to make that happen.

"Well, all right then," the Chief says, "I guess I'll be able to make my class. Which is good, because today we're practicing heel hooks, and that's not something I can afford to miss."

"One second, Chief," Garabelli interrups. "I hate to possibly make you late for your . . . your . . . hooking lesson, but I'd like to move that, in addition to granting the case, we also issue an opinion summarily reversing the Third Circuit Court of Appeals and holding that the Pledge of Allegiance is manifestly constitutional. I think this approach would send a clear message to the lower courts that we will not look kindly on the type of radical church-state separation position endorsed by the ACLU and some of these other liberal groups that have completely misunderstood the original meaning of the First Amendment."

The Two Musketeers are delighted by Garabelli's suggestion, and they grunt their enthusiastic assent in unison. The Chief, too, though she is miffed at the delay and also seriously considering smacking Garabelli in the ear for the hooking comment, has to agree that a summary reversal is the right course for the court to take in the case. Since it takes five votes to decide a case one way or the other, however, and since it's clear that the four solid liberals on the court either think the lower court was right or was at least maybe right, the decision to summarily reverse comes down to Ed. Everyone instinctively knows this, and so, as soon as Garabelli's suggestion sinks in, all eight of the other justices turn their attention to Ed, who is busy doodling a picture of a rhinoceros.

Ed looks up, and there they all are, staring at him. He puts his pen down. The rhinoceros is only half-finished. It has a horn, an ear, the top of a head, part of the body, but the drawing runs out toward the back of the animal because Ed can't recall whether rhinoceroses have tails or not. He was about to try drawing it both ways.

"What do you think, Ed?" the Chief asks. "I think Tony, pain in the ass that he may be, has it right here. Should we just reverse this thing? It's hardly a prayer, of course, and as we've always suggested, and as everyone in his right mind knows, the 'under God' phrase is just an acknowledgment of the importance of religion in the nation's history."

"Right," Epps pipes in. "And if we just substituted 'under Buddha' or 'under Allah' for 'under God,' I'm sure that the religious right would be fine with that."

"Let's not forget," Justice Leibowitz squeaks, "the phrase wasn't added to the Pledge until 1954, and it was clearly put there to distinguish us from the godless communists."

"So what?" Garabelli says. "Who cares what it was put there for? Nobody is forced to say it. A kid whose parents have forced him not to believe in God can just sit there quietly while his classmates engage in this time-honored political exercise. No harm to anyone at all. This is the easiest case of the year."

"Oh yes," Stephenson offers. "Children usually feel quite comfortable sitting quietly in a room while their peers join in a group activity. Your understanding of the pre-adolescent psyche is remarkable, Justice Garabelli. Where did you do your graduate work in psychology again? I forget. Oh, wait, I think I remember. Wasn't it *Nowhere University*?"

Before Garabelli can reply, the Chief once again takes control. "Okay, okay, no need to hold oral argument on the case right here. Ed, what do you think? And no 'abstaining' this time, either."

Ed looks down at his half-finished rhinocerdoodle. He keeps thinking that they must have tails, to swat away the flies, but then he realizes he's probably mixing up rhinoceroses with hippopotamuses. But then how would rhinoceroses keep the flies away? Although Ed may not know what a rhinoceros looks like, he knows the arguments on both sides of the Pledge issue inside and out. The court just heard practically the same case not so long ago, after all. It's true that back then he was willing to rule for the state, but even at that point he wasn't one hundred percent sure. And now he's even less sure. In any event, he certainly doesn't want to "send a message" to the lower courts not to decide cases however they want to decide them.

"I vote no on the summary reversal. Let's hear the case like any other one. This doesn't merit any extraordinary treatment in my view."

Garabelli throws his hands in the air in disbelief. The Chief is disappointed but not surprised. "All right, then, we'll set it for argument in April. What fun it will be," she says. "Meeting dismissed."

***

Ed spends the rest of the day working industriously in his chambers. Because he doesn't like to let anything he's working on go unfinished, he starts with the matter of the rhinoceros; a quick Internet search reveals that the horned creatures do in fact have tails, so he completes his drawing accordingly. Not bad, he thinks, making vague plans to do a full-sized sketch later when he gets home. After the drawing is done, he focuses on the cases, and it turns out to be one of those days like those of old when he loses himself in the work. He edits Rick's draft on a majority opinion he has to write on an important issue of civil procedure and then turns to preparing for the two tax cases the court will be hearing on Monday. Ed generally finds tax cases difficult, but with the help of an expert memo prepared by Sasha, who for some reason wants to be a tax law professor some day, it takes Ed only about two hours to work his way through the two cases, stopping only for about ten minutes in between them to practice "Yesterday" on his ukulele.

When the tax cases are prepped, Ed's next task is to decide whether to agree to do a college commencement address this year, and, if so, what invitation he should accept. He's been doing graduation speeches pretty much ever since he's been a judge, but only since becoming a justice have the speeches been in front of the entire college or university instead of just a law school. He's never much liked the full university speeches. At least when he was talking to law students, he felt like he could provide some useful advice, even if that advice were limited to how the kids should pursue their legal careers, practical stuff like pay attention to the details, do pro bono work, don't ignore your family (advice he himself never followed well). But when he speaks to the full university—the poets, the astrophysicists, the anthropologists studying ancient civilizations—he has always been at a loss. What advice, after all, can he be expected to give to a twenty-one-year-old student of Slavic Literature, a newly minted dentist? This year, though, he feels differently. He is actually looking forward to giving a university commencement address, and he wants to make a splash with it. Maybe he'll play a little tune for the students on the uke; he will, almost certainly, quote from the *Chuang Tzu*.

But whose invitation to accept? He received about ten over the course of the fall, and now he's whittled it down to three: William & Mary, Elon, and Stanford. In the past, he's favored smaller colleges to the larger universities; at least that way, there are fewer people and no graduate students in the audience. If he followed this model, he would probably choose Elon, a small but prestigious college in North Carolina with allegedly the most beautiful campus in the country, and a place he's never been before. But this year, he's leaning toward Stanford, where his old fraternity buddy Ray is now the president. If he's got something to say, maybe it's worth saying it somewhere big. He takes a look at the Stanford website. He's been there a handful of times—a conference here, a moot court there—and it's such a beautiful place, palm trees on the side of the road and the smell of flowers in the air. Certainly there's never any harm in visiting northern California. Maybe he could combine it with a trip to the wine country, San Francisco, Yosemite.

Ed picks up his phone and prepares to call his friend at Stanford to accept his offer. He gets through the "1-650" when he hears Linda call out "Freddy? Freddy?" from next door. Her voice is usually reserved, so when he hears the obvious concern in her call, he knows something's going on. He puts the phone down and heads out to the main room of the chambers, where he finds Linda shaking a bag of treats and scouring through the file cabinets, apparently looking for their new office cat.

"What in the world are you doing?" Ed asks.

"We can't find Freddy anywhere," she answers. "Nobody's seen him in hours."

"And you think he might be in the file cabinet?"

"This was open for a while when I was looking for something. He might have jumped in."

"He's not a salamander. Isn't he kind of big to be in a file cabinet?"

"You clearly don't know anything about cats. I'm not sure you're qualified to have a cat. They can fit in extremely small places. They're very clever and flexible."

"Well, all right, then, why don't you check inside some of the file folders? Maybe he's in the one labeled 'Correspondence'."

Linda stops her searching and shaking to give Ed a scathing look. He is sufficiently shamed.

"Okay, okay, let me help. Where haven't you looked?"

"I don't know. I think we've looked everywhere. Go check with the clerks."

"Fine."

Ed walks through the open doorway that separates Linda's lair from the set of offices where the clerks do their work. He enters the relatively spacious common area and sees Dawn standing on one of the several long wooden tables in the room, peering over the top lip of a high bookshelf overstuffed with legal treatises on almost every imaginable subject. This room is invariably a mess, which is why Ed doesn't venture back here very often. He steps over a pile of United States Reports and pirouettes past the substantial green-carpet-covered cat tree he purchased for Freddy's amusement a few days ago, just barely avoids stepping in the cat's inadequately cleaned litter box, and lets himself down butt first on the ancient leather couch with bronze studs that's probably been court property since the days when Justice James Clark "No Jews Please" McReynolds would start reading a newspaper anytime Justice Brandeis walked in the room.

"Are you looking for Freddy up there?" Ed says, peering up at Dawn's long bare legs, her heart-shaped ass, which is barely, just barely covered by a frightfully short black skirt, and then turning his gaze away before an erection can expose him for the creepy horny old man that he is.

"We've looked pretty much everywhere. I don't know how he would have gotten up here, but who knows, cats are pretty resourceful."

"Where are the others? Are they looking for him too? Is anyone doing any work today?"

"They're both looking around their offices I think," she answers, and then inches over a little farther toward the wall, steps up on tippy-toes and sings "Freddy? Freddy? Where are you?" in a sexy voice that just about gives Ed a heart attack.

"Hmm, all right," Ed says, standing up and walking over to Rick's office—each clerk has a small individual office off of the common area—where he finds his employee on all fours, head buried in a cabinet.

"Any luck?" Ed blurts out and a startled Rick bangs his head against the top of the inside of the cabinet.

"Ow," he cries out.

"Oh my god, I'm sorry," Ed says, although he's actually smiling and stifling a laugh. "Are you all right?"

"Yeah, yeah, I guess," Rick says, pulling his head out of the cabinet and rubbing it with his left hand. "The cat's not in there anyway."

"Has he disappeared before?" Ed asks.

"There have been a couple of times when we couldn't find him for a while, but he's always shown up once we shake the treat bag. This time Linda's shaken that thing in every nook and cranny of the office, but no luck."

"Could he have escaped out of the office maybe?"

"I think we've kept the door closed the whole time. But I don't know. Maybe, I guess."

Dawn and Sasha both arrive in Rick's office to hear what's going on. "Could he have scooted out when McLaughlin came in with the cert pool list?" Sasha queries, referring to the kid who works as a messenger for the Chief and brings around the list of petitions that each chamber is responsible for analyzing.

"I guess it's possible," Dawn says. "Oh shit."

The four of them look at each other with increasingly horrified expressions as they realize that their cat might be wandering free around the Supreme Court building. It's a big place. Freddy could be anywhere. Right now, Ed imagines, the cat could be sitting on Justice Arnow's desk, taking a dump on his draft opinion in the Fourth Amendment fence case. On second thought, Ed reflects, maybe that wouldn't be so bad. Hell, it might make the opinion better.

Ed realizes he has to take charge. "All right, let's split up," he says, leading them into the main room of the chambers where Linda is still shaking the bag of treats and combing through the file cabinets. "I'll head toward the East and West Conference Rooms. Sasha, you go upstairs, check the hallways up there, the Reporter's office. Rick, why don't you take the exhibit hall and the cafeteria, that area. And Dawn, go up to the library, maybe the gym. If anyone finds him, text the others. Is it a plan?"

"It's a plan," Rick says. Dawn and Sasha nod their assent as well, and the search for Freddy commences.

***

Ed strides down the long gilded corridor toward the East Conference Room, an ostentatious cathedral of a place that the justices and others occasionally use for public functions. Ed doesn't come here often; the last time he remembers stepping foot in the room was for a dinner the justices held for a group of judges from the European Court of Human Rights the previous spring. Vaguely, Ed remembers guzzling a thousand glasses of wine to survive an unbearable conversation with the Danish husband of one of the judges who insisted on critiquing every conceivable aspect of the American political system while punctuating his points with an obnoxious laugh that sounded like a goat being constricted to death by a reticulated python.

Ed glances to his left and right to confirm that nobody is watching him and then steps softly onto the plush red carpet that covers the room's entire floor. "Here, kitty, kitty. Here, Freddy," he says softly, but no cat appears. Ed wants to do this quietly, so as not to attract the attention of any staff members or colleagues who might be wandering by the room's entrance—he would rather not have to explain why he's hunched over in an empty room, seemingly talking to himself in a sing-songy voice. He's already decided that if someone catches him, he'll say he's looking for a lost cat-shaped cuff link and hope that does the trick. The harder part will be what to say if someone catches him with an honest-to-goodness cat in his arms. He doesn't know whether animals are allowed in the building, and even if they are, surely they can't be allowed to run wild amongst these exalted rooms with their precious historical objects like Rembrandt Peale's famous portrait of Justice John Marshall that hangs over the room's now-quiet fireplace. Ed cringes at the thought of little Freddy leaving scratch marks on the Baldwin piano that sits in the corner of the room and which Ed now approaches, as it seems like perhaps a good place for a cat to hide. Ed looks all around the priceless piece but sees no sign of any cat near or underneath the piano or its bench. He wonders whether to lift the cover of the piano and look inside. Is Linda right that cats can get into almost anywhere?

Ed decides to leave the cover of the piano alone and goes in search of the cat elsewhere in the wide-open space. A dozen or so ancient and hideously upholstered chairs line the sides of the room, and the tall windows are draped with what looks to Ed like sets of bloomers that a ninety-year-old woman might have worn in the late eighteenth century. He looks under the chairs and behind the drapes the best he can, but the room is fairly dark, and Ed has trouble seeing; he wonders whether it's possible to turn on the two ornate chandeliers, imported from Czechoslovakia, when there was such a thing, that are hanging from the gold-glazed ceiling, but he decides against it. Surely if Freddy were in the room, he would have made himself known by now. Wouldn't he?

It's while Ed is on his way from the East Conference Room to its twin on the west side of the building that Ed runs nearly head-on into the Chief.

"Ed!" the Chief exclaims. "Just the guy I want to see. What are you up to?"

Unwilling to reveal the real reason he's wandering around the court building—if anyone would frown on keeping a cat in chambers, it would have to be Janet Owens—Ed fumbles for something to say. "Oh, I, umm, uhh, I'm not looking for anything or anything—just walking around, trying to clear my head, think through these tax cases," he says.

"Yeah, God, those things are a pain in the ass. I hope I get to assign them—I'll give them both to Tony. That'll teach him to make another 'hooking' wisecrack."

Ed smiles at the thought of not having to write either of those two opinions. "That would be his just desserts, all right. Just as long as you don't assign them to me. I don't know the Internal Revenue Code from the . . . from the . . . well, I don't know," Ed says, unable to come up with a phrase that sounds anything like "Internal Revenue Code."

"You know, on the subject of what you *can* do for me . . ." the Chief starts, but she is interrupted by a jingly jingle coming from Ed's front pocket—the sound that lets Ed know he has received a text.

"Oh, sorry, hold on a sec, will you?" Ed asks the Chief. "I need to look at this."

The Chief isn't thrilled about "holding on a sec," but she has no choice, so she holds on a sec while Ed checks his phone. The text is from Dawn, and it says "found freddy—mission complete."

"Oh, phew, she found him," Ed says, under his breath.

"Found who?" the Chief inquires.

Ed realizes his flub. "Oh, umm, nothing, it's just one of my clerks— she found, uhh, the precedent I was looking for. The case."

"You refer to cases as people these days?" the Chief asks.

"No, of course not, umm . . ."

"Look, Ed, I need to talk to you about something," the Chief says, putting her hand on his upper arm and steering him down the hallway away from the Conference Room. She starts walking, and he falls in step. "Capitol Hill is giving me no end of grief on this whole cameras in the courtroom thing."

Ed grimaces. "You know how I feel about this, Janet. It's a terrible idea. And with these showboat colleagues of ours trying to get laughs all the time—the place will turn into a circus. I wouldn't be surprised if Cornelius starts using a ventriloquist dummy to ask his stupid questions."

"I know, I know. I'm quite versed in your views on the issue. And I basically agree with you. But I'm starting to think we have no choice. The word from the Speaker is that they've got the votes for a bill to require us to televise."

"That's clearly unconstitutional, you know that."

"I know it, and you know it, but what are we going to do—review the law ourselves and hold it unconstitutional? We'll look ridiculous. Not to mention whiny and pathetic. You know how precarious our position is with the public. I don't think we can afford to make ourselves look bad if we can help it."

"I say we take our chances," Ed urges. "In the end I doubt they'll end up passing such a thing."

"Well," the Chief answers, "I think you're wrong about that. And, frankly, I think I'm in a better position than you to know what they're going to do. But, there is a compromise possibility."

"What compromise?"

"The word is that if we agree to a pilot program—televising one or two arguments per sitting for the next couple of terms, they'll hold off on the bill, see how it goes. By the time the experiment is over, everyone will probably realize how completely uninteresting it is to see us on TV, and pressure for us to let cameras in will go away."

"Ugh," Ed says. He hates the idea of any of their hearings being broadcast on television, particularly now that he's realized how great it is to be anonymous. How will he be able to take a sketching class at the adult education center in peace or pretend he's Ralph at the Chuang Tzu meetups if his face is broadcast to millions six days a month? "What do the others think?" he asks.

"Well, of course, the three of them who are already in favor of televising are on board," the Chief answers, referring to Cornelius, Arnow, and Epps. "And Garabelli and Stephenson seem at least to be intrigued by the compromise. I'm going to be pretty comfortable green-lighting this thing if I get a two-thirds majority. I'm just asking that you think about it."

Ed shrugs. What can he do? "Okay, I'll give it some thought."

The television conversation has distracted Ed, and he only now realizes that the Chief has been leading him back to his own chambers. The recognition comes only a split-second before Dawn turns the corner in front of them, cradling Freddy in her arms.

"Justice!" she exclaims, "I found the little rascal. Skittering on the spiral staircase of all places. Oh, hi Chief. Oops."

"Ahh, hello Dawn, great, thanks, terrific," Ed says. For a moment, the three of them stand quietly in the hall. The Chief looks at Ed, then the cat, then back at Ed.

"Okay, then, back to work," Dawn says, and extends Freddy out to Ed, who has no choice but to take him. Dawn ducks quickly into the chambers and disappears, leaving Ed, now holding the mewing cat, alone with the Chief.

"What, umm . . ." the Chief starts, but Ed is fast to interrupt.

"So, anyway, I'll be sure to give some thought to the television thing. I'll get back to you pronto. Great talk, Chief. See ya," he says, and then he himself steps into the chambers and closes the door behind him. The Chief, now alone in the hallway, unsure what to do, shakes her head, turns the other way, and heads back to her chambers.

***

Freddy safely stowed away in the clerk's wing, not one but two closed doors now between the frisky feline and the corridors and spiral staircases of the nation's highest court, Ed pats the cat's head and returns to his office to call his daughter. Miraculously, she picks up.

"Hi, Dad, what's up?"

"Hey there, I just wanted to say hi. I haven't talked to you in a while. How are things?"

"Oh, I don't know. I'm thinking about adding a 'tuber of the day' selection to my menu. What do you think? Rutabaga, turnips?"

"Are sweet potatoes tubers?" Ed asks. "If so, then I support the idea."

"I think so. I'm going to run it past my sous chef. What are you doing?"

"Our new office cat just escaped from chambers and ran around the building. One of my clerks caught him on the spiral staircase. She brought him back right when the Chief was in the doorway. Do you think I can be impeached for having a cat in the court?"

"You have a cat?" Katelyn asks, irritation in her voice. "Since when have you wanted a cat? You don't like cats. I asked to have a cat my entire childhood, and you never let me. Even though you were never home."

"Yeah, sorry about that. I let you have a fish, though. Several fish, if I remember correctly. You kept letting them die."

"That's because I didn't want any fucking fish. I wanted a cat. I wouldn't have let the cat die, if that's what you're insinuating."

"I'm not insinuating anything. Why don't you get a cat now? Oh, right, Bill's allergic, I forgot."

"Actually, I think we're going to break up. So maybe I will get a cat after all."

"What? Really?" Ed says, and his delight is evident.

"Not that you have to be so transparently giddy about it."

"What? No, I'm not giddy," Ed says, trying hard to straighten out the smile that has involuntarily formed on his face. "What, umm, happened? Do you want to talk about it? Are you okay?"

"Yes, I'm okay. And no, I don't want to talk about it. I think we're just realizing that we don't like each other much anymore. And it's become clear that he definitely doesn't want kids."

There's that smile again. "Well, kids are good, I'll vouch for that. And I'm always here if you want to talk, you know, et cetera, et cetera."

"Yes, yes, I know. Thanks, Dad. So, what about you? Have you seen that professor chick you're into? Or are you still playing hard to get?"

Ed, of course, hasn't told Katelyn about either Tammy or the Chlamydia. "You and Greg Bash, it's like the two of you are trying to get me shacked up. I'm not playing hard to get. I just don't think it's a good idea to be seeing anyone right now. You know, among other things, I've got to decide whether the government can censor pornography. Which is kind of a big burden for one person to shoulder, if you ask me."

"It sounds to me like you're just back to being a hermit again. The same way you've been ever since you and mom split up. You came out of your shell for three months, and now you've crawled back inside."

Ed is quiet. She's right, of course. But look what happened when he came out of the shell. *Cousin fucker. STD getter.*

"I don't know what Greg Bash is thinking. I mean, who could possibly know what that guy is thinking? But I'm just saying that when you talked about her, you sounded different, that's all. Like it was somebody who made you feel something. Which is no easy task."

"Hey, what's with the lashing out at your old man? If I am cut, do I not bleed?"

"Ha. Hey, speaking of cutting and bleeding, I almost cut my index finger off yesterday trying to de-bone a goose."

"Ouch, that sounds awful. Are you all right?"

"I needed a couple of stitches, but nothing a seasoned chef like myself can't handle. Actually it gives me some street cred with the cooks—it's been a while since I almost cut something off my body. These guys were starting to think I was getting soft."

"That's good, I suppose. Hey, why don't we eat swans?"

"What?"

"I mean, we eat ducks, geese, turkeys, chickens, game hens, partridges, pheasants. Why not swans?"

"I don't know. Maybe because they're big, mean motherfuckers?"

"It's interesting. You should look into that. Be the first restaurant to serve baked swan. You'd get lots of press."

"Maybe I'll also serve a roasted capybara. With cheese sauce. Or boiled owl."

"Why not? Speaking of horny birds, by the way, how's your mother?"

"Nice one. This weekend is her second anniversary, you know. At least she's not in a shell. She's going to Hawaii."

"Ugh, kill me," he says, and he actually does feel bad for himself. Not that he really misses his ex-wife, but like anyone in his situation, he doesn't enjoy falling so behind in the happiness race. He tries to cheer himself up by remembering what a bozo her new husband is, but it doesn't help much. They had met one time, before Sarah had actually married the guy, at a misbegotten Thanksgiving dinner that Katelyn put together at her cramped Brooklyn apartment to recreate some sort of family normalcy for herself. Ed had spent the entire afternoon cringing through conversations about Bill's leveraged buyout deals and his ex-wife's new Vanyasa yoga practice while Harry and Katelyn traded excruciating stories about organic cantaloupes and free-range ducks. When it turned out that drinking a bottle and a half of Chateau Palmer didn't work to relieve the discomfort, he left early, before Katelyn could serve up Harry's mincemeat pie, claiming some sort of vague sinus-based ailment that involved lots of fake sneezing.

"Sorry, but you asked."

"I know, I know. My fault."

"So, any more thoughts on your momentous career decision? Let me guess, you're going to quit and go back to grad school in biochemistry? Try your hand at writing screenplays?"

"I don't know. I go back and forth. Today was actually a good day. I worked through the cases, no problem, found them pretty interesting, just like old times. Maybe I'll stay here for the next thirty years. Die of a brain hemorrhage right on the bench like Harlan Stone."

"Sounds great. I'll look forward to that. It will be very dramatic. Look, I have to go—my pastry chef just showed up, fifteen minutes late I'll add, and we have to get to the bottom of Eclairgate before anyone else contracts salmonella. I'll call you this weekend."

"All right. Bye. And, that's disgusting."

***

Ed works throughout the afternoon, confirming the Stanford speech, making some preliminary notes about it, tweaking a couple of draft concurrences for cases argued in the fall, reading the problem for a moot court competition he's going to judge at Cornell next week, a few other items. Before he knows it, night has fallen, dinnertime has passed him by, Linda and his clerks have gone home for the night, and he is alone in his chambers, wondering what to do next. He could go back to his little apartment, of course, but that's not such an attractive option, given the lack of comfortable furniture, no semblance of adequate cable television, and an elusive mouse that's been living in his kitchen cabinets and eating his potato chips. The uke is on the couch, and Ed walks over and picks it up. He's been getting better, made real strides this week in his spare time. The instrument is not so difficult. He strums the super easy C chord a few times, then switches to the F—one great thing about the ukulele is how simple the F chord is compared to playing it on the guitar, which Ed used to do a little bit back in college, poorly—then to the G-7 and finally back to the C, and that's practically a tune right there. Just have to add some words, Ed figures, to make his first song, and so he does: *I'm a Justice,* he croons, *at the Supreme Court. My job is kind of boring* . . . He pauses, tries to think of something to rhyme with "court" on the final C. *I should probably take . . . a big dose of St. John's Wort.* He is pleased.

In the clerks' wing, now vacant except for Freddy, Ed closes the door behind him and says hello to the cat, who has made himself comfortable on the middle level of the cat tree. *Hi there, Freddy,* he sings, *how are you today? You are cute . . . and you like to play.* Freddy gets to his feet and looks up at Ed, who is standing there strumming and singing this refrain over and over with a pained expression on his face, like a guy who can't sing trying to come across as Paul Simon or Chris Martin, and he meows. "Yeah, sing along," Ed says, but when he sings the verse again at a higher and somewhat scary volume, Freddy jumps off the cat tree and scurries under a desk.

Ed takes the uke with him as he leaves his chambers and walks the silent corridors of the mostly empty court building. A few clerks are probably huddled away in their offices researching obscure lines of argument in some case or other, and there are a handful of security officers wandering around somewhere as well, but Ed doesn't see anybody, as he strums the instrument quietly and pads his way on the plush carpet to the grand and now dark courtroom. Hunting around on the walls at the side of the room, he locates a couple of dimmable lights that he turns on just a little bit, softly illuminating the chamber. He climbs the small set of stairs leading up to the bench and sits down not in his own chair, but in the Chief's.

Damn, the Chief has a nice chair, Ed thinks, as his ass sinks deeply into the seat's soft leather. Maybe he should stick around and try to get appointed Chief so he can have the great chair. Also he would get to open every session and say "the case is submitted" after every argument. "The case is submitted," he says, aloud, and then plays an F chord before deciding that it would probably be prudent to keep the volume down. He leans back, plays a little of his new St. John's Wort song quietly on the uke, and tries to take in the scene. What's he trying to do here? As if playing a ukulele while sitting in the Chief's chair in a dark empty courtroom at midnight on a Tuesday is going to somehow magically help him make up his mind whether to retire? He thinks about what he would do if he did step down. This is something he's been thinking about a lot. It wouldn't be worth quitting if he ended up working at the Cinnabon in Tyson's Corner, now would it? What he thinks he really wants to do is travel. Not the kind of travel you do when you're a justice of the Supreme Court—riding in chauffeured cars and eating at state dinners (come to think of it, he may actually have eaten boiled owl at one of those state dinners somewhere), but something real, maybe with a backpack. He's backpacked before, but that was during college, when he was a different person, a half-lost philosophy major with long hair who smoked weed and had his own jazz show on the college radio station and blurted out anonymous cruelties at pretty girls who hadn't noticed him. India. He should go to India. He's never been there. Not even in the chauffeured car, state dinner way. How can somebody say they've lived a life, he wonders, without ever having been to India?

India-a-ah, he sings, lightly playing an A-minor chord. He closes his eyes, tries to think of India, but all he comes up with is the Taj Mahal, some vague image of the Ganges River, Mother Theresa tending to the Calcutta poor. *I suck*, he thinks: *one of the greatest countries on earth and I can only imagine three things about it, one of which is a nun.* Opening his eyes, he looks around, and suddenly the strangeness of what he's doing becomes apparent.

"Shit, I've got to get out of here," he says to himself, and then he does.

NINE

EARLY IN THE EVENING ON FRIDAY AS HE'S LEAVING THE building, Ed runs into the Chief, who is about to do the same. They are in the corridor near the elevator that descends to the parking garage under the building. Ed says hello, and then when the Chief presses the down button, he tells her that he'll see her next week and starts to walk away. This surprises the Chief.

"Don't you want to go to the garage to get your car? Or do you have plans in the District tonight?"

Ed doesn't want to linger, get caught up in a conversation about the cases or, even worse, about whether they should allow cameras in the courtroom, but he feels he should explain. "Actually I have a place nearby where I'm staying these days."

"Don't you live in McLean? I know you live in McLean. I've been to your house. More than once."

"I'm selling that place. It's too big for one person, and I've decided it makes more sense to live in town. In the meantime, I've rented an apartment on C street. Northeast."

"Oh yeah? That's interesting. I've been thinking about doing something similar, actually. Downsizing, that is. Not moving to the District. God knows I would never move to the District. Hey, do you mind if I walk with you for a bit? Maybe you could show me the place. I haven't been outside all day. I could use some fresh air. And I have something I want to talk about with you."

Ed would prefer not to take a walk with the Chief "for a bit," but what can he say? "Sure, I guess. Why not?"

They are outside, crossing from the court to the other side of Second Street, when the Chief brings up the television issue. "Made any progress on the television issue?" she asks.

Ed cringes. He hasn't thought about it a single time since their embarrassing encounter the other day. "Oh, I'm sorry, Janet, I just haven't had a chance to give it any thought."

"No?" the Chief wonders. "Because Bill—you know, the head of security—told me today that you were spotted the other night walking around the halls playing your ukulele. I thought you might have been thinking about it then."

Fuck, Ed thinks. "No . . . yeah . . . well, no. I guess I was playing the . . . but I was thinking about something else."

"Are you sure everything is okay, Ed? You've been acting very strange. The ukulele, the glasses, that wacko question during the pornography argument, the mysterious missing cat. Is there anything I can do for you? Do you need some, I don't know . . . resources?"

"No, I'm fine. I'm totally fine. I just took up a new instrument to relax, that's all. And I'm keeping a new cat in my office just for a short time—his name is Freddy, by the way—until I can get permission from my landlord to let him in my apartment. The rest is nothing, just little hiccups, nothing to worry about at all. I'm completely normal, I assure you."

"Okay, if you say so," the Chief replies, as they walk slowly down Second Street, avoiding the occasional ice patch that has formed on the snow-surrounded sidewalk. "But if there's anything you need, just let me know."

"I will, I promise. But I'm fine. Totally fine."

Rounding the corner toward Constitution Avenue, they run almost head on into a short Asian man wearing a trench coat and multicolored beanie with a bright yellow propeller on the top. The three of them do an awkward side-to-side dance as they all try to make it past each other. The Chief is irritated. Ed, mortified at having run into Mr. Wong while walking with the chief justice of the United States, turns his face to the side, hoping that Mr. Wong won't get a good look. It takes a second or two, because Ed is not wearing a baseball hat or his glasses, but then Mr. Wong recognizes that the guy wearing the expensive suit and cashmere scarf is his fellow Chuang Tzu devotee. "Ralph? Ralph, is that you?" he says, embracing Ed in a bear hug. "What's going on, buddy? Where are your glasses? Ralphie!"

The Chief looks at Ed, then at the weird little man with the propeller beanie, then back at Ed. "Who is your friend with the funny hat, Ed?" she asks.

"Ed? Who's Ed?" Mr. Wong says.

"Janet, this is my friend Mr. Wong," Ed says. "We know each other from the . . . from the neighborhood."

"Oh, okay. Hello, Mr. Wong. Very nice to meet you," she lies, and puts out her hand for a shake.

"Very nice to meet you, ma'am," Mr. Wong says, but instead of shaking her hand, he spins his propeller. Awkwardly, the Chief retracts her hand and places it in her coat pocket.

"All right, then. We've got to get going. I'll see you around, Mr. Wong," Ed says.

"Okay, dude. You going to the next meeting? It's going to be so totally cray-cray. We're going to talk about whether CT can know the pleasure of a fish even though he's not a fish. An zhi yu zhi le, man," he says in Chinese that Ed doesn't understand.

"I might make it. To the meeting. Neighborhood meeting. I'll see you there. Maybe," Ed responds, and then starts walking forward.

"All right. Bye, Ralphie-Ed," Mr. Wong blurts, "nice to meet you, miss." And then, for apparently no reason at all, Mr. Wong breaks into a sprint and runs away, waving his hands over his head like a madman.

Ed and the Chief are quiet. The stillness lasts only a few seconds, though it seems to Ed like five minutes, perhaps an hour. Finally, the Chief breaks the silence. "As I said, if you need any help . . ."

"Yeah, yeah, yeah, I know," Ed says, and starts marching off in the direction of his apartment.

***

A few minutes later they arrive at the front door to his building, an unassuming four-story brick structure with a vertical strip of entry buzzers next to a faded olive green front door with the number "242" on it.

"Are you sure you want to see this? It's nothing special," Ed says. "Actually, it's kind of a hovel. I just needed a place to stay near the Court. I've barely moved in any of my own stuff. It came furnished. There's a mouse."

By this point, the Chief has clearly become so intrigued with Ed's odd behavior that she very much wants to see his new shitty apartment. "Absolutely," she says, wrapping her arms around her body. "I want to see this place. Come on, open the door, I'm cold."

Ed sighs, takes his keys from his pocket, opens the door, and lets the Chief in to the building before him. He leads her up one flight of stairs, takes a left, and walks halfway down a short corridor, where he stops before another green door, this one with a gold-plated "2C" on it. Taking hold of a different key, he opens both the top and bottom locks, pushes the door open, and says, "here it is—come on in."

Standing in the tiny, pock-marked-wood-floored living room, the Chief takes a long look around the place while Ed hangs up his coat. She is not impressed. Peeling gray radiators, an old brown couch like something out of an eighties' family room, a folding table topped with old newspapers and two used coffee cups. This does not look like the home of anyone with a steady job, much less a Supreme Court justice. "Are we paying you enough?" the Chief asks. "Do you have a gambling problem or something?"

"I told you that it's just temporary while I'm putting the house up for sale. I've been going to open houses on Sundays. I like this neighborhood. I'll probably end up buying something here."

"Well, all right, if you say so," she says, and she, too, takes off her coat, which surprises Ed, who figured she was just coming in for a second and then leaving.

"Do you have any booze in here?" she asks, throwing her coat over the back of the grungy couch. "I could use a drink."

Ed does have some booze. A bottle of eighteen-year-old Talisker, to be exact. Several times over the past months he's thought about breaking the seal, but it hasn't happened yet. This might be just the time. "I have a bottle of scotch. Good scotch."

"Scotch, huh? I prefer bourbon, but if that's all you've got, why don't you bring it over? Do you have any glasses? Maybe a paper cup or two? Or should we just drink it out of the bottle?"

"No, I've got cups," he says, making his way into the narrow kitchen. "Have a seat, make yourself at home."

"If I wanted to make myself at home I'd have to burn everything in here first," she replies, though she does take a seat on the far side of the couch. Soon Ed returns, holding the bottle and two mismatched small glasses, which he places on the small wooden coffee table in front of the couch. He opens the bottle, pours two healthy portions of whiskey into the glasses, and hands one to Janet. "Here's to not having cameras in the courtroom," he says, and clinks her glass.

"It's going to happen, my friend, whether we want it to or not," she declares, taking a sip of the scotch, nodding in reluctant approval. "It's just a matter of whether it's every argument or just a few."

"I say we call their bluff. We tell them to go ahead and pass the bill and that as soon as it's passed we'll sue them in district court. They'll cave."

"They're not going to cave. McGready has got a bug in his ass over this issue," she answers, referring to the majority leader in the Senate and taking another drink, longer this time. "This scotch is actually pretty decent. I didn't know you were a scotch drinker. I think I've only ever seen you drink wine."

Ed takes a long drink from his glass. He can't believe how good it tastes. This is in fact the first drink other than wine he's had in months, and it is delicious. The liquid warms his throat, coats his stomach, makes him immediately feel three times better. "Wow, you're right, it is good," he says. "I do like scotch. So much. Scotch is my friend. I've been trying to drink less recently, and it's been a long time since I've had any, so this is good. Very good."

The Chief looks at Ed, cracks a smile. "Scotch is my friend—I like that. So why have you been trying to drink less? Health problems? You look pretty fit."

"No, it's just, I don't know, I don't always make the best decisions when I drink."

"Hmm. I know you've been making some bad decisions on the cases lately. But I didn't get the sense that you were drunk at conference."

"Hah. No, I've considered bringing a flask to oral argument a few times, but no, never been drunk at conference." He pulls the cork on the bottle and pours them both full glasses. "It's more, shall we say, romantic decisions that are the problem."

"Aha, interesting," she says, drinks some more. "Romance. I remember romance. Sort of."

Ed thinks about the Chief's late husband. Robert Owens. Bob. They had always seemed like an odd couple. Her: tall, rugged, tough; him: small, almost delicate, a pediatrician. He died of a sudden heart attack maybe five years ago. Ed remembers the funeral, how Bob died on a Thursday and Janet was back to work, running the conference, on Monday. Since then, whenever there's a public function at the court—a party, a dinner, whatever—she comes alone, just like he does.

"Have you, umm, been involved with anyone since Bob passed away?" Ed asks. It's strange having a personal conversation with the Chief, especially in this spartan apartment of his, but why not, he figures. He hasn't had a real conversation with anyone other than Katelyn or Bash in months.

"Off and on," she says. "An old friend who lives in San Francisco. We don't see other very often. It's not like I'm going to get married again. You?"

"No. My daughter says I'm a hermit."

"Do hermits own cats? Do they play the ukulele?"

"Sure, why not?"

"I guess."

They pause. It's a little awkward, but neither of them mind. They drink. "So, do you have plans to watch the Super Bowl?" she asks. In two days, the Ravens and Seahawks will battle it out in New Orleans for the championship. The Ravens are a touchdown favorite. "You probably aren't a football fan."

"What? Of course I'm a football fan. Kind of hardwired to root for the Patriots, but I'll be pulling for the Ravens on Sunday. Alone. Here. But still rooting."

"Hmm, I hadn't taken you for someone who likes sports."

"How long have you known me?" he asks, finishing his scotch, pouring two more. "It's strange, isn't it, how we can all work together for years and years and know hardly anything about each other? All of us cloistered away in our chambers, coming out only to talk about cases. I played football in high school, you know? Starting tight end, actually."

Ed notices an immediate change in the Chief's expression—softer, her blue eyes dialed up one shade brighter. "Come on, you're kidding, right?"

"No, I'm not kidding. I wasn't great or anything. Our team wasn't great. I think we finished my senior year season at something like 3-7, but yeah, I played."

"I'm impressed, Tuttle. I guess I've figured you wrong all these years. Who knew you were such a jock? To high school football," she says, puts her glass forward for a clink.

"To the Ravens," Ed says, and they clink, a new understanding forged over pigskin.

***

And so the justices of the Supreme Court sit on Ed's tattered, second-hand couch, drinking whiskey and talking, for an hour, two. They avoid speaking of work, focus on the topics that friends meeting at a party might discuss. Ed talks about his daughter's restaurant; Janet mentions that her son is an oceanographer, her daughter an investment banker. Janet asks Ed about where he grew up, what he studied in college; Ed inquires as to whether Janet has been to India. She has not, she replies, and has no interest in visiting.

"But can you really say you've lived a life if you haven't been to India?" Ed asks, and Janet replies: "Yes. Yes you can. Absolutely."

Between topics, they sip—by now the whiskey bottle is half empty—and Janet once again marvels at the notion that Ed played football. "Are you sure?" she asks, reaching over, squeezing his bicep, grimacing. "I'm not so sure."

"I'm pretty sure, yes. In fact, I'll show you something," he answers, then bends over and pulls up his left pant leg so half his calf is revealed. Now it's Ed's turn to grimace, as he gets a look at his hairy old leg peeping out between his wool pants and cotton socks. No part of a man, Ed has always believed, is more horrible, more hideous than the pant/hairy-leg/sock combination. He pulls the pant leg up a little more and finds what he's looking for—a deep scar, jagged, stretching diagonally across about a third of his leg's circumference. "Here it is," he says, putting his leg up on the coffee table and displaying it to Janet, a task made more difficult than it should be by his drunken condition. "I got this my junior year in the second quarter of a game against Everett. Defensive back crushed me into the safety. Missed three games."

Janet leans over and looks carefully at the scar. "As a lawyer—well, let me rephrase that—as a human being with the capacity for rational thought, I think you'll agree that this scar does not prove that you played football."

"No. Well, of course. But . . ."

"But I believe you. I believe you, I do." She drains her glass. "But take a look at this."

The Chief unbuttons the cuff of the right sleeve of her button-down blue-and-white-striped blouse and pushes the fabric of the shirt up over her forearm and elbow to reveal a scar almost as long as Ed's on her inner arm, near the bicep. She's explaining how she got the scar—something about a pickup basketball or hockey game during law school, or maybe elementary school, Ed's not sure what she's saying, because he's looking at Janet's forearm, her delectable forearm, much less aged than he'd expected, just lightly freckled and fuzzy, and as he stares at it, his penis grows, within seconds unfurling into half, maybe two-thirds of an erection. *Goddamn these forearms*, he thinks, *why can't they let me be?*

Suddenly he starts wondering whether he might fuck the Chief, something he hadn't thought of a single time, even as a joke, over their years of working together. But she's not half bad looking, he decides, if you look at her the right way. And by the "right way" he means the right *places*—stay away from the crooked nose, focus on the blue eyes instead, keep your gaze on the forearms, avoid the thick calves, it's hard to see her ass on the couch, and he can't remember much about it, but he can see the curve from where he sits, and it seems acceptable, something he wouldn't mind sinking his teeth into a little bit. Don't bite that mole on her cheek, though. Her hair is on the longish side and brown, almost certainly dyed, her light blue skirt clings to her upper thighs, the smallest hint of a slip peeping out beneath it. The erection has definitely matured into the two-thirds stage now. Plus, he has to admit that her power is kind of titillating. He's never been with a woman more powerful than he is; there aren't many out there who *are* more powerful. Maybe Hillary, but she's taken and out of reach. Oprah, too, seems ungraspable. But the Chief, well, she's here, she's in his apartment, and she's more powerful than he is, if only slightly. She swears in the Pres, carries out *administrative responsibilities*. And, of course, he hasn't been in anybody's pants—hell, *near* anyone's pants, in months.

"So, are you?" he hears her say.

"What? I'm sorry, I wasn't focusing. Maybe I'm a little drunk? What now?" He starts to lean back, then realizes the trouser-tent that will result. He stays bent forward a little, tries to think of his grandmother. The erection recedes slightly.

"The scar," she says. "Are you impressed?"

"Oh yeah, absolutely. That thing is *very* impressive."

She stares at Ed, wonders whether she's got a good read on him or not. "Does this place have a bathroom, by any chance? Or is there like a latrine out back or something?"

"Let me get you the shovel," he says, and when she laughs, he notices her smile isn't half-bad either. She's certainly kept up her oral hygiene, probably flosses twice a day. Hardcore conservatives can be like that. "It's around the corner."

Janet gets up, smooths the blue skirt, and turns toward where Ed is pointing. The vantage point is now excellent for an ass-of-the-Chief-view, and Ed takes full advantage. It's pretty decent, he decides, happily, the wool of the skirt clinging tautly to the ample bottom—ample but shapely! Plus, is that the slightest of panty lines he spies as she walks toward the bathroom? *Wow, the Chief wears panties*, he thinks—not that this isn't obvious or anything, it's just that he's never thought about it before, but of course, why not? He wonders what they might be like. Silky and lacy? Solid and sturdy? Pink? Gray? Better keep thinking silky and lacy, pink. He contemplates on the panties some more, even the word *panties*, he says it over and over in his head, *panties, panties, panties,* and his erection is now at full blast, the idea of sleeping with the Chief starting to seem like a real possibility. But would she be interested? They work together, right? She's his boss? Sort of. But she invited herself to his apartment, made that crack about missing romance, squeezed his bicep. Definitely, she'd be interested, he concludes, then pours another extra-large shot of whiskey and drinks it down in a single gulp.

Standing up, he thinks *grandma, grandma, grandma*, and the erection subsides some, enough for him to walk quietly in the direction of the bathroom, which is next to his bedroom, the one where he sleeps on a used futon like a nineteen-year-old unpaid intern. He turns the light on in the bedroom, pretends to be scanning a bookshelf for something or other, but really he's listening to the Chief pee in the room next door. *The Chief pees!* He rests his forehead against the wall separating the bedroom from the bathroom and listens, tries to focus, whoa is he drunk, thinks about what he will do, then forgets what he was thinking about. In a minute, the Chief emerges, and Ed snaps to attention, resumes pretending to look for something on the bookshelf. Janet nearly walks by the bedroom on the way back to the couch when she realizes that Ed is in the bedroom with the light on. She enters, looks around, sees the shabby futon, notices an alarm clock and lamp sitting on a concrete block, scowls.

"Is this your bedroom?" she asks, incredulously, but Ed, who now steps to within an arm's length of the Chief, hears something like "Hey there, sexy handsome man, nice bedroom!" He places his hands on the outside of her upper arms, right below the shoulders, and flashes a smile that he deliriously thinks makes him look like George Clooney. "Umm, Ed? What's going on?" Janet asks, right before Ed leans in and kisses her full on the mouth.

"What the fucking hell?" the Chief screams, and the punch that she instinctively delivers to Ed's midsection hits like a truck and knocks him flat out on the futon. *Oh my god, I've miscalculated*, he thinks, and he tries to offer an apology, but the noises that come out of his mouth sound nothing like words: "ahheeeaa," "urrrrghh," "blurrrp." The Chief has crushed the wind right out of him. "Jesus, what the fuck were you thinking?" he hears her say, and again he tries to answer her, but instead he squeals, grasps desperately his shattered solar plexus, writhes on the futon like a seal that has just been clubbed on the head. She leaves the bedroom, keeps yelling: "You are a fucking idiot. I thought for a minute that maybe you weren't a fucking idiot, but it turns out you're even more of a fucking idiot than I had originally thought."

"Geerrrrp," Ed moans.

A minute later, she returns to the bedroom, this time with her coat in her arms, and looks down, disapprovingly, as Ed struggles to sit up, his hair askew, face red with drink and the effort. "I think you'll agree," she says, "that we will not speak of this to anyone, ever, including each other."

He nods, sort of.

"Oh, and one other thing," she adds, disappearing from the bedroom and opening the front door of the apartment. "I will be counting your vote on the television issue as an enthusiastic *yes*."

***

An hour passes. Ed sits on the couch, a tiny bit more sober, his physical pain dissipated, the humiliation still hot in his throat. He tries to tell himself that what he's done is no big deal—a misunderstanding that nobody will ever know about, except for one other person, who will realize it was just a drunken error, one that he'll apologize for first thing Monday morning. Well, not Monday morning, maybe, because they have oral argument in the morning, but sometime on Monday. Or soon, anyway. For a moment he feels all right, even laughs a little at his own wildness. What the hell was he thinking? Fuck the Chief? Talk about cray-cray! Then the embarrassment of it all sinks in again, and he feels miserable. *I tried to kiss the Chief Justice*, he thinks, and wants to cry. How can he possibly work with this woman again, look her in the eye, disagree publicly with her views? *Kiss my ass*, she'll say, *oh wait, you already tried that, and I punched your lights out*. His colleagues will mock him, the reporters will pity him, the audience in the courtroom will erupt not in "laughter" but in "merciless laughter." Stupid, stupid, stupid. Plus she's going to assign him the crappiest possible opinions—as if the job weren't depressing enough already, now he's going to have to write the two tax cases, he just knows it. He buries his face in his hands, takes a deep breath, shakes his head, wishes he could get a do-over on the night, the year, his life.

After a while, he turns on the radio, tries to listen to an NPR story about the difficulties facing almond farmers in the Central Valley—drought, competition from abroad, a younger generation not enthralled by growing nuts. It is hard to concentrate. He sees the whiskey bottle, still uncorked on the coffee table, and figures, what the hell, the damage is done. He drinks directly from the bottle this time. As his tank-topped grandfather used to say, why put lipstick on a pig? Gulp.

The radio show is killing him. Who the fuck cares about the almond market, anyway? He turns it off, listens to the sounds of drunken youngsters yelling loudly in the street. On the coffee table sits his stack of Chuang Tzu books—the original orange one, but also a few others, alternate translations, some commentary. He picks up one of these secondary sources, apparently a classic in the genre, the author a Brit, one of the giants of his weird little field. Ed tries to focus on a passage from an early chapter on "Spontaneity" that he's underlined, marked with several stars in the margin:

> *For Chuang-tzu the fundamental error is to suppose that life presents us with issues which must be formulated in words so that we can envisage alternatives and find reasons for preferring one to the other. People who really know what they are doing, such as a cook carving an ox, or a carpenter or an angler, do not precede each move by weighing the arguments for different alternatives. They spread attention over the whole situation, let its focus roam freely, forget themselves in their total absorption in the object, and then the trained hand reacts spontaneously with a confidence and precision impossible to anyone who is applying rules and thinking out moves.*

Through a haze of inebriation and shame, Ed ponders the passage the best he can. As the marginal stars indicate, it's a passage he's thought about a lot these past few months. Sometimes he finds the message profound, other times it seems banal, like one of those geometric patterns that looks convex until you look at it long enough, then it turns concave, and back again. He trades the secondary source for Diana's orange volume and opens it to the title page, which has her name written on it. Why hasn't he tried to talk to her? He's been an idiot, a coward, he knows now—hell, he's known it for months, but he just hasn't been able to admit it to himself. Tracing her signature with his index finger, he lets himself think of her. Sometimes you *just know*, isn't that what they say on the talk shows? What has he been doing throwing himself at his pebble-hearted, mud-brained ugly boss, when he should be trying to win back the mirthful Chinese philosophy professor with the delectable lips?

He looks at his watch—it's ten o'clock. Too late to go over there now? Bring her back the orange book, confess his ass-ness, tell her how he feels? But what if she's out or in bed or hosting a dinner party? Better wait until tomorrow. No, be Chuang-Tzuian about it, be spontaneous. *Go.* Oh, but what if her kid is home for the weekend or something? That would be awkward. He doesn't know what to do. Should he be spontaneous, or not? He considers getting out a pad of paper, making two columns, and comparing the pros and cons of being spontaneous, going so far as to rise out of his chair to get a pen, before realizing how incredibly fucking stupid that would be and smacking himself, a little too hard perhaps, upside the head. He grabs Diana's book, slips on a pair of loafers, picks up his coat, and leaves the apartment without another thought, off to Union Station to get himself a cab.

***

Although he's been to Diana's townhouse twice, it's been a while, and he can't quite remember exactly where she lives. He has the taxi drive up and down a few of the narrow Georgetown streets before he's certain that he's found the place. Light is peeking out of the curtains that cover the living room window, and no light is visible anywhere else. This leaves him mildly optimistic. At least it would seem she's not hosting a dinner party or something of that sort, and the light in the living room could mean that she's reading or working in there. Ed pays the cab driver and steps lightly on the walk leading to the front door, where he takes a deep breath and knocks three times with a solid fist.

Nobody answers, nothing stirs. Ed sighs, figures that she must not be in the living room, probably she's asleep or out. He's crestfallen, this isn't how his spur-of-the-moment romantic whim is supposed to turn out—she should throw the door open, break into a rainbow of a smile, embrace him in a hug like a grizzly bear in heat. He knocks again, readies himself for the inevitable silence. But no—this time he hears something, someone stirring, a step or two on the staircase. Her voice: "Hello? Is someone there?"

Ed knocks again, his spirits lifted, his heart thumping heavily in his chest.

"Hi, Diana, it's me, Ed. I, umm, brought your book back. You know, the Chuang Tzu book you lent me?"

A few moments pass. The upper lock turns, the door opens a crack, Diana's face appears in the opening, her hair messed up every which way, glasses missing. "Ed? Ed? What in the world are you doing here?"

He's delighted to see her, no matter how disheveled. "I'm sorry, I know it's late. I just needed to see you, to talk to you. Look, I know I've been such an ass, but I really like you, I think about you constantly. I don't know what . . ."

"Do you know what time it is?" She rubs her eyes, squints, tries to get a better look at him.

"Yeah, umm, as I said, I know it's late . . ."

"And . . . your phone is broken?"

"No. Umm, no," Ed mutters, starting to realize that this is not going well. He holds up the orange book. "I brought your book back. Is there any way I could, you know, come in?"

"This is not a good time for you to come in," she says, and then, just as might happen on a television melodrama from the mid-nineties, a man's voice bellows from upstairs. "Diana? Is everything all right down there?"

"Everything's fine," she calls back.

Oh shit, Ed thinks, curses Chuang Tzu under his breath, that stupid moron sage. "Oh, I'm so sorry," he tells Diana, his hopes crushed. "I had no idea, I'm an idiot, I'll leave, I'm sorry."

The man's voice is closer now, maybe halfway down the staircase. "Are you sure? I can get a baseball bat or something if you want. Maybe a table lamp? I'm an advanced orange belt in Tai Kwan Do, everybody here should recognize. I know eighteen ways to kill a man."

The voice is familiar to Ed. It takes a second, but then it dawns on him. "Bash? Bash, is that you?" he yells, trying to poke his head into the doorway to confirm what he knows is true. *Diana is fucking Bash.*

"Ed? Ed Tuttle?" Bash yells, clomping down the steps to the foyer. "What the fuck are you doing here?"

"What the fuck am I doing here? What the fuck are *you* doing here?"

Diana is embarrassed, confused. She tries to get the men to settle down, but it's no use.

"I'm on a date, is what I'm doing here," Bash says, appearing in the doorway, wearing only an ill-fitting pink silk kimono that he found in Diana's closet. "Well, I don't know if we're technically still in the date stage at this point. We are, after all, naked. Is sex after a date still part of the date? I'm not sure."

Ed's anger boils. It has been a bad night. He turns to Diana. "I can't believe you're actually sleeping with Big Balls over here. Have you seen the size of those things, they're disgusting."

"What?"

"Yeah, he's got big gross balls."

"Aren't big balls a good thing?" she asks.

"No," Ed yells. "They're not good big balls, like manly big balls, they're old diseased big jaundiced disgusting balls."

"Why do you know anything about his balls, anyway?"

"Wait a second here," Bash interrupts. "My balls are not the issue. The issue is why are you here at eleven o'clock at night without calling first? I see that your 'no drinking' phase has come to a close."

Ed turns back to Bash. "No, the issue is why are you sleeping with my . . . with my . . . ?"

"With your *what*?" Diana exclaims.

Ed knows he has no answer. What's he going to say, *with a woman I went on two dates with three months ago and then cheated on with my diseased ex-step-cousin?* He looks at Diana. She's as pretty as he remembers. Even all defiled by his nasty friend, he still wants to reach out and kiss her increasingly angry lips. The situation is killing him. He turns back to Bash, who has now replaced Diana in the doorway. "I know why you did this. I do. You've always been jealous of me. Ever since your career flatlined and mine skyrocketed you've resented my success. You think you would have made a better judge, I know that's what you think. And maybe you're right. But you know what? Presidents do not choose crazy people to put on the bench. Crazy people like you do not get to be judges. Crazy people don't get put on the Supreme Court!"

Bash shakes his head. "You have absolutely no idea what you're talking about. So, here's what we're going to do. I'm going to close the door, and then I'm going to go back upstairs where—hopefully, if you haven't fucked it all completely up already—I will resume having sex, and you, my mixed-up friend, are going to go home and go to sleep. We can get together sometime soon for you to apologize and beg my forgiveness. Okay? Now I'm closing the door."

"Don't close the door, you big balled jealous asshole," Ed yells, and although he puts his hand lightly on the door as Bash closes it, he makes no effort to keep it open. In a moment, Ed finds himself alone, in the dark, on the landing, his face inches from the now-closed door, a tear forming in his left eye. He could easily wipe the tear away, but instead he leans his forehead against the door and lets the tear drip onto Diana's straw welcome mat. That's when he realizes he's still holding the orange book. He looks at it, then turns away from the door. "Screw you, Bash. Screw you, Chuang Tzu," he yells as he heaves the book into the road in front of Diana's house, where it lands with a thud. Ed stands on the landing for a minute, wondering what he should do next, when an old Honda comes screaming past the house and runs the book over, scattering its well-annotated pages this way and that across the cold, quiet street.

APRIL

TEN

IF THERE IS ONE THING THAT ED TUTTLE HAS ALWAYS ESPECIALLY liked about living in the Washington area, it would be the reliable punctuality of spring. Unlike in New England, where he grew up, went to college and law school, and worked his first real job clerking for a federal judge in Boston, unlike in these places, where winter stays late, refusing to leave, like a lonely party guest who remains planted on the couch spinning uninvited stories long past the time when any reasonable person would know to go home, here in the District, by late April, winter has left the premises, and spring has come to stay. Ed reads in his office with the windows open, the mid-afternoon breeze lightly wafting in, a pleasant perk of his exquisite workplace, right up there with the basketball court and the two-storied library staffed by the best "information specialists" in the land. Only one week of oral arguments remains, though on Monday, only four days from now, the justices will hear the Pledge of Allegiance case, which is turning out to be the term's most controversial piece of business.

"The Court in the Balance" announces the *Wall Street Journal*'s editorial page, and Ed cringes. He leans back in his chair and skims the piece—he's back to reading the papers these days, but he's afraid that if he reads one more overwrought article about how the future of the First Amendment rests on his shoulders, how the integrity of the nation's constitutional democracy teeters perilously on the tips of his fingers, he might blow chunks right into the seventeenth-century porcelain urn that sits on the eighteenth-century oak cadenza where he's currently resting his feet. He closes his eyes, then opens one slightly to peek at the editorial. "Will this be the court that relegates our great nation's religious character into the dustbin of history?" the author asks. "Will five unelected justices decide that the rights of lascivious smutmongers trump the will of the people to keep our children safe from vulgar sexual imagery? In two months, we will know the answers to these questions, and along with them, whether this remains an America that our brilliant and courageous founders would have recognized."

"What do you think about this, Freddy?" Ed turns and asks the cat, who is napping in the corner of the couch. At the sound of Ed's voice, Freddy opens his eyes and looks at Ed, who poses a follow-up: "Do you think that I should relegate the religious character of our great nation to the trashbags of smutmongers?" The cat makes a squeaking noise, then stands up, turns around, and lies down again.

"No, I didn't think you'd have an opinion," Ed says, folding up the paper and relegating it to the trashcan of his office. "Unfortunately, neither do I."

Having caught up with the news as much as he can bear for the moment, Ed refills his coffee mug and then turns to his main work of the afternoon—writing a response to the draft concurring opinion that Tony Garabelli circulated yesterday in the *Sexy Slut* case. The Chief had sent around her opinion last week—a relatively straightforward, somewhat narrow opinion finding that Texas had not violated the First Amendment by prohibiting the sale of the specific magazine with all the penises on the cover but by no means massively expanding the government's power to regulate porn. Although he still doesn't know what he's ultimately going to do—for one thing, he's waiting for Stephenson to circulate his opinion, and the old guy is notoriously slow in getting these things out—Ed appreciates the Chief's effort to court his vote, and he thinks the opinion is at the very least a reasonable one.

Not so Garabelli's infuriating separate screed. The first several sections of the short concurrence are bad enough, with their inflammatory language about the weakness of the Chief's moderate position and the dangers of even the most benign of sexual imagery, but the part that especially gets Ed's proverbial goat is the last section, the one where Garabelli insists on citing his conservative religious beliefs as support for his radical constitutional views. It's the same kind of thing that sent Ed into a tizzy in the gay marriage case a few years back, and if he weren't so agitated that the old right-wing nutjob is at it again, he might be able to find some pleasure in imagining how pissed Janet must be that Tony still insists on writing this kind of alienating stuff, jeopardizing her ability to get a court for her opinion. The Chief might be an old right-wing nutjob herself, but she is about a thousand times more politically savvy than Garabelli and his two idiot musketeers, both of whom have already emailed their intention to join the concurring opinion.

Garabelli might be a political dipshit, but he's no dummy. With degrees in philosophy and theology in addition to law, and a background as a law professor at Pepperdine for a dozen years, he knows his stuff when it comes to the question of whether it's legitimate for a judge to rely on his or her religious beliefs when reaching decisions on controversial moral and constitutional issues. Ed reads from the concurrence's penultimate paragraph: "As philosophers and legal scholars have long understood, the notion that a judge can ignore his or her deepest religious or moral convictions when deciding how to interpret and apply a vague and open-ended constitutional provision to a severely contested moral issue is simply impossible. Those judges who purport to ignore their religious and moral views in cases like this are deceiving themselves, the judicial system they represent, and the citizens they serve. By making my religious views explicit and explaining why I think they lead me to the result that I have outlined in this opinion, I am simply making transparent what others choose to hide and obscure." When put in this way, Ed realizes, Garabelli's position sounds reasoned, even plausible, especially with the footnote that takes up almost two full pages with citations to law journal articles and philosophical treatises that support his point. What Ed plans to do in the little memo he's going to write and circulate to the rest of the court, however, is point out that if Garabelli can get all Catholic on the nation's most controversial issues, then nothing's going to stop Ed from getting all Chuang Tzu-ian on those same issues, and if Ed chooses to do that, well, that's going to fuck everything up royally, now, isn't it?

It was the *Chuang Tzu* as much as anything that had helped him recover from the "Great Debacle," as he now refers to the night he tried to fuck the Chief and then cried on Diana's stoop. At first, he could barely get up in the morning without wanting to tie an anvil to his ankle and throw himself into the Potomac River. One weepy weekend afternoon, though, he opened up a translation of the *Chuang Tzu* that he had bought himself and read it for hours while slowly depleting what had been left in the bottle of scotch he'd shared with the Chief. The marathon study session had left him with one basic message, which was: *Lighten up, Tuttle.* In the days following, Ed found himself enthralled more than ever by the quirky philosopher's refusal to embrace the usefulness of logic, the authority of language, or the reliability of rationally derived distinctions—the essence, in other words, of his daily work. "What is It is also Other, what is Other is also It. Are there really It and Other? Or really no It and Other? Rather than use a horse to show that 'a horse is not a horse' use what is *not* a horse. Heaven and earth are the one meaning, the myriad things are the one horse." Ed has come to love this stuff, and although he realizes that he's not prepared to live according to it completely, he likes to think that he can embrace it at least somewhat in his everyday life. As for spontaneity, Ed has decided that he will try to embrace that too, but never again in a state of half-blind inebriation.

He turns to his computer and, with a smile widening across his face, starts writing the memorandum, which, like all correspondence among the justices, is addressed to "The Conference":

To: The Conference
From: Ed Tuttle
Re: Justice Garabelli's Concurrence in Sexy Slut

I have received and reviewed, as I'm sure you all have, Justice Garabelli's draft concurring opinion in Texas v. Sexy Slut Magazine. *Although I have yet to decide if I will be joining the Chief's draft opinion circulated on April 10, I am taking the unusual step of responding to the draft concurrence because I believe the opinion seriously misapprehends the judicial role by citing the author's religious beliefs as support for its conclusions. Later in this memo, I will outline the response that I am considering taking if the relevant section of the concurrence is not deleted prior to issuance.*

As we all know, because Justice Garabelli has been so kind as to include a two-page footnote filled with supporting evidence, a number of legal scholars and political philosophers (to say nothing of high court judges sitting in theocracies around the globe) have argued, in good faith and with decent enough logic, that judges may, should, or even must *consult their religious views when deciding deeply divisive issues which cannot be decided through recourse to legal sources alone. Although I will spare you a similar footnote (if you're interested, feel free to ask me for the details, I'd be happy to share), at least as many—probably more—philosophers believe that exactly the opposite is true. But I hope you will agree that it doesn't really matter who can line up more scholars behind their position. What matters is whether the court can maintain its legitimacy in the eyes of the public and the other branches of government. We're on thin ice as it is, lacking as we do any method to enforce our own judgments. And if you'll recall from the general reaction to Justice Garabelli's papal-inspired harangue in the* Vogel *case a few years back, talking about religion in our opinions does not, shall we say, play well outside a few pockets of reactionary religious fanatics that lie far outside the mainstream of American public opinion.*

So, what should we do? If it is true (as I sincerely doubt, but let's just grant it for the sake of argument) that Justice Garabelli simply cannot make up his mind about how to vote in a case like this without consulting his religious beliefs, then there is little I or anyone else can do about it. But in my view, discussing these beliefs explicitly in an opinion, far from serving the interest of "transparency," in fact imperils both the short- and long-term authority and legitimacy of this court. I strongly urge, and hope that I can prevail upon some of you to join me in this urging, that Justice Garabelli rethink his commitment to quoting Bible verses in his opinion, to say nothing of actually reprinting the Lord's Prayer in the opinion's conclusion.

But we've heard all this before, haven't we? As we were deliberating Vogel, *some of us made similar points, although some of us (not me, but some of us) were not quite as insistent as maybe we should have been about the matter. So let me, if you will, up the ante this time around.*

Have any of you read the Chuang-Tzu? *If you're not familiar with the eponymous book, it is a famed Taoist tract from the fourth century BC in which the author, through the use of both philosophical argument and some super silly stories, suggests that reason, logic, and language are all inadequate tools for living an authentic life. If you haven't read it, you should check it out—it's terrific (Justice Leibowitz, you in particular I think would get a kick out of it!). Anyway, I have been reading the book recently—quite a lot, actually—and I've started taking it to heart. You may have gotten a sense of this from the question I asked during oral argument in this very case. That was not meant as a joke. I was truly curious how the Texas solicitor general would answer a question about the adequacy of language to convey meaning (and, come on, we all know how useless oral argument usually is, so what's the harm of a little experiment?).*

Why am I talking about Chuang Tzu? Well, I figure that if Justice Garabelli is justified in writing about his Christian views in his opinion, nothing should stop me from writing about Chuang Tzu in my opinion. What's good for the goose, and all that, right? I haven't decided yet what I might write about, but lots of possibilities have come to mind. Maybe a little section about language? I like Chuang Tzu's point about how maybe words are nothing more than the cheeping of small birds. That would be an interesting thing to talk about in a Supreme Court opinion! Or maybe his position on distinctions? A horse is not a horse or maybe it's a non-horse, or maybe everything is really a horse? A chair, you know, is a horse. Also potato salad. Or I could go another route, write a bit about the giant fish named K'un who turns into a bird called P'eng and flies out to the South Ocean? Maybe I could write about all three of those things! Of course, as you all know, in a 4-1-4 case, it's the opinion written by the one justice that counts as binding precedent. That would sure confuse them down in the lower courts, don't you think?

But hopefully it won't come to that. I look forward to seeing all of you and perhaps talking more about this at tomorrow morning's conference.

Ed reads over the memo several times, makes some small changes here and there, then decides that it's done. He is overcome with excitement. This is some unprecedented shit, right here! When he first got the idea to write something like this the evening before, he figured it would simply be an exercise in catharsis, something he'd tear up like an angry letter to an unfaithful lover, nothing he would actually send to his colleagues. But working through it, he changed his mind. Why *not* send it to them? Who's going to stop him? What could anyone possibly do to him? Plus, it's fucking Garabelli's fault—somebody has to stop that guy, and it sure doesn't look like any of his brethren are up to the task. Yes, the memo will go into each justice's permanent files, and then ultimately, after every one of them who is currently on the court has died, those files will be opened up to the historians and scholars who will learn what a lunatic Ed was, but what does he care—by that time, he'll be nothing more than a pile of dust who won't give a rat's ass about his own legacy or anything else.

Ed prints out the memo and, since the justices unfathomably still have not gotten around to using email to communicate with each other, he brings it to Linda and asks her to copy it onto the usual heavy cotton paper for circulation to the Conference. Then he grabs his coat and rushes for the court's exit before Linda can read the thing, and before he has the chance to change his mind.

***

At about six o'clock, Ed arrives at The Greedy Llama, where he is meeting Katelyn and her new boyfriend Chris for an early dinner. Since he's about fifteen minutes late, they are already sitting and chewing on some steaming beef hearts when he shows up. He apologizes for the lateness, gives Katelyn an enthusiastic hug, shakes Chris's hand with gusto. Ed has been looking forward to meeting Chris for a while now. Everything Katelyn has told him about the guy—a former Foreign Service officer turned high school history and government teacher—has sounded promising, and indeed Ed likes him right away. Chris is, of course, nervous to meet Ed. It's hard enough meeting a new girlfriend's father even when he's not a Supreme Court justice. That's probably the reason Chris and Katelyn are already halfway through their second Pisco Sours.

"You look like you're in a good mood," Katelyn says to Ed, having noticed a rare gleam in her dad's eyes and little extra zip-a-dee-doo-da in his step. "What's going on?"

"I wish I could tell you," Ed says, picking up Katelyn's drink and sipping it. "Someday, long after I'm dead, maybe you'll find out. But for now, I need to get one of these."

"That's lovely, thanks," she says, and Chris laughs, leans over and kisses her softly on the cheek.

Ed gets his drink, and they order another round of appetizers. Munching on fried yucca and corn on the cob slathered with cheese, they talk about Peruvian seasonings, Chris's favorite student, Ed's impending Stanford speech. Katelyn marvels at the simplicity and delectability of the corn and considers adding something like it to her menu. Ed answers questions about his romantic life and asks whether either of them has ever speed dated. Chris says that he has, that he in fact met a prior serious girlfriend that way, but when Katelyn jokingly, or maybe not so jokingly, refers to Wendy as a "two-bit skank of a ho-bag," he changes the subject.

All the while, Ed delights in seeing his daughter so happy, and although he's participating in the conversation, he's at the same time thinking of her as a child, wishing he had been around more but also remembering the times he had been there, taking her to the bus stop in the morning, trying to focus on whatever game or television character she was interested in through the fog of his own thoughts about clients, cases, arguments. One family vacation stands out for Ed—a long weekend in Fort Ticonderoga, of all places, taken when Katelyn was maybe nine or ten. Somehow he had managed to fully engage in their activities, his mind focused for once on something other than work. Perhaps he had just submitted a long brief or settled a big case and hadn't started the next project. In any event, he remembers touring the fort, dressing up as a Revolutionary War soldier with Sarah, having a picture taken of the three of them straddling an eighteenth-century cannon. They'd eaten lunch at an open-air café overlooking Lake Champlain, the northern range of the Green Mountains at their backs, and he clearly remembers Katelyn insisting on ordering a salad featuring apples and bleu cheese, candied walnuts. He'd tried to dissuade her, but she was always headstrong, and when she ate the cheese, which must have been the first time she'd ever tried such a thing, rather than being disgusted as any other kid would have been, she was enthralled. And now he's sitting here watching her with a man she seems to adore, and she's talking to him about rare Peruvian spices like paico and huacatay, and he doesn't know what the hell she's talking about, but he's drinking the Pisco Sour and nibbling his own cheesy corn cob, and for a moment, a short moment, a fleeting one, yes, but undoubtedly a real one, he finds himself feeling truly, supremely, surprisingly content. *Damn*, he thinks, *I should come to The Greedy Llama more often.*

Unfortunately, his reverie is interrupted by the ringtone of his phone, a bit of a song by the band Cake, which is not the sort of band he'd know anything about except that his clerks were listening to the song one day and he liked it. Katelyn flashes him a look that says she is impressed by the breadth of his musical range, which she had assumed (reasonably, correctly, pretty much) was limited at this point to jazz and maybe an old Fleetwood Mac record, and Ed gives her a wink of acknowledgment before he looks down at the phone and learns it's Linda who's calling him. He was half expecting her call, and although it would probably be prudent to take the phone outside, he decides to answer it right there at the table.

"Linda, how's it going?" he says. "What's up?"

"Is this memo serious? You don't really want me to send it out, do you?"

"Absolutely I want you to send it out. You haven't sent it out yet? You need to hurry up or nobody will read it before the conference tomorrow."

"Why are you writing about Chuang Tzu to your colleagues?" Linda asks, butchering the philosopher's name so that it sounds like *Shh-huaaaaang Tuhzoooo*. "And who is Shhhuaaaang Tuhzooo, anyway?"

"I thought I made that clear in the memo. He's a fourth-century BC Taoist sage. And my fellow justices would all benefit a lot from reading him. You'd like him too. I'll buy you a copy of the Inner Chapters."

At that, Chris and Katelyn look up from their whispering. *Why is my father talking to his secretary about a Taoist sage?* his daughter wonders.

"No thanks," Linda says. "I'll stick with reading my erotic romances."

Ed shudders. "All right, then. Can you please circulate the memo as soon as possible?"

"You know that the Chief is going to be livid."

"I know what makes the Chief livid. Believe me, I know. I've given this thing a lot of thought. I know it seems bizarre, but I'm sure about it. Someone's got to throw down the gauntlet at this crazed maniac before the court gets written off as a mental asylum. And that someone is me."

Linda sighs. She's watched her boss slowly losing it all term long. She thought maybe the ukulele and the fake glasses were going to be the low point, but now she realizes that those weren't even close. She reminds herself that she's got plenty of retirement money sacked away and could take her four cats and move to her summer home on the Outer Banks at a moment's notice, if it comes to that. "Okay, then," she says. "If you say so."

"I say so. Thanks, Linda."

Ed turns off the phone, returns it to his pocket, drains the Pisco Sour. He looks up to see Chris and Katelyn regarding him with expressions that straddle the line between confusion and deep concern for the nation's future. Ed raises his eyebrows and smiles at them. "Tomorrow's conference should be pretty interesting," he declares. "Let's order."

***

Ed arrives as late as he possibly can for the morning conference so he doesn't have to talk to anyone before it starts. When he enters the room, the justices stop their chatting and turn to look at him. He gives them a little wave, plops his papers and files on the table, and takes a seat.

"Thanks so much for joining us, Justice Tuttle," Justice Cornelius says. "Some of us thought you might have retreated to a Nepalese mountaintop to live out the rest of your life eating insects and bark."

"Why would I have done that, Alan? Chuang Tzu's not from Nepal. You know where China is located, I assume? Shall I procure a globe from the library?"

Garabelli has been steaming all morning and cannot keep his anger under control for any longer. The very sight of Ed puts him over the edge. He stands from his chair, places his hands on the table, bends forward in Ed's direction. "If you think that your little shenanigans are going to stop me from expressing my opinions in any way that I damned well please, you are sorely . . . hey, what do you think you're doing?"

Fully expecting a Garabelli outburst early in the meeting, Ed is ready with his counter, which is to chirp and tweet in Tony's direction, flap his hands like a tiny sparrow, request a small handful of birdseed to hold him over to lunch.

"Do you have a small handful of birdseed?" Ed asks. "To hold me over to lunch? Chirp. Tweet."

Garabelli is apoplectic. Nobody chirps at Associate Justice Tony Garabelli like a small bird and gets away with it! Yet, since nobody has ever thought to chirp at him before, he's not sure how to react. His ears redden, muscles contract, teeth clench. He picks up a book—a big book, some kind of case reporter, maybe a recent edition of the *U.S. Reports*—and hurls it across the table at Ed. "You shitbag!" Garabelli hollers, the book hurtling through the air at Ed's head. Ed flashes a look not of worry or fear, but of surprise; he squawks vociferously and blocks the book with his hands/wings. The volume falls harmlessly onto Arnow's lap directly to Ed's left.

"Okay, okay, can we please settle down?" the Chief insists, like an exasperated fourth grade teacher. "If we could perhaps not resort to intra-bench violence for the first time in the history of our esteemed institution, I would very much appreciate it. We have a lot of business to get through, and I think it would be best to put off Ed's threat to insert Chinese mysticism into our jurisprudence until the end of the conference."

Garabelli huffs deeply, stares Ed down with bulging angry black eyes. *Cheep?* Ed says, quietly, and he can see Tony's rage immediately return. "Enough!" the Chief screeches, and at that, Tony takes a seat, Ed retires the bird act, for the moment anyway, and they both look down at their notes.

"Thank you. I don't want to have to give anyone detention today, so let's try to focus, okay? First off, I want to remind everyone that the cameras will be back in the courtroom for Monday's arguments."

A collective groan. Even the justices who theoretically support having cameras in the court don't particularly like actually having them there.

"I know, I know," the Chief says. "But this is the last day of them for the term, and if the reaction tomorrow is anything like the first couple of times, we might be able to put this whole idea to bed for good."

"Rumor has it that the Speaker fell asleep while watching last month's argument in the FTC case," Stephenson says.

Arnow adds: "I think the editorial page of the *Times* called that argument *more boring* than watching paint dry."

"Why would anyone in their right mind want to watch one of our sessions?" Ed pipes in. The Chief stares him down. They haven't traded a word about their implicit post-punch "agreement," and Janet is definitely not going to tolerate any backsliding now. "What?" Ed asks, looking down sheepishly at his notebook. "I'm just sayin'."

The Chief keeps her gaze focused on Ed for a couple more uncomfortable seconds before returning to her own notes. "Obviously, this is our last week of oral arguments for the term, after which we've got about two months to get out the rest of our opinions. We're doing well so far with getting out decisions from the earlier sittings. All the cases from October and November are done. December is almost done. John, how's it looking on the right to counsel opinions?"

"In due time, Chief. In due time," Stephenson responds, unwilling to be bullied into doing his work any faster than he wants to.

"Yes, well, *do* spend some *time* getting those things circulated, won't you?" the Chief responds, and both Arnow and Cormelius chuckle lightly. "So, this brings us to the long list of petitions for discussion. It looks like next term is going to be a blockbuster."

As they talk and vote, it becomes clearer and clearer that the Chief is right—this term might have some important cases, but next term is going to be a doozy. A case about the president's pardon power, one about the constitutionality of the Smithsonian, yet another obscenity case, not one but two cases about the Third Amendment. *The Third Amendment*, Ed thinks, as he finishes off a rough sketch of the great eighties boxer Marvelous Marvin Hagler. *What is the world coming to*?

When they have finished working through the petitions, the Chief returns to Ed's controversial memorandum. "So, if anyone would like to discuss Justice Tuttle's memo from yesterday evening, now would be the time. And I'd like to emphasize here that when I say 'discuss,' I mean *discuss*, not *throw a book* or *chirp like a bird*."

Garabelli is still livid, but he has regained his composure. "What I object to most strenuously in this memorandum is the mockery of my religious beliefs. This is over the line. It's beyond the pale. I call for Justice Tuttle to be officially, I don't know . . . *rebuked*." He looks at the Chief. "Do you have some procedure for rebuking around here?"

"I'm not mocking your religious beliefs," Ed responds. "How could you read that memo to be a mockery of your beliefs?"

"I also thought it was a mockery of his beliefs. *My* beliefs. Beyond the pale," Arnow interjects.

Rebecca Leibowitz says something, perhaps involving the word "agree" or "disagree," but she is so quiet that nobody understands what she says, and Garabelli interrupts her anyway: "It's a mockery because you're suggesting that my belief in Jesus Christ and the Holy Spirit is silly. Silly like a belief in some . . . some Chinese sage who believes a horse is potato salad."

"That part was kind of funny," Epps adds, from the back end of the table.

"Now who's mocking whose religious beliefs?" Ed exclaims. "You just said that my beliefs are silly. You only think I'm mocking your beliefs because you think my beliefs are a joke. But they're not. I believe in Chuang Tzu. Just like you believe in Jesus. It just happens that believing in Chuang Tzu is a little harder to square with applying logic and precedent to decide legal disputes."

"Nobody believes in Chuang Tzu! You're ridiculing me, and I won't have it." Garabelli insists.

"I'm not ridiculing you. I do believe in Chuang Tzu. I've just demonstrated the weakness of your position, that's all."

"All that you've demonstrated is that you're a lunatic. There's nothing wrong—and everything right—about consulting one's deepest convictions when making what is essentially a deeply contested moral decision."

"Well, my deepest conviction is that a horse is a potato salad and all words are like the cheeping of tiny birds. Why can't I consult *that*?"

"Because . . . because . . . because it's fucking *retarded*, that's why! You shouldn't be a judge if you think that language is just the tweeting of tiny birds."

"But that would violate Article VI of the Constitution, which prohibits any religious test as a qualification to any office or public trust under the United States. And please, Tony, let's watch our language. 'Retarded' is not the preferred nomenclature. 'Mentally disabled' please."

Garabelli is practically growling at this point. Like a rabid dog. There's drool.

"Look," Ed says. "I'm sorry that I've proven your position untenable, but that's just . . ."

"Untenable? Un*ten*able? I'll give you *untenable*—right in the head," Garabelli bellows.

He stands up and is about to launch himself over the table at Ed when DeLillo, who likes Tony about as much as he likes getting food poisoning, gets up and grabs the old guy from behind in a bear hug. This sends Garabelli into a fury, and he instinctively starts throwing elbows, one of which lands squarely on DeLillo's nose. DeLillo's head spins to his left. The blood that spurts out of his proboscis showers Epps, who shrieks, stands up in shock, and then trips clumsily over the legs of his chair. Ed shimmies out of the way as Epps falls to the floor, and when Epps puts out his left hand to break his fall, the fall instead breaks Epps's left hand, or at least hurts it enough that the junior justice doubles up on his shrieking, which now sounds like something out of a *National Geographic* special on hyenas getting devoured by Zambian lions. Meanwhile, freed from DeLillo's grasp, Garabelli thinks again about diving over the table at Ed but is stymied by Justice Cornelius, who tries, gingerly, for fear of meeting the same fate as DeLillo, to restrain his right-wing mentor by grabbing his arm at the bicep and pulling the struggling Garabelli back away from the table, all the while saying things like "he's not worth it" and "don't stoop to his level" and "whoa, look at all the blood that just splashed on Epps's face!" Tony pulls forward, Cornelius pulls back, and eventually the tug of war sends them both toppling toward the floor. As he starts to fall, Garabelli's foot lands awkwardly on the edge of the eighteenth-century rug and twists like a screw cap on a pickle jar. He yelps and collapses, chopping Cornelius off at the knees and sending him tumbling face forward onto the carpet. When their fall is complete, Cornelius is draped over Garabelli's substantial girth, his gray-wool-clad ass sticking up into the air, while Garabelli continues moaning and trying to grab his ankle, which he cannot reach because it is blocked by Corenlius's left thigh.

The Chief stands and surveys the scene. What a fucking mess. DeLillo is screaming and wailing and trying desperately to staunch the bleeding from his nose with a torn-out page of a *Federal Reporter*. Epps is rolling around, grabbing his left wrist, spreading DeLillo's blood all over both the rug and the room's original wooden flooring. Cornelius and Garabelli are all tangled up, their limbs intertwined, as Garabelli calls Cornelius a "moron" and demands his immediate freedom so he can tend to his twisted, probably sprained ankle. Cornelius squeaks "sorry" and lets out a worried fart. The Chief can do nothing. She looks over at Ed, who is also standing, trying to stay clear of the spinning Epps, and he looks back and shrugs. "I guess this means the conference is dismissed?" he says to her, and then he gathers his files and papers, steps carefully over Epps's head, and leaves the room.

ELEVEN

ED ARRIVES AT THE DOWNTOWN TAPAS RESTAURANT AT exactly the same time as Greg Bash and his three fresh-faced, nervous students. Greg introduces the students to the Supreme Court justice, and Ed tries to remember their names. It won't be easy: Nate he'll remember without much trouble, but Keiko and Shamaila will be more challenging. The host shows them to their table, where they ask for still water and plates of olives and exchange chit-chat—where are you from, what did you do before law school, that sort of thing. It's Saturday, but on the early side for dinner, so the restaurant is fairly empty; Bash's booming voice echoes uncomfortably around the main dining room as he regales the students with one of his favorite stories from law school—the one about Ed and Greg's section-mate Paul, who dominated their first semester with endless comments and questions and answers to all the professors' inquiries, all of which made everyone else in the section both furious and insecure, but who then disappeared after grades came out, never to be heard from again.

"Remember the time he told Babcock that he had written a letter—and sent it to her through the mail—outlining his views on promissory estoppel?" Bash asks Ed, a glance of delighted amazement in his eyes, as though the astounding event happened just yesterday.

"Of course I remember," Ed says, only slightly less excited than Bash at the ridiculous memory. "He told Babcock to 'feel free' to get back to him anytime it was convenient. Babcock looked at Paul like he was an alien from Neptune who had just inexplicably landed in her contracts class."

179

The students can't believe what they're witnessing. Hearing their constitutional law professor yapping with a justice of the Supreme Court about old law school memories is almost more than they can handle. Nate hopes that the sweat seeping through his shirt won't also saturate the armpits of the blazer he bought just for this evening. Shamaila feels dizzy and eats three olives in quick succession to head off a fainting spell. Keiko concentrates so she doesn't have another projectile vomiting incident like the one during her first semester torts exam. The three of them won the dinner at the law school's public interest auction a couple of weeks earlier—an event that the law school holds every year to raise money for students who take unpaid jobs during the summer. Ed and Bash do this regularly, and it always brings in a lot of cash for the auction, although Ed doesn't realize that Bash typically puts in a good deal of his own money to ensure that his con law students win the prize.

Although they have exchanged several emails filled with all sorts of apologies and explanations, this is the first time that Ed and Bash have met face to face since the Great Debacle. In mid-March, as the auction was approaching, Greg asked Ed if he wanted to forget about the dinner this year, but Ed was insistent, and now he's glad he was. The dinner is fun. The kids are interesting (the things young people do these days before going to law school—Teach for America, graduate school in English, the Peace Corps in Armenia!), the food is delicious, and the sangria is flowing as quickly as Ed and Greg's banter. Ed remembers now why they've been such good friends for so long. It's a cliché, the thing they say about how true friends can pick up after months, even years of not seeing each other, as though they had never been apart, but for him and Bash it's true, and this, for Ed, is rare—indeed, he can't think of another friend that he can say it about.

The two of them tell tales from their relative youths—petty controversies at the *Law Journal*, the summer they spent working at the same firm, the party that same summer where Ed passed out in the bathtub. Ed is a little worried that Bash might go too far with the stories—the drug use, though testified to, in general terms, at his confirmation hearing, is not something he wants to talk about with these kids, and the college girl he got pregnant over 1L Christmas break is definitely off-limits—but Bash stays well clear of these topics, if for no other reason that he knows what Ed could counter with. Among other things, the prospect of the Georgetown Law student body learning about his own arrest for public urination, not so long ago really, suffices to keep Bash careful on that score.

Soon the dinner is over, the garlic shrimps and bacon-wrapped dates and white anchovies all devoured, the cups of dessert flan emptied, the thin glasses of after-dinner sherry that the two old guys introduce to the students who are used to drinking Natty Light drained. The kids have had the time of their lives, a night they'll treasure and think fondly upon during long nights of mind-numbing litigation discovery at whatever lifeless corporate law firm they find themselves at after graduation. Everyone shakes hands, the kids' wet palms like soft lizards in Ed's jaded grip. Greg puts the students in a cab and sends them on their way. The two friends stand awkwardly on the sidewalk outside the restaurant. Neither wants to head home, but at the same time both are unsure what to say to the other now that they're alone. Finally, Ed suggests that they have a nightcap, and since the Willard Hotel and its Round Robin Bar are close by, that's where they head.

***

Scotches ordered, tall glasses of cool water and plates of gourmet nuts placed in front of them, Ed launches into an apology, one he's been meaning to offer for months. "Look, I know I've said this by email, but I want to say it face-to-face. I'm sorry about what I said that night at Diana's. It was, you know, as Tony Garabelli might say, 'beyond the pale.' I was jealous, and upset, and drunk, and the Chief Justice had just punched me in the stomach, and, I'm just totally and completely sorry."

Bash's eyes narrow at the mention of the stomach punching. A bushy eyebrow lifts toward the ceiling. "Umm, well, first of all, apology accepted. Of course. Second of all, regarding the Chief Justice, *what?* And third of all, you were right, you know. About what you said that night on the stoop."

"What? That your balls are jaundiced and diseased?"

"Yes, that too," Bash laughs. "But I mean what you said about me being jealous of you. I am. I mean, not all the time, and it's not like debilitating envy or anything, but of course I'm jealous that you're a justice of the fucking Supreme Court. How could I not be?"

"Really?" Ed asks. "You never act jealous. No one could possibly tell."

"And how easy do you think that is? Not only am I jealous, but I have to act like I'm not jealous all the time, or how could we ever stay friends, right? What a pain in the ass." Bash takes a drink.

"I never thought of it that way."

"Well, think of it from my perspective. Thirty years ago, you and I were in basically the same exact position. Top of the class, law review editors, both clerking at the court, precisely identical potential for legal greatness, right? Maybe I was a little smarter, but other than that, the same. So I go off to academia, start writing a bunch of silly articles that nobody reads, and you go the law firm to make some money to buy a boat or whatever it is you said you wanted . . ."

"A Jaguar E-type, actually," Ed interjects. "Which I never bought, by the way."

"Whatever. Who the fuck cares? Anyway, you go to the firm, become the biggest litigator in the city, and the next thing I know you're on the court of appeals. And I'm still writing silly articles that nobody reads."

"Oh, come on, your job is great. You make more money than I do and you work like three hours a week."

Greg laughs. "True, it's not very onerous. I could probably write a novel on the side and nobody would bat an eye."

"Well, I don't know about that."

"Yeah, maybe not. Still, though, my point is that you were right about the jealousy. Even if you were a little mean about it."

"You'll recall that you were having sex with a woman I might have been half in love with, even though I somehow thought it was a good idea not to talk to her for three months. It's my own fault, I'm a moron. But you can understand why I might have been upset."

"I tried to tell you that you were being a moron. Several times. I honestly thought that you had written her off. So, you know, when the opportunity presented itself, I took it." Bash pauses. "Not that I wouldn't have taken it if I hadn't thought you had written her off. I was out-of-control horny."

"How many times did you two sleep together? Was it just that night? Oh, hell, don't tell me, I don't want to know."

"It didn't last long, let's put it that way. I'm pretty sure she doesn't want to have anything to do with either one of us ever again," Bash explains. "And in about a month she's heading off to Shanghai for her sabbatical anyway."

"Well, lesson learned, I guess," Ed says, sipping from the glass of scotch. Lately, he's been trying to drink more slowly, but he's not very good at it. "You know, I'm thinking about retiring at the end of the term."

This startles Greg. "Really?" he asks. "Are you serious?"

"Completely. This First Amendment stuff is putting me over the edge. Between you and me, what the fuck do I know about whether 'under God' should be in the Pledge of Allegiance? What about me or my background suggests that I should have any idea about how to answer that question for the whole country? I really can't stand constitutional law."

"I never understand you when you say that. What other kind of law is there?"

"You see, this is where we're different. When we were young, all everyone talked about was constitutional law, the juicy controversies about abortion and race and religion and speech and all that. Except for me. I never liked constitutional law. It's barely law at all, in my view. It's just politics, filtered through a few vague phrases in an old document written by people who couldn't possibly fathom what the world looks like today."

"Okay, granted. And that's what makes it so interesting," Bash interjects.

"No, that's what makes it suck," Ed answers. "For me, anyway. I was much happier deciding administrative law cases at the DC Circuit. Or better yet, litigating them."

"Wow. You're truly thinking about stepping down. How odd," Bash says, genuinely surprised. "What would you do?"

"I don't know. Travel? Write a screenplay? Learn how to bake? Take a class in astrophysics? Plus I can always sit on a lower appeals court whenever I feel like it. Hear some ordinary cases—the ones I actually like. Souter does that all the time these days."

"Oh, no, don't be like Souter. That guy is such a weirdo."

"You don't know the half of it."

"Is it true that he was a Star Trek fanatic?"

"Never missed a convention."

The two friends are quiet for a moment, nibbling on nuts. All this talk about the past has rendered Ed pensive, nostalgic, a little melancholy. Finally, he breaks the silence. "Remember how we used to go to Atlantic City when we were in law school?"

"Are you kidding, of course I do," Bash answers, a wide grin stretching out across his face. "That place was such a dump. I loved going there."

"Drinking, smoking, and gambling, all at the same time—it was the vice trifecta—the complete opposite of studying torts and evidence."

"Remember the time we pooled our last five dollars at like two in the morning so we could put down a ten-dollar chip on a number in roulette, and it came out?"

"Number thirty. Always my lucky number."

"That might have been the greatest moment of my life up until that point. Maybe even up to this point."

"I remember we were so excited that all of a sudden out of nowhere we each had a hundred and eighty bucks so we could keep gambling. That number probably bought us two more hours of excitement."

"And free drinks."

"God, we were so stupid. We had no money. Less than no money, if you counted the loans, and we'd spent the last of it playing craps instead of, like, buying a sweater or something."

"When was the last time you were there?"

"Atlantic City? Probably our third year of law school. Unless we went while we were clerking. I think maybe we did once or twice. So, maybe a million years ago?"

"We should go again," Bash says.

"Maybe we should. That would be fun. Maybe that's what I'll do after I retire. Learn how to count cards and park myself at a blackjack table at the Tropicana."

"No, I mean we should go right now. Tonight."

"I'm sorry, what?" Ed asks. "You want to go to Atlantic City right this instant?"

"No," Bash answers. "I think first we should finish our scotch. And then we should go to Atlantic City. Why not? What else do you have to do?"

Ed pauses, considers the possibility. "Nothing, I guess. I've got arguments on Monday morning, but I'm ready for them. Ready enough, anyway. How would we get there?"

"Why, hitchhike, of course. How do you think? One of us would drive. I'll drive." Bash lifts his glass and drains the rest of the whiskey. "I've always been a magnificent drunk driver."

"I don't know. It's kind of crazy, isn't it?"

"Yeah, a little bit. But so what? Come on, let's do it. In three hours we'll be smoking cigars and playing craps. And this time we have all the money in the world to spend. No desperate ten-dollar bets at the small change tables. Gotta bet big to win big."

"Scared money loses," Ed says, one of the mantras of their youth. He's smiling and nodding his head. The idea has gained traction. He wants to do it. "Can we swing by my place so I can get my hat and fake glasses? And maybe a toothbrush?"

"Absolutely. Let's go." Bash stands up, fishes two twenty dollar bills from his leather wallet, and places them on the bar. "And on the way, you'll tell me about why the Chief Justice punched you in the gut."

***

Somewhere around one in the morning, Greg pulls his sleek new Acura with the "BLT MMM" vanity plate into the valet parking lane at Caesar's Atlantic City and hands his keys over to an eager attendant. Ed gets out of the car and stretches. The drive, at three and a half hours, was longer than he expected and made worse by Greg's near-constant taunting of him for trying to make out with Janet Owens. Several times during the course of the trip up Route 95 to Philly and then off to the east through New Jersey on the depressing Atlantic City Parkway, Ed decided that this outing, which had seemed like such a good idea while sitting in the warm embrace of the Willard Hotel, was in fact going to be a huge mistake. As someone who has been making huge mistakes nearly constantly this past year, Ed had not been happy about the prospect of making yet another one. It had been the sea air, seeping through the barely cracked windows, that had lifted his mood as they'd approached the shore. Now, having finally arrived at their destination, and looking forward to nothing but gambling, drinking, and maybe swimming a lap or two in the hotel pool for the next eighteen or so hours, Ed is content. Excited even.

The lobby appears oddly similar to Ed's workplace. Enormous white marble pillars jut out of the tile floor and stretch up to the ceiling, which is painted like an autumn sky, light blue and cloud-covered. Some of the pillars have statues of Roman gods and heroes standing upon them. Caesar himself looms tall in the center of the lobby, his left hand holding up a toga and grasping a staff, his right extended upward, pointing to the heavens, as though he's in the middle of performing a disco dance from the mid-seventies. Ed has made a reservation from the car, so he and Greg check in, leave a few things in the room they don't expect to spend much time in, and head directly downstairs to the cling-clang-clanging of the never-sleeping casino.

They decide to start with craps, stepping into two open spaces at the end of a twenty-five-dollar minimum table. Each sets down five hundred dollar bills and gets a neat stack of red and green chips in return. It takes Ed a couple of minutes for the game to come back to him—the pass line, the odds bet behind the line, purportedly the best bet in the entire casino, buying the numbers, the come bet, ten on the hard six, *press the yo*. Soon they're both betting with gusto, and since the old guy directly across from them with the brown pants pulled up to his nipples keeps throwing fours and eights and sixes and pretty much everything other than a seven, they quickly find themselves up and up big. The game moves too fast to do any counting, but Ed figures that by the time he finally receives his first scotch and soda from the Roman-clad, short-skirted waitress with the red hair and bewitching perfume, he's already made as much dough as he tended to lose during entire trips back in law school.

Inevitably, though, their luck starts turning south and sevens are popping up all over the table like dandelions on a poorly groomed lawn, so Greg and Ed demonstrate the wisdom of their years and decide to leave before things worsen. They color up and give the dealers handsome tips, hoping they will bring karmic rewards before the day is through. Ed feels mighty as he pockets three purple five-hundred-dollar chips.

"Now what?" he asks.

"Why don't we get cigars," suggests Bash.

"Cigars!" Ed affirms.

They find a convenience store that sells a small selection of cruddy cigars and buy two of the least terrible ones they can find. Strolling down the boardwalk listening to the waves crash quietly against the shore, they puff away, pretend they're young, try not to cough too much. They last about ten minutes. It is cold out, too cold, so they make their way back to Caesars, put out the cigars, and head inside. When Ed yawns, Greg insists that they both drink giant cans of Red Bull before heading back to the tables. Ed has never drank a Red Bull in his life, though his clerks sometimes seem to be practically mainlining the stuff, but he agrees because it's after three and he sees no other way to stay awake. The SweetTart flavored beverage gives Ed a boost. They wash it down with a shot of whiskey each and then try to figure out what to do next.

"Maybe we should play a little roulette," Ed suggests.

"Ugh. I hate roulette. It's a game designed for the mentally disabled and stroke victims," Bash answers.

"No, it's fun. The ball spins around. *Zip zip.* Then *clunk, clunk, clunk,* it falls into place. And the chips are so colorful!"

"What are you, a six-year-old girl? I'm not playing any game where old people sit around and keep notes on what random numbers have come out before so they can predict what random number will come out next."

"All right, fine. What then?"

Bash looks around. He sees a game called "Let It Ride" that he's never heard of before. Two middle-aged, relatively attractive women are sitting at it, and there are two empty chairs next to them. It's an easy decision.

"Let's try this thing," he says, striding over to the table and sitting down before Ed can weigh in on the choice. "Hello, ladies," Greg says, taking out a purple chip and changing it for some smaller denominations. "Is this table hot?" he asks, double-entendre-ly.

Ed rolls his eyes and takes the seat next to Greg, changes in his own purple chip. The women are definitely good looking—mid-forties, mid-thigh skirts and black tights, lots of jewelry, one a fake blonde and the other a brunette—but probably cougars more interested in men half Ed and Greg's ages. And Ed is not in the mood for anything remotely romantic here at three in the morning, his hair slightly matted, breath smelling of tobacco, whiskey, and sugar-free carbonated energy drink.

"It's going okay," the blonde says, listlessly, to Greg.

"All right, how do you play this game, anyway?"

The brunette, who is sitting to the blonde's left, and so two seats away from Greg, is somewhat more welcoming than her friend. She introduces herself as Cindy, her friend as Maggie, and gives the men a quick overview of the rules. It's like a mini-poker-type deal, except that the players start by putting forward three equal bets. The dealer deals two common cards face up and then gives each player three cards face down. After the dealer turns over one of the player's cards, the player can choose either to take back his first bet, if the card sucks, or to *let it ride*, if it looks good when combined with the common cards. This is repeated for the second face-down card. The third bet stays no matter what. After all the cards are turned over, any pair of jacks or better gets paid. A full house, for example, gets paid fifteen to one. Greg observes that the payout odds are only slightly better than, say, a state lottery or a contest from the side of a cereal box. "Yeah, that's true," the blonde says, "but it's kind of fun—you feel sort of like you're in control, and it takes a long time to lose everything you've got."

They play for a while, drink another glass of scotch, win some and lose some. The game is terribly boring. Ed is exhausted; he's seeing spots before his eyes and feels like his head is going to fall off and roll across the casino floor. Greg is still chatting with the ladies but if he's trying to get one of them to give him a blow job or something, he's not making much progress. When it becomes clear to him that his charm is not working, he comes up with a new plan.

"Hey," he whispers to Ed, leaning over in his direction, "can I tell them you're a Supreme Court justice?"

Ed is mortified. He's not wearing his hat, but he is wearing the fake glasses, and there is no way he wants to reveal his identity. "Absolutely not," he tells Greg.

"Come on," Greg urges. "If they find out you're a Supreme Court justice, we'll probably get laid. Do it for me. Do it for your buddy."

"I don't want to get laid right now, and it wouldn't work anyway, and also, *no you may not tell them I'm a Supreme Court justice.*"

Greg leans back toward the women. "You know, my friend is a Supreme Court justice."

Ed can't believe it. Actually, he can.

"I'm the Queen of England," says the brunette.

"And I'm Sally Ride," the blonde adds.

"No, no, he is. Tell 'em, Ed."

Ed stands up and gathers up his chips, puts them in his pocket, drains his drink. "I'm not a Supreme Court justice," he says. "And I'm going to bed. Good night."

"No, no, you can't go," Bash calls after Ed as the Supreme Court justice walks away. "God save this honorable court. Oyez, oyez. Come back here." But Ed doesn't look back as he makes his way to the elevators, ultimate destination the queen-size bed in their ninth-floor room.

***

When Bash makes his way upstairs a half-hour later, Ed is already asleep in the bed by the window. Ed throws the blankets over his head to block out the light that Greg thoughtlessly turns on and to dampen the racket he makes taking off his clothes and settling into the other bed. The lights finally go off, and Ed pops his head out of the covers just as Greg starts farting like an elephant. Greg's farts fill the night. Squeaking, rumbling, odiferous, horrible farts, aimed almost exclusively in Ed's direction. *Why can't he at least turn his asshole the other way?* Ed sleeps fitfully, dreams of swimming in a Mumbai sewer, wakes at about eleven and wonders whether the toilet has overflowed. He sits up in the bed and immediately retreats back under the covers. His eyes water from the stink. *Has someone released a tear gas canister in here? Am I in the middle of a 1967 campus riot?* Ed peeks out from beneath the blanket. Greg is sleeping on his stomach, snoring like a truck, drool washing over the side of his pillow like Niagara Falls after a rainstorm. Ed throws a balled-up dirty sock at his friend's head and tells him to wake up. Greg turns on his side and farts.

It takes a while, but by one o'clock they're up and dressed and fed and caffeinated and back at the craps table. Ed gets lost in the game, piling up bets on all the numbers, pressing them when they're rolled, brushing it off when he loses. He bets the hardways, despite the terrible odds, urges on the shooters with gusto, throws the dice with pizzazz when it's his turn, delivers a round of high-fives when someone hits the point. It's the communal aspect of craps that sets it apart. The gamblers at a hot table are like a family, celebrating their successes with toasts, helping each other get through the occasional unwelcome *seven out*. At one point, a novice shooter gets on such a roll, brings so much joy to the nine gamblers who stand around the table drinking their beers and cokes and gin and tonics, each one of them from some different place, heading back before long to their jobs inside cubicles and under cars and on the top of roofs and behind long oak benches, that Ed wants to freeze the moment, embrace them all in a group hug, set up a Facebook page and plan their five-year reunion. He plays all day, outlasting even Greg, who after a few hours leaves the table to go bet on horse races. When they reconvene at seven and head to Hooters to dine on buffalo wings and leer at the waitresses, Ed is up over three grand.

After dinner they return to the casino, where time has stood still, the buzzing of the crowd and blinking lights the same as when they left, when they were here at three in the morning, when they visited thirty years ago. He can't be sure, but Ed suspects that the old lady with the oxygen tank who is shoveling coins into the jangling slot machine next to the blackjack tables is the same one who was shoveling coins in there sixteen hours earlier. They start playing again, alternating between ordering black coffees and light beers, and even though they're standing next to one of those failed men for whom the craps table is their only forum for exercising power—he makes overly complex bets for no reason, throws his chips far from the dealer's grasp, waits for the last possible moment to demand five on the field—they fall right back into their winning ways, and before they know it, they are both up over five thousand smackers, and it is midnight. Oral arguments start in ten hours, so Bash suggests they should get going, but Ed dreads trading in Caesar's Palace for his marble one and demurs. Three hours pass before Ed finally admits that they have to leave; he will get some shuteye in the passenger seat while Greg makes the three-plus-hour drive back home, landing Ed back in the District with a few hours to spare before taking the bench in the most important case of the year.

***

Ed falls asleep in the passenger seat of Greg's Acura almost as soon as they hit the highway, the stale air of inland New Jersey replacing the light sea breeze through the window that Greg keeps open to help him stay awake. Though buoyed somewhat by the gallons of coffee he sucked down back at the craps table, Greg can hardly keep his eyes open as he pilots the car through the nearly pitch-black night. They are only half an hour into the drive when a deer bounds into the road in front of them with no warning; it's a buck, huge, with many points. Greg swerves first to the left, a testament to his diminished reflexes because the deer is moving from right to left. He realizes his mistake and immediately swerves back to the right, clipping the deer in the rump. The deer scampers wildly away while Greg tries to bring the car back on course by swinging it back to the left. In this endeavor, he is only mildly successful; he gets the front of the car aimed in roughly the right direction, but the vehicle's forward momentum takes them off the side of the road, where they slam side-first into a ditch and then flip over, coming to rest upside down, the car's wheels spinning, useless as the legs of an upside-down cockroach.

TWELVE

"ARE YOU OKAY?" BASH SAYS, A FEW SECONDS AFTER THE CAR has come to rest on its roof.

A moment passes. "Mmm, yes, I think so. I think I'm all right." Ed checks his body the best he can in the crumply space. His limbs move. There's some blood. From a cut in his face, he thinks. "What, uhh, happened?"

"Good. You're okay. There was a deer."

"There was a deer."

"Am I okay?"

"I don't know. What do you think? Ow, I think maybe my face is bleeding."

"I'm not sure. My arm seems kind of fucked up." Bash looks over at Ed. Ed's face is indeed bleeding. Not too badly, but it does make him look a little like a monster. "You're bleeding."

"I know."

"Goddamned deer."

"Yeah," Ed says, straining his neck to look at his watch, whose face is now turned away from him. "Hey, do you know what time it is?"

***

The police arrive and help the two men out of the car. The Acura is totaled, no doubt about it, but Ed and Greg are more-or-less all right. A paramedic tends to the deep gash in Ed's left cheek, while his partner checks out Greg's arm, which appears to be busted in some way. The paramedics explain that they have to take both Ed and Greg to the hospital to get checked out by a doctor. Ed objects, tries to explain that he is fine, that he's never felt better, that he needs to get back to the District as quickly as possible because he has "some very important cases to decide," but this just serves to increase the paramedic's worry that Ed has suffered some possibly irreversible brain trauma. Slowly, and with exaggeratedly precise diction, the paramedic makes it clear to Ed that seeing a doctor tonight is not optional.

The hospital is ten miles from the scene of the accident, but with the ambulance's sirens blaring, it takes them only seven minutes to get there. The paramedics escort Greg and Ed into a waiting room, where they are given water to drink and forms to fill out. Ed has about six hours to get back to the court for the beginning of arguments, so from a corner of the waiting room he calls the court and, without providing too much in the way of details, asks that a car be sent immediately to the southeastern New Jersey dump where he's being held captive to pick him up and transport him directly to One First Street. When the car is successfully arranged, Ed breathes a sigh of relief and tries to relax, maybe even get a little more sleep, so that when he finally does arrive at the court later in the morning, he won't start sawing logs right in the middle of some question about James Madison and the First Amendment.

He is just dozing off when a nurse calls his name. In a small examination room with pictures of koala bears on the walls, a young doctor—maybe a resident, perhaps a sophomore pre-med at South East New Jersey State—puts four stitches in his face to close up the ugly wound. Later, once again just as Ed is falling asleep on the examination table, a more senior doctor arrives to run a battery of neurological functioning tests, like standing on one foot and reciting the alphabet backwards, both of which Ed finds difficult, not because his brain has smashed into his skull but because he is as tired as that guy in *Clockwork Orange* who is forced to watch violent films with his eyelids held open. The doctor decides that Ed is okay—okay enough to leave the hospital, anyway—and he sends him off with some things to look out for (dizziness, cloudiness of vision, persisting in the idea that he needs to "adjudicate disputes") and instructions to see his personal doctor within a couple of days. Back in the waiting room, discharge paperwork complete, Ed reunites with Greg, who is now sporting a bright red cast that reaches from the fingers on his left hand all the way up to his bicep.

"Atlantic City," Ed says. "That was sure a good idea."

"Shut the fuck up."

They finally do get a bit of sleep—uncomfortable sleep, draped over several plastic chairs under the harsh glow of the waiting room's florescent lights, several of which blink maddeningly—before Ed gets a call alerting him that the car will be arriving within minutes. When the car pulls into the entrance of the hospital, it is almost exactly half past six in the morning. Ed and Greg pile into the backseat and tumble off to dreamland as the car leaves the hospital grounds, zooming off as fast as it can practically go toward the nation's capital.

***

The eight men and women who march out to hear arguments in *Philadelphia v. Downey* are probably the motliest group of justices to take the bench in the history of the United States Supreme Court. Garabelli hobbles in on crutches. Epps sports a cast on his left hand and forearm. DeLillo's face is purple and swollen. The Chief looks exceptionally grumpy, even for her. The audience gasps. The journalists look at each other, confused and bemused. Farkas scratches his bald head. Julie Anderson nervously twirls her finger in her hair. The guy from the *Journal* doesn't know what to think. *What the hell?* says a woman from *USA Today*. *Did these guys play a rugby match against the Senate Judiciary Committee?* The justices take their seats, and that's when everyone realizes that Ed Tuttle is not present. More gasping. Attentive court watchers have come to expect odd behavior these days from Tuttle, but this seems particularly ominous. Given the condition of some of the other justices, many in the gallery wonder whether Ed has maybe lost a leg, or had his spleen removed, or gone to the great marble palace in the sky.

***

The car carrying Ed and Greg comes to a screeching halt in front of the court's back door on Second Street at just about ten minutes after ten. Ed bolts out of the back seat, sleep goop crusting the corner of his eyes, his unwashed hair shooting out of his head in all different directions like a clown's, the smoky smell of Atlantic City still clinging to his clothes. Thirty minutes ago, he called the Chief and let her know that he'll be late, hoping that she might delay the beginning of the session for a bit, but she refused, so Ed has no choice but to run to his chambers, gather up the materials he needs for the argument, and get to the courtroom as fast as he can. The Chief is swearing in some new members of the Supreme Court bar before the arguments start, so it's possible that he will make it without missing too much back and forth about the Pledge of Allegiance.

He sprints by the security guards who stand by the back door, ignoring their greetings and inquiries, and runs down the long carpeted corridor toward his chambers. Ordinarily, with all the tennis he's been playing, a four-hundred-yard dash wouldn't be overly taxing, but in his current state—somewhere between a sleep-deprived zombie and a gash-faced Frankenstein—he feels like he might just collapse before he gets to his office. But no—he makes it, throws open the door of the chambers, rushes to his office, and collects the bunch of papers and briefs and files that are stacked on his desk. He turns and sprints back out the doorway, stray pieces of paper floating out of the pile and trailing behind him as he runs. He's huffing and puffing as he gets to the area where the justices keep their robes. It is right next to the curtain that drapes behind the courtroom bench, and through it he can hear Justice Leibowitz asking Philadelphia's lawyer how a polytheist fourth grader might feel about saying "under God" at the beginning of the school day.

Ed puts down his stack and struggles into his robe. It's a little crooked across his shoulders, but this is no time for sartorial perfection, so he leaves it that way, picks up his materials, and steps through the split in the curtain, Johnny Carson like, making his sudden appearance directly behind the Chief Justice. The lawyer at the lectern, who is in the middle of explaining to Justice Leibowitz that there's probably never been a fourth-grade polytheist in the history of the nation and that even if there were one, he or she could simply choose not to say the Pledge, shrieks like a banshee at the unexpected sight of wild-eyed, face-sliced, crazy-haired Justice Tuttle. The Chief, who has been completely focused on the details of the argument and hasn't noticed Ed's sudden arrival, is startled by the lawyer's shriek. She screams. Justice Arnow, who has never before heard the Chief scream, tosses his pen up in the air in surprise and then watches it as it bounces off of Justice Epps's head. Instinctively, Justice Epps throws his broken left arm up in the air to catch the pen and yelps with excruciating pain.

The Chief hangs her head in disbelief. *This was not a good day to let cameras in to the courtroom.*

"Excuse me, sorry, I'm very sorry, excuse me," Ed says, shuffling down the bench to take his seat. "Very sorry. Please carry on. Something about fourth-grade polytheists?"

It takes a minute or two for the ruckus in the courtroom to come to an end, for the gallery to stop laughing and whispering, for Justice Epps's whimpering to die down. The Chief calls things back to order, thanks Ed for making time in his busy schedule to come to the argument, asks for the discussion to resume. Justice Arnow, who sits on Ed's immediate right, inches his chair a bit toward the Chief to escape the fetid smell of Ed's armpit. The city's lawyer advances her final point in response to Justice Leibowitz's hypothetical fourth-grade Greek god worshipper.

From there, the argument proceeds more-or-less normally. The liberals pepper the city's lawyer with questions about why Congress added "under God" into the Pledge, whether the Pledge could just be rewritten without the phrase, how counsel can possibly say that leading students in declaring their allegiance to a single Creator doesn't count as "advancing" religion in violation of the First Amendment. When Justice Stephenson brings up an amicus brief filed by several Buddhist organizations in opposition to the Pledge, Ed considers asking what the Taoists might say about it but stops himself, figuring that he has already caused problems for the morning and should probably try to keep a low profile for the rest of the session. The plaintiff's lawyer gets up next, and this time it's the conservatives who do the peppering. *Isn't it just a political exercise? If nobody has to say it, how can it be unconstitutional? Isn't it simply an acknowledgment of our religious heritage?* At first Ed finds himself cringing through this line of questioning, and then he tunes out, fingers the sutured cut on his face gingerly, starts sketching a craps table on the back of the city's brief.

He looks up only when there seems to be a bit of a commotion in the back of the courtroom. People in the last row are actively whispering, turning around and pointing at something—there's some giggling, a tiny *eeek* of surprise. As the lawyer explains that no, pressuring eight-year-olds into saying they believe in a single god is not just an acknowledgment of our national religious heritage, the commotion grows. A no-nonsense security officer makes his way toward the area of the courtroom where it's taking place. More chattering and giggling. Soon, half the courtroom is looking back to see what's going on. Even the lawyer stops and turns. Ed has no idea what's happening. He surveys the scene and is surprised to see his law clerk Dawn on the side of the room waving wildly in his direction. Ed turns and looks behind him to see if she might be trying to get someone else's attention, but there's nobody there, and who else could she possibly be trying to communicate with anyway? He looks at her, shrugs, raises his hands in the air to signal that he has no idea what she is trying to say. Dawn recognizes that Ed is confused and gets an idea. Quickly she takes a green highlighter and writes something on a manila file folder and holds it up so he can see it.

FREDDY!

Oh shit, Ed thinks, *shit, shitdog, shitbag, shitcake. I must have left the chambers door open.* He flashes Dawn a wide-eyed expression of horror, which she returns. She points to herself, as if to ask whether he wants her to get the cat. He shakes his head no—this is his responsibility, he'll take care of it. He stands up to get a better look right at the moment that a frightened Freddy scampers from beneath the last row of seats into the center aisle where everyone can see him. The security officer strides angrily toward the cat, as though Freddy has made some sort of conscious decision here to violate the rules of the courtroom by showing up in the middle of an argument without a ticket. Ed sees the officer approach Freddy, and a sense of terrified doom overtakes him— he imagines the guard stomping on his cat with his heavy black boots or pulling out his revolver and shooting Freddy's head off. There's no time left. Ed has no choice.

"Freddy," he yells. "I'll come save you!"

The entire courtroom turns its attention from the cat to the justice, as Ed hoists himself onto the bench, stands up, and then leaps off, his robe billowing out behind him like a superhero's cape. He lands hard, goes down to his knees, then springs up and approaches Freddy, bends over and calls out to him. "Hey there, Freddy. Hi Freddy. Come here, kitty. You can't be in the courtroom. Courtrooms are off limits for cats." The members of the gallery are flabbergasted. Many gasp. Ed turns to one side of the room and explains calmly: "He's my cat. I keep him in my chambers. He likes to escape. Crazy, silly cat." Freddy does not seem to recognize Ed—it could be that he's too afraid, having stumbled into this chaotic room filled with people, or it could be that it's the robe Ed's wearing that throws the cat off, or it could just be that Freddy's brain is the size of a garden pea. In any event, when Ed walks over to the cat, Freddy bolts toward the back of the courtroom. Ed stands and sprints wildly after him, yelling *Freddy, Freddy, Freddy* until the justice smacks straight into one of the two cameramen who are filming this argument-turned-carnival-sideshow for broadcast around the world. The cameraman goes flying into a row of spectators, the camera crashing to the ground, a seventy-four-year-old woman on the aisle displeased by the sudden appearance of the man's ample buttocks in her lap. Ed recovers from the collision, twirls, regains his stride, only to find the second cameraman right in front of him, filming the tail end of the crash. Ed looks directly into the camera. "My cat is loose. I'm sorry. I'm going to take care of it. The argument will resume shortly," he says to the viewing audience, then ducks under the camera and continues his pursuit.

Freddy is against the back wall of the courtroom, looking at Ed, who is still fruitlessly trying to talk to him, waiting for an opportune time to leap forward and grab him, wishing he had a feather toy or handful of catnip to make his life easier. Everyone in the courtroom is straining to see what's going on. Even the justices still on the bench are standing, craning their necks for a view. When he thinks the cat has become momentarily distracted by a floating piece of dust, Ed lurches forward to grab him, but Freddy is too quick. He dashes off to his right, toward the area where the clerks sit and where Dawn has been attentively watching and waiting, hoping to be able to help resolve his nightmare somehow. Here's her chance! Freddy runs right at her. She reaches down with the dexterity of a two-time all-conference college field hockey left winger and gets a tenuous hold on Freddy's backside. The cat tries to escape, skitters to his right, his fuzzy paws working a mile a minute but making no traction against the polished floor. She tightens her grip on the cat, lifts him to her bosom, declares the chase to be over. Panting, Ed walks over to Dawn, thanks her profusely, and takes the cat in his hands, lifting him into the air to show the crowd. "Freddy the cat is captured!" he bellows, and the entire court-room—minus the three or four justices who wish Ed would just die already—bursts into applause. The cameraman who is still able to walk approaches and directs his lens at Ed, Dawn, and Freddy, broadcasting the celebratory image of the group to each and every one of the forty-three people currently watching on C-Span 4, as well as the 3,432,695 people who will view it on YouTube over the next few days.

Ed hands Freddy back to Dawn, asks her to bring the little bugger back to chambers and lock him up behind four or five closed doors. The cat delivered, Ed walks back down the center aisle, past the plain-tiff's lawyer, and up the stairs on the side of the bench that leads him back to his seat. Before sitting down, he looks out at the crowd. "Okay, then, Pledge of Allegiance," he says. "Take three."

***

In the conference room, the justices sit around the table and look at each other in silence. These have been a bad couple of days. Although most of them are unhappy with more than just one of their colleagues, almost all the justices—Justice Leibowitz excepted, for, as it turns out, she is a cat lover and has twice already mentioned that she'd like to pay a visit to Ed's chambers to pet Freddy and maybe give him a toy—are focusing their ire on Ed. The Chief, in particular, has been staring daggers at him since she took her seat two minutes ago. Ed notices and recoils. It's like she is trying to recall what it felt like to punch him in the stomach. Suddenly, a satisfied smile breaks out across her face, and a quiet growl escapes her lips. *BLAM!*

"All right, then," she says finally, opening the thick binder where she keeps all her case information. "Not that anyone is going to take our edicts seriously ever again, but I suppose we ought to decide these cases." She starts with the second case that was argued—a controversy about whether corn on the cob is a "vegetable" for purposes of a statute administered by the Food and Drug Administration. The justices half-heartedly debate the question—Justice Epps taking the hardcore "corn is a grain, what are you nuts?" position against Justice Cornelius's "ask any average person on the street, and they'll say it's a vegetable, I mean you buy corn in the frozen vegetable portion of the supermarket, for heaven's sake" view—for ten minutes or so before they come to a 7-2 conclusion in favor of calling corn a grain. Observing that the opinion will be one of the more boring ones of the term to write, the Chief assigns it to Ed with a self-pleased smirk.

They next turn to the Pledge case, and, as with *Sexy Slut*, everyone's attention turns to Ed. The rest of them are split four to four, and so once again, and to nobody's surprise, the future of the First Amendment comes down to him.

Ed looks up from his sketch of the guy at the craps table with the brown pants hiked up to his nipples and glances around the table at his colleagues. "I look forward to reading your draft opinions," he says. "Hopefully one of them will be convincing enough for me to join."

Silence. Seething. Sketching. The Chief slams shut her binder and leaves the room without saying a word.

THIRTEEN

SEVERAL WEEKS LATER, ED IS RIDING A RENTED BICYCLE around Palo Alto. May on the Peninsula is glorious—as glorious as October is there, as glorious as January, as glorious as always. The smell of blossoming flowers fills the late-spring air, as Ed pedals in his crisp khaki shorts and royal blue polo shirt and sandals newly purchased at the ritzy Stanford mall near his hotel. He glides through manicured neighborhoods, passing modest-sized multimillion-dollar homes with immaculate lawns inhabited by Internet moguls and tech tycoons and surrounded by fragrant trees growing persimmons and lemons and who knows what other types of fruits. Mangoes? Do mangoes grow in northern California, he wonders, as a beautifully restored 1938 Packard slowly passes on his left? They must—doesn't every possible kind of fruit grow here? That, after all, is what everyone in the Bay Area talks about most of the time. The fruit trees, they can't shut up about them! Even his friend Ray, the president of the university, when they met earlier in the morning to discuss the weekend, wouldn't stop yammering about the kefir limes he picks from the trees in his yard to use in Thai soups and top-shelf margaritas.

Graduation is tomorrow. Ed's speech is in the late morning at the general convocation, where graduates of all the colleges across the university—both graduate and undergraduate—will gather with parents and families and loved ones in the football stadium under the bright sun to be ushered into the next stages of their lives. His words are ready, all nine pages of them, filled with exhortations to be unique, to be generous, to live life to the fullest, to pursue professional dreams, to spend a year on the beach, to default on a mortgage if necessary, to serve the public good, to relax under a rainbow, to amass mountains of cash and give some of it to the arts, to perform great acts of kindness, to invent a new kind of stapler that consistently works, to backpack around India, to build towering structures in the sky and paint them orange, to save the whales. Some of the advice, Ed realizes, involves things he hasn't done himself—yet anyway—and a lot of it is contradictory too, but that's okay—he kind of wants the audience to leave confused. Not enough confusion in commencement addresses these days, he'd decided, in the early days of drafting the address. Hell, if he's confused about life, then why shouldn't they be too?

And confused—well, he is certainly that. By now he's read the drafts on both sides of the *Sexy Slut* case, and he still doesn't know whether he should join one—and if so, which one?—or if he should write something himself. Same with the Pledge case. His colleagues—Leibowitz on the side of striking it down, Garabelli on the side of upholding it—circulated their drafts remarkably soon after the argument, but Ed remains uncommitted. His house has sold—that's nice—but since he doesn't know what he's going to be doing come the fall (talk about confusing decisions!), he hasn't bought anything new with the 1.4 million, or even looked much. The only thing he knows for sure is that he's not keeping any more cats at the court. The day after Freddy got loose, Ed moved him into his Capitol Hill apartment, figuring that his landlord's unhappiness, were he to learn of the cat's presence, would be nothing compared to the fury of the Chief.

He rides onto the Stanford campus. Past the medical buildings, the engineering complex, he arrives at the top of Palm Drive. On his left, the iconic view of the palm trees stretching the length of the loop road back to town. On his right, Memorial Church and the main quad. He pedals into the square, a weirdly blank and uninspiring space surrounded by squat adobe-colored buildings with red roofs and arched doorways. It reminds him more of an old person's home in a Phoenix suburb than the primary gathering place of one of the world's great universities. He circumnavigates the square a couple of times to make sure he hasn't missed anything, then leaves and finds his way to the center of campus, a more inviting place with its marvelous trees, always the trees, sweet mother of God the trees, where he pauses to rest on a fountain in front of the bookstore. The campus is filled with milling families who have come here from everywhere—from Boston, Florida, Minneapolis, Oslo, Tel Aviv, Shanghai—to celebrate the achievements of their children, their grandchildren, their nieces and nephews. Ed smiles and thinks of the rumpled Williams sweatshirt that he bought at Katelyn's graduation eons ago, as he watches the proud relatives enter the bookstore empty handed, emerging thirty minutes later carrying heavy bags overstuffed with cardinal red gear of every possible stripe.

The sun is going down now, the disappearing light turning the sky several shades of marvelous purple. The students are out, some dressed for dinner at a fancy restaurant with their parents, some still playing Frisbee or hacky sack despite the late hour. Suddenly there appears from nowhere the Tree, the Stanford band's one-of-a-kind mascot, a man in an eight-foot pine tree costume, googly eyes and a big red smile. Students and parents alike congregate around the loony figure, who every once in a while breaks out into a small dance for no reason other than because dancing is fun, especially when you're a batty-looking tree. Families erupt with joy and take pictures with the thing, post the images on Facebook within minutes, collect "likes" by the hundreds. Ed has always admired the Tree, and today he admires it more than ever. Could it be possible, he wonders, that the meaning of life lies completely within this arboreal mascot's idiotic grin? They should let the Tree give the commencement address—it could stand there silently behind the microphone for twenty minutes, wiggling, smiling its static smile, periodically spinning around in place. There'd be more wisdom communicated in that speech than in the speech he's going to give tomorrow, Ed thinks, Ed knows—*that* he can be damned sure of.

***

The next morning, Ed arrives at the appointed place at the appointed time in the bowels of the football stadium, where he is quickly surrounded by security guards. Assistants help him into his bright red regalia, place an awkward mortarboard on his head. He meets the university's top brass—the provost, the dean of Arts and Sciences, the football coach—and makes chit-chat about the Japanese constitution with Haruki Murakami, who is here to receive an honorary degree. Soon, someone from the AV team comes to set Ed up with a super high-tech wireless mike that will broadcast his words of encouragement to the farthest reach of the grandstands. With nothing left to do before giving his speech, Ed takes his notes out of his pants pocket and sits down in a comfortable chair to review them one last time. He is about halfway through the notes, making minor, last-minute changes to the text with a pen, when Ray the President comes over to say hello on his way to start the ceremonies. Ed stands up to greet him, gives him the manliest handshake he can muster. They've come a long way, Ed ponders, since the days of drinking bad beer in the basement of their Dartmouth frat forty years ago.

"Ready to inspire the next generation?" Ray asks.

"Oh, yes, absolutely," Ed answers.

"As part of the speech, you're going to reveal to all of us how the court is going to decide those First Amendment cases, I hope."

"No, sorry, no luck there," Ed says, "but I think I might announce my retirement from the bench."

Ray laughs, though it's a forced laugh, because it is not clear from the way Ed delivered the line that he was joking. "All right, then, see you out there," Ray says. He pats Ed affectionately on the shoulder and strides off to take his place on the podium that's been set up on the field upstairs.

Ed has just retaken his seat when the AV guy from before comes rushing over to him and whispers at Ed to take the microphone's receiver out of his suit jacket pocket and hand it to him. Ed complies. The AV guy looks at the receiver, grimaces, and flips a switch. "Shit," he says, handing it back. "This thing was on. Apparently your small talk was being broadcast across the stadium. Hope you didn't say anything too confidential."

"Yikes," Ed replies, putting the receiver back in his jacket. "Glad I didn't take that call from the chief justice."

"Yeah, guess so," the AV guy chuckles.

Ed returns to reading over his speech. Outside, Ray yammers to the graduates about hope and perseverance and student loans, then introduces the undergraduate student speaker. Caroline Brewer, a dual English and engineering major from Salinas, talks earnestly to an inattentive audience about how to reconcile the humanities with the hard sciences. Ed is listening to the boring speech, wondering how this young woman could possibly have been selected as her class representative, when his phone vibrates in his pocket. "I should turn this thing completely off," he says to himself. "Don't need my inner thigh to start tickling during my address." Reluctantly, though, he takes the phone out and looks at it. It's a text from his daughter: "You're retiring??? WTF??" *Hmm, that's weird*, Ed thinks. Then he thinks again, worries. "What R U talking about?" he texts back. Nervously, he awaits her response. "Did u just announce your retirement at Stanford speech? Look at Twitter. u r trending." *Uh oh.* He stands up, starts pacing, brings up Twitter, where he's been a bit of a celebrity since the Freddy incident. He himself is not on Twitter, but he knows where to go to see if anyone is talking about the court, and, well, there you go, look at that, they're all talking about *him.* The Twitterverse is playing the kids' game Telephone with his words here in the basement of the stadium. *Tuttle retiring. Tuttle announces retirement at Stanford speech. Tuttle makes graduation speech all about himself, ignores students. Who will be the next justice? Tuttle gives commencement address naked.* He looks at what's trending, and although there are two sports stars and #leggingsarenotpants in front of him, he is indeed right up there. *Holy fucking shit,* he thinks. And then he starts to laugh.

He laughs and laughs and laughs and laughs like he's never laughed before. He laughs like a hyena, like a clown on nitrous oxide, like a guy who's just seen Richard Pryor open for Louis C.K. He thinks of everything that's happened this past year, and what else can he do but laugh? He cannot stop himself. The security guards ask him if he's okay. He tries to reassure them, but it's hard when you can't talk and tears are streaming down your face and you're kneeling on the comfortable chair with your head on the back of it and laughing like SpongeBob SquarePants after smoking a brick of pure Moroccan hash. The joy of laughing so hard, so uncontrollably, so *magnificently,* the release of it all, Ed laughs even more thinking about how he can't stop laughing, and when he finally, finally is able to control himself, to speak for more than two seconds without breaking back into hysterics, he realizes that he has perhaps never been happier than at this precise moment. Which is good, because it's time for him to give his speech.

Still chuckling lightly, he emerges from the runway of the stadium, climbs the stairs to the dais, and takes his place behind the podium. The crowd is going wild. Ed may have underestimated the fame that his incident with the cat has brought him among the 18–22 set. Apparently, the late night talk shows had been running bits on it for a week, but he had been too embarrassed to watch them. Now the applause goes on and on. Students hold up signs that say "I Love Freddy" and giant pictures of cat heads on sticks. As Ed tries to get them to settle down so he can begin, they start chanting *Fred-dy Fred-dy Fred-dy*. A girl to his right screams *Don't Retire* as loud as she can, and this brings even more cheers. When the din finally subsides, Ed thanks the crowd profusely. If it were possible for him to be happier than he was five minutes ago, he would be.

"Umm, you might have overheard me say that I'm retiring," he says. The same girl, and a handful of others too, voice their displeasure. *No. Don't do it. Freddy for President.* "I guess," Ed continues, a sudden burst of inspiration hitting him like a thunderbolt, "that I let the cat out of the bag on that one."

Pande-fucking-monium. Ed's never seen anything like it. The *Freddy* chants are louder and longer this time, the cat heads on sticks bouncing up and down even more wildly than before. Looking out at the frenzied crowd, he thinks about what to say next. It would be easy enough to dispel the retirement rumor that's taken over the Internet. All he'd have to say was that he was joking, that of course he wasn't retiring, that he'd be insane to give up a job like the one he's been so lucky to have had for these past eight years. The kids would go on Twitter and Facebook, and the news would be over just as quickly as it started. It would be simple. But as he looks around at all these kids on the brink of starting their new lives, he starts to think that maybe he won't dispel the rumor. Maybe instead he'll confirm it. That would be just as easy. He could say it, then give his speech, and it would be over. Tomorrow he could go to India. Tomorrow he could learn to play the trombone. Tomorrow he could write a kids' book about a cat that won't stay put. Tomorrow he wouldn't have to worry about deciding any cases involving *Sexy Slut Magazine.*

He looks around some more at the students with their tans and big smiles and fresh faces who are still yelling about Freddy, and then he spots the Tree, standing by itself on the football field, a bit off to the side of the students. It too has a cardboard cat face on a stick, and it is waving the stick around and dancing and twirling, and then Ed knows. He is as sure as he's ever been about anything. Standing behind the podium, he is the perfect carpenter, the master angler. He is Cook Ting, and he's cutting up an ox like nobody has ever cut up an ox before. *Zip, zoop.* This is it.

"Well, I certainly hadn't planned on announcing this here today," Ed says, when the noise dies down. "But it is true. I am retiring from my seat on the Supreme Court. Effective immediately, I guess."

The crowd *ooohs* and *ahhhs.* A few more screams of *No* go up, but mostly everyone is taking pictures and texting and tweeting and instagramming this moment when they've witnessed history. He knows ten seconds after he's done it that there's no going back. And that's just fine. "But this day isn't about me," he says. "It is about you, and I have some things that I want to tell you."

And so he does. He tells them what he knows. He spreads out his notes and gives them the speech. He tells them to be unique, to be generous, to live life to the fullest, to pursue professional dreams, to spend a year on the beach, to default on a mortgage if necessary, to serve the public good, to relax under a rainbow, to amass mountains of cash and give some of it to the arts, to perform great acts of kindness, to invent a new kind of stapler that consistently works, to backpack around India, to build towering structures in the sky and paint them orange, to save the whales, to be on the Supreme Court someday and then retire before it's too late to do anything else.

To a final burst of applause, he turns from the podium and walks away, and as he takes his seat on the dais next to his old friend, the chanting continues, the cheers go on, and he listens to them, and he shakes a little, and he knows that, for better or worse, it's over: He is no longer a sitting member of the United States Supreme Court.

SEPTEMBER

FOURTEEN

WHEN SHE BRINGS HIS STACK OF PANCAKES AND SIDE OF bacon, the waitress at the diner in this tiny town near the western border of South Dakota also pours Ed another cup of coffee, which he is definitely going to need because he has a long drive ahead of him. According to the Internet, it takes a couple of hours to get to the Wyoming border from here, although the exact location of the border is actually kind of the question. For the past couple of weeks, Ed has been working as a special master in a long-standing dispute between the two states over their precise border. The chief justice appointed him to the position in late August. She was reluctant when he first asked her for the gig but ultimately decided that giving him the job would be prudent. Not that Ed had actually come right out and said that he might tell the guy profiling him for *Vanity Fair* about how she had once punched him in the gut, but with Ed's recent erratic behavior still fresh in her mind, she'd decided it would be best to stay on his good side.

Ed finishes eating, but he's still got half a cup of coffee left, so he takes out his phone and flips through the pictures he's been taking these past couple of months. He sips the weak brew and lets the photos take him back to his travels. He now has far more than three images of India in his head—the Taj Mahal surely lived up to his expectations, but he is thinking far more of the people, so many people everywhere, and the poverty and the traffic, and the food, *God* the food, and the temples, the idols to every imaginable god, and the smell of spices in the markets, the street-side stalls selling fried puffy things doused in ghee and hot syrupy sweet globes covered with nuts that he usually avoided but once in a while risked, luckily avoiding somehow contracting cholera or dysentery or any other major gastrointestinal nightmare. He hadn't backpacked exactly, but he wasn't staying in five-star hotels either (though admittedly he did eat in them once in a while). He hired local guides and chatted with the taxi drivers, gave rupees to starving children, took yoga classes, and finally learned the rules of cricket after living sixty-two years in the dark on the subject.

"Any more coffee for you?" the waitress asks, seeing that his cup is empty.

"No thanks," Ed says, realizing that he should probably get on the road. "Just the check, please."

"Sure thing, sweetie."

While he waits for the bill—nothing happens too quickly around here—he pulls up the *Times* on his phone and re-reads Farkas's story about the upcoming battle in the full Senate over the president's nominee to replace Ed on the court—a former bigwig government lawyer for the Dems, now dean at NYU—whose views on constitutional interpretation some Republicans think are too radical for the bench. Since this is the guy who's probably going to have the final say on all sorts of critical legal questions, not least of which include the regulation of obscenity and the Pledge of Allegiance when those issues inevitably make it back to the court (the two cases from last term were, as they say, "affirmed by an equally divided court" in Ed's absence, meaning they have no precedential value), everyone is looking carefully at this guy. Among other things, they want to be sure he is not a closet lunatic. Indeed, the first question asked of him during the Judiciary Committee hearings earlier in the month was, "Sir, do you own a cat?"

Ed pays the bill and buttons up his coat, heads out to the Jeep he's rented for the long drive. The mornings here are cool, but he knows that by mid-afternoon the temperature will rise into the seventies. He's got plenty of bottled water and snacks for the road, a turkey sandwich packed in his backpack which he'll hopefully eat when he gets to where he's going. He drives west toward the Cowboy State on the narrow empty road, the low sun at his back, and thinks about the life he's left behind—the briefs, the arguments, the opinions, the paper, all that paper everywhere in stacks and folders and binders, in his briefcase and on the windowsill, paper coming out of his ears—and he realizes that he almost never misses it, at least so far anyway. The NYU guy can have it. Ed does miss having the cavernous office a little, that's true. The offices they give the retired justices in the Federal Judiciary building down near Union Station are nothing like what you get in the court itself, and he plans to spend as little time as possible there. When he needs to work, like when he's preparing the report on this case or when he's sketching illustrations for "Freddy and the Justice," under contract for publication from Little, Brown Young Readers next Christmas, he'll do it from the unassuming row house he's recently purchased in Capitol Hill.

At the point where the road runs closest to the border between the two states, Ed pulls the Jeep into a small, currently empty parking area maintained by South Dakota. From here a trail of about two miles leads toward the creek bed that may or may not be the actual dividing line from Wyoming, depending on a complicated set of factors that Ed has been considering, work that has required him to spend long days poring over nineteenth-century maps and deeds and various other antiquated legal instruments in the hotel room that he's rented back in town for the past two weeks. Wyoming has argued that the border is defined by a longitudinal line that is about five miles west of the creek bed; South Dakota has always maintained that for the ten or so miles that the creek bed exists, it is the border. Ed is pretty sure that he will recommend that the court adopt South Dakota's view—it's not one-hundred-percent conclusively correct, but based on everything he's read and studied, Ed thinks it's the better position.

He does not really have to see the creek bed in person to decide how the case should be resolved, but he wants to. After all, if he had wanted to spend all his days indoors looking at papers, he could have stayed a Supreme Court justice! So, he straps on his backpack, makes sure he's got enough water for the four miles of hiking he's got in front of him, takes the straw hat that makes him look like a weirdo but which is necessary given that the sun is now warm and high in the sky, and heads off.

As he walks, he thinks about his life back home. He hasn't spent much time in Washington recently, but he plans to spend most of the fall there, with the exception of the week in early December when he will be traveling to New York for Katelyn's wedding. He got the news by email in his hotel room in Mumbai at three in the morning while he was trying to adjust to the time difference, and he had immediately celebrated despite the strange hour by drinking two bottles of Kingfisher from the hotel room mini bar. It's going to be quite an affair—these kids have plenty of money of their own to spend and no children (yet) to spend it on, so they are sparing no expense. Already there's talk in the elite chef circles about this being a culinary wedding for the ages—rumors abound that Matsuhisa will be preparing the main course, that Laurie Jon Moran is baking the cake. Ed is just looking forward to giving his daughter away, giving a toast, not using a microphone this time. His ex-wife Sarah will be there, of course, with her dipshit of a husband, but that's okay. He'll be so happy for his daughter it won't matter, and he's thinking that if things go like he hopes with Monica, the fifth-grade teacher in her late forties whom he met speed dating and has been seeing for the past couple of weeks, he might end up having a hotter date for the wedding than Sarah will be able to handle.

He comes finally to the creek bed. It's dry, as it almost always is, mostly just dirt and rocks, but very clearly a place where water might flow, or has flowed, or could flow again. He takes his camera out of the backpack and takes pictures of the creek; he will include these in the final report he makes to the court next month. Putting the camera away, he steps down into the creek bed and starts walking south. The bed is only about three feet deep and maybe five feet across. As he walks, though, the creek gets narrower and narrower. About a quarter of a mile from where he first jumped in, the distance from one side to the other is maybe a foot and a half. Ed gets an idea.

He climbs out of the creek on the South Dakota side and backs up maybe six feet. "I'm in South Dakota," he says, aloud, to nobody, then runs and leaps to the other side. When he lands, he pumps his fist in the air and exclaims, "Now I'm in Wyoming!" He does this several times, trying to jump as far as he can, taking off the backpack so he can get more lift. *Wyoming, South Dakota, Wyoming, South Dakota.* Even though he is tired from the long hike, he can't get enough of it. On the South Dakota side, he backs up about twelve feet from the creek because he figures he will be able to jump further with the longer running start. "On your mark, get set, go," he says to himself and then goes. He's right. He soars over the creek bed, jumps longer than he has before, but this time when he lands, he comes down awkwardly on his ankle, which twists slightly but painfully and causes Ed to hit the dirt. *Oh, fuck*, he yells, and grabs his ankle, rubbing it, rolling on the ground, his clothes now covered with dirt, the hot sun baking him from above. The ankle hurts. It hurts. It hurts so much. But Ed doesn't care.

He is in Wyoming now.

ACKNOWLEDGMENTS AND AUTHOR'S NOTE

I AM SO DELIGHTED THAT THIS BOOK IS IN PRINT THAT I FEEL like thanking pretty much everyone I've ever met, but space is short, so my biggest and sincerest thanks go to:

My outstanding editor Jon Malysiak and my terrific agent Allison Hunter. Without both of these wonderful people, this book simply would not exist outside the C drive of my laptop.

Sarah Gannett, my friend of now over 30 years (!), who not only read several drafts of the book and gave me great comments, but who was also a constant source of encouragement.

Lexa Edsall, Sarah Freitas, Sasha Natapoff, Diana Winters, and Ben Winters, all of whom were kind enough to read a draft of the book and point out where and how it needed to be better. Without their generous help, this book would have been very bad.

Jon Warner, who after reading my short story about Ed Tuttle's summer vacation in Jackson Hole ("The Adventures of Ed Tuttle, Associate Justice") encouraged me to expand the story into a novel.

Alan Childress, who agreed to publish that original short story in a book of questionable sanity with his awesome Quid Pro Books press.

The editors of the fantastic *Barrelhouse* magazine, who originally published the short story.

And last but not least, my wife Karen and son Walter, who have tolerated me talking about this guy Ed Tuttle for far, far too long.

One quick note: Although I have attempted to depict the law and the Supreme Court as accurately as possible throughout the narrative, there are moments here and there where I felt that the needs of the story outweighed precision, and in those cases the story won out.